deadly cravings

CRIMSON COVEN
BOOK 1

ALLIE SANTOS

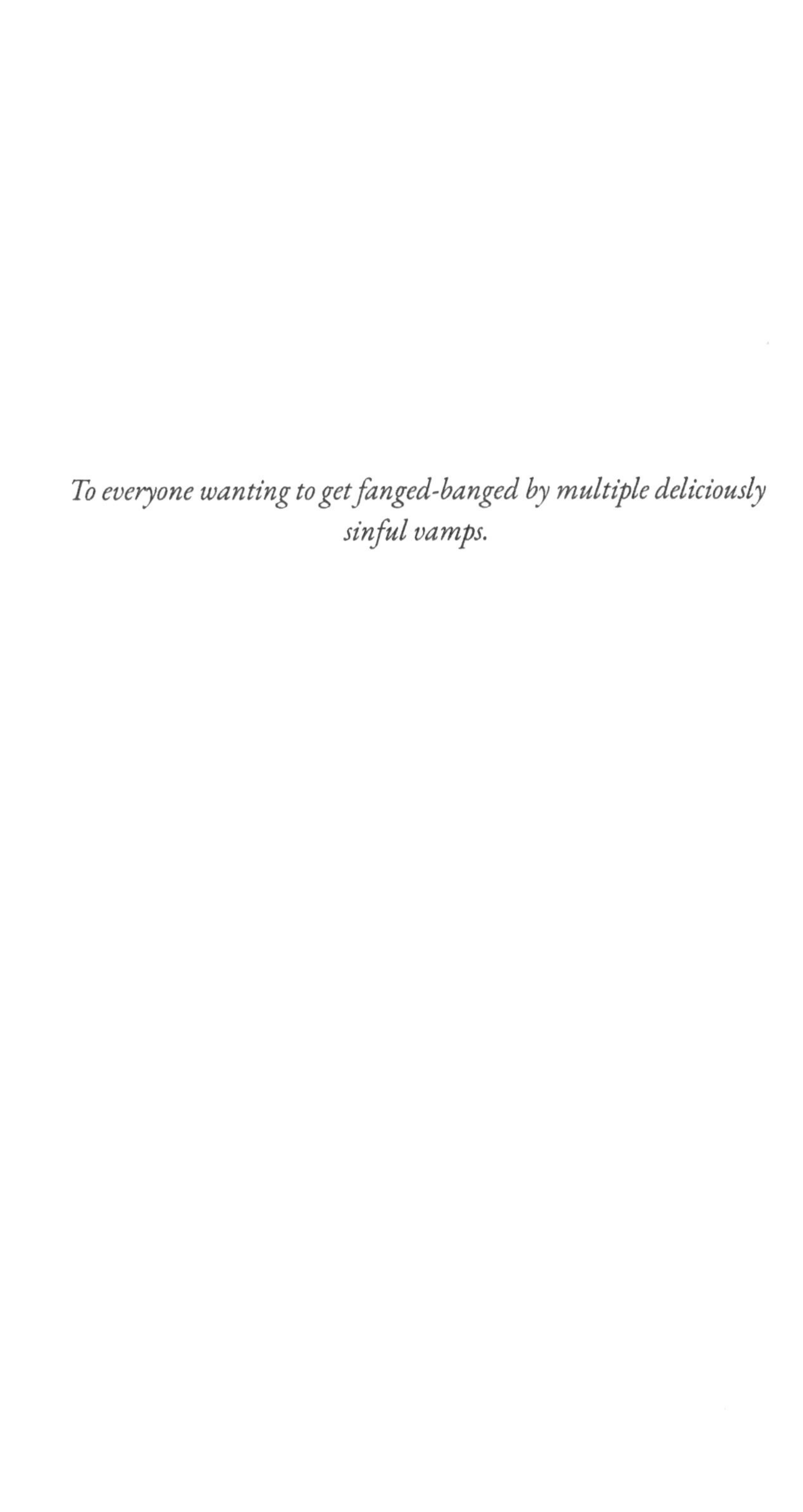

To everyone wanting to get fanged-banged by multiple deliciously sinful vamps.

a note from allie

I have an unhealthy obsession with vampires. That's it, that's my note to you haha. I hope you enjoy my why-choose vampire romance. Don't forget to recommend Deadly Cravings, it's the best way to help me move releases forward!

I have a history of reading something and then saying it incorrectly, so I'll include the following for anyone like me:

- Tobias: Toe-bye-us
- Calliope: Kuh-lie-uh-pee

Love,
Allie 🤍

content warnings

Violence, Mention of Past forced Sodomy, Murder (on page), Descriptive Sex, Foul Language, Descriptive Murder Scenes, Non-Con Biting, Bite Play, Nyctophobia, Somnophilia

Please be advised that the following trigger and content warnings contain spoilers for the story and plot of the novel.

DEADLY CRAVINGS is a Why-Choose Paranormal Romance. The main character's past trauma of being held captive and sodomized is referenced throughout the story. Deadly Cravings contains adult content, and these vampires oftentimes display cruel, manipulative behavior. The main characters partake in rough, bloody sex. At the end of the novel some of the heroes treat the heroine cruelly. Disclaimer: The series will progressively contain darker themes.

Deadly Cravings is set in a mythical world and all contents are purely fiction.

ONE

catalina

THERE WERE ONLY a few more boxes to bring in and I would be done. I just needed to push a *tiny* bit more. Crouching, I set the box down in my new bedroom. It thumped on the floor.

I pressed my palms to my chest, catching my breath from the nerves already nipping at my heels. The sun had already set, much sooner than I expected since it was still early. All I wanted to do was hunker down inside the house.

I rolled my neck; I didn't have time for that. Once I brought in the rest of the boxes, I needed to head into town to pick up my cell phone, brand new screen and all. With it being the first day and me being new to the city, I needed to get going before it became even later. Being out at night went against everything I believed in, but the shop wouldn't be open on the weekend, and I couldn't go that long without it.

I trudged down the hall, toward the front door where a nice breeze drifted inside. I clocked all the spiderwebs gracing the corners of the high ceilings and narrowed my eyes at them. *You won't stay there for long, you little creeps.*

An itch started at my arms like it did every time I saw spiders, or anything related to them. Those multi-eyed, voyeuristic fuckers were done for. As soon as I got my ass to a store, I'd spray them into oblivion.

Wood creaked loudly under my foot, and I froze in the hallway leading to the front door. I slowly slid my eyes shut and dragged my fingers through my hair before crouching.

I tipped my head back and groaned. It hadn't simply creaked, the dang thing had cracked. I poked my nail into the surface and squinted. I could see the cement beneath it. Of course this happened. It was my luck swooping in again like a little bitch. I didn't know what I'd done to offend lady luck, but she had a hard-on for me.

I pursed my lips as I frowned at the crack in my new-to-me flooring. Snapping my fingers, I smiled.

I knew exactly how to fix it.

I'd laid the slab of carpet over in the hallway leading to the living room. Gripping the edge, I dragged it over the floorboard. As I brushed the dust off my hands, I studied the plush, swirl patterned carpet now covering the worn cracked wood.

That worked.

Okay, back to getting my boxes from the car. I had to wiggle the door to get it open and the hinge squealed a little too loudly.

Another thing added to my fix list. I rubbed my forehead with my thumb and forefinger. So many small things I had to do.

But, on the bright side, if I didn't want to fix it, it could be like a little security system too. It wasn't like I ever had visitors . . .

Wow, that seethed with self-pity.

Being alone was a hundred percent intentional. One, I didn't have time for friends, because I was writing as much as I could. And two, I didn't want to put anyone in danger.

Even if I wanted to get close to someone, I had to move within a few months, so the effort wasn't worth it.

At my van, I bent in to get a grip on a box. I'd pulled out the back seats so I could lug everything with each move and although it was beat-down, I thanked it every day for its service. Maybe with my next advance check, I could splurge on a nicer car, it should be enough for me to have money left over after covering my costs.

The box dug into my palm and I heaved it into my arms.

The hair on the back of my neck stood, sending a shiver down my spine. A crow's caw ripped through my ear drums, much too close. I shot up so fast I thumped my head on the roof of my car, dropping the box.

A dull pain spread through the back of my head. I whimpered and carefully backed up. Lifting my palm to my head, I rubbed as I swept my gaze across the front of my rental.

The one-story town house structure was solid, but a bit run-down. The beams were all intact and the roof was good. So what if it was tilted to the side and the mansion next door made my little rental look like an abused Barbie house? It was a roof over my head, and more importantly, it was cheap.

In comparison, the sprawling Gothic structure perched on an incline ostentatiously looming over my place made my situation seem worse. It was the only other home on the barren street right outside of Seattle, yet it was still *too* close to my place —to the point that it made my house seem like some servant quarter extension of it, even outside of the wrought iron barrier.

I was unsure if I saw the outline of someone at the window, since it was too high to make out clearly. *Was someone watching?* My brows furrowed as I stared up, squinting to try to make out the details. No way, that was impossible. The place was abandoned, according to my landlord.

It must be nice to have such a place, but it was nowhere in my future, even if I lived long enough, which was a big question mark. If I lived to see Peter graduate and I no longer had to pay his tuition, maybe . . .

I shook the nonsense thoughts away and refocused on that odd sensation of being watched. There was no one around. Everything was clear and that was all that mattered . . . it wasn't *him*.

My throat tightened thinking about the deranged vampire.

Before my memories got me twisted up in knots, I plucked the box up, and I refocused on my opportunities, as basic as they may be. I couldn't be too picky about any of it, since the owner had given me a huge discount if I fixed up the rental. It worked for me, after all, I may not be here long enough to finish, and it gave me somewhere to stay for a few months.

Plus, this was a lot better than some places I'd stayed at before, especially that seedy apartment in Los Angeles I'd barely afforded.

But sometimes the depression got to me, and I just wanted to be taken care of—babied—something. I wanted to dress in the nice clothing I saw at the stores I couldn't afford to splurge on. Buy the nice bags—the whole, spoiled nine yards. But that would never be my future for many reasons—at least for now. It wasn't that I didn't have nice things, but the guilt that accompanied each purchase weighed on my shoulders. Fortunately, I may be able to treat myself with my next royalty check. Based on the contract I signed, it was larger than I'd ever received before.

A little wiggle of excitement burst in my chest at the accomplishment. Things were starting to turn around and I had my fingers crossed I could stay here a little longer than my usual couple months.

This was a fresh start—another one. The vampire that had attacked me so many years ago hadn't found me after four years, so I was seeing the light at the end of the tunnel. I'd been hopping from place to place, getting farther and farther from Maryland, and now I was in Washington.

I dropped the box at the threshold and returned to my van. A crow rested on the hood, its head twisting side to side. It looked freaky perched there with the moon framing it. Once I was a few feet away, it beat its wings and took off to perch on one of the windowsills of the mansion next door. No lights shone through the shadowed structure other than whatever light the moon reflected off the pane. I rubbed my arms. If I were being honest, that was the type of place I could see vampires living in, but I was the only person on this street.

This was my first opportunity at attempting to rest in one place for longer than usual, but eventually, I would have to move again. As nonsensical as it may seem, fear kept me bouncing from state to state. After extensive research, I'd found the low crime rate here pointed to a possibility of normalcy, but as soon as I caught a hint of vampires, I would be long gone.

TWO

asher

I RUBBED my sensitive fangs with my tongue. They'd popped out as soon as I'd seen the delicacy hop out of her van with a grin on her face. My gaze dropped to her thick, lush thighs, and I kneaded my palm against my hard cock. I'd been watching her since she'd arrived, going in and out of her house as she dragged box upon box out of her vehicle.

The sway of her walk enthralled me, and that ass was unmatched. I couldn't wait until I got up close and personal with those legs and buried my face between them. Even from a distance she seemed like such a treat that lust may overcome me, and she'd end up dead. After all, it wasn't like I'd seen anyone else move in with her, so no one would find her drained corpse if I fucked her to death. My dick twitched and I unbuckled my belt before sliding the zipper of my jeans down.

There was no way she'd see me rub one out since I was on the third floor of the manor . . . and she was down there . . . in that teeny tiny speck humans considered houses.

Freeing my dick, it bobbed, hard and ready, the mushroom head red from the blood that had rushed there. A bead of red-tinted cum formed at the tip of my cock. Groaning, I wrapped my hand around the flesh.

Eyes narrowed on the human, I watched her bend over. That ass bouncing on my cock would be phenomenal. I'd slam into her so hard, her fragile human bones would snap. I sucked a breath between my teeth and more cum spilled on my hand.

Mercy.

My lips parted as she popped out of the van and tilted her head up, looking directly at me again. A flush warmed my face, heat spreading down my neck. There was no way she could see me, but I fucking wanted her to. I wanted her eyes on me as I rubbed my thick cock in her honor. I ached to know the color of her eyes. To watch the light flee as she gifted me her life's blood. The moonlight caressed her skin, highlighting a long, beautiful, sun-kissed neck perfect for me to sink my fangs into.

I moaned, picturing how well she'd react to me dipping into her warm pussy as I stole her blood. I'd never left my lovers wanting, even as they greeted death.

My cock twitched, jerking hard as the orgasm hedged over, causing my head to drop forward as I placed a palm on the windowsill to brace myself.

Warmth spread down my spine and metal creaked from a door opening as my cock spasmed in my hand, drenching me with my undead little swimmers.

My heart raced from sucking up the blood in my system. I groaned. *Shit.* That was a hard one for it being a handy. I would need to feed soon to replenish my strength.

"Don't fuck the neighbor. Even better, don't even think about fucking the neighbor."

I tugged a handkerchief from my pocket to swipe myself clean and shoved the sullied cloth into my pocket.

"You're no fun, brother." Licking my lips, I tucked my dick into my jeans and zipped the big guy up before he got any more ideas and started to harden again then faced Jax.

We were the spitting image of each other, if you ignored the scowl that never failed to mar his face. His lowered brows spasmed as irritation flashed across his features.

"You're going to have her at our door like all your other whores. And we don't need any more, especially living right next to us. Not when we need to keep this place quiet."

I pouted. "I always convince them to . . . forget our rendezvous, that is unless they die, I don't get why your panties are in a twist."

Jax stared at me, silent and unbending. "We're planning in the living room," he spat, and the echo of his heavy steps were heaven to my ears.

Killjoy.

Taking my time, I strolled across the large 'family room' encapsulating the left of the staircase, splitting the west and east sides of the home. I descended with my thoughts fixated on the woman next door. Females went crazy over meet-cutes, but how to set one up . . . *hmmm*? I trailed after Jax, taking the stairs two at a time.

Perhaps I should go over and offer my services—*not yet, Asher, step by step*. And if that wasn't cute enough for her to obsess over, I'd have to sneak over . . . I'd never resorted to sliding into a woman's bed in the thick of the night to fuck her. One look at my face and they fell like flies, but if she proved unruly, I'd be capable. After, I could compel her to forget and that was that. None of my coven had to know.

"Why are you grinning?"

Tobias's eyebrows were lowered. Downer number two,

except this one's moral compass surpassed all *humans* I'd encountered. He was an oddity, the only vampire I knew to care about humanity, but he needed to get with the program. Humans were toys, correction, *everything* was a toy meant for us to play with.

"Have you seen the morsel next door?" I licked my lips. "I can't wait to get my dick and fangs in her, you'll think the same as soon as you lay eyes on her—okay, maybe *you* won't." The British vampire was the oldest of all of us and yet, he was as untouched as a nun—or priest. I chuckled under my breath.

"Let's stop discussing cunts," Jax hissed as I dropped in the parlor recliner.

I kicked my feet up, crossing them at the ankles, admiring the glint of my Dior Derbys.

"I'm going to the club on Thirty-Sixth Avenue to see if I can get to the restricted area." Tobias crossed his arms.

Ah, that's why he was all dressed up.

Ren had been gone for a few weeks. A blink of an eye really, I don't know why they were up in arms about it. My bets were that he'd worn down that vamp bitch he was obsessed with, and they were fucking away like little rabid bunnies.

I dampened my grin before my next words. I couldn't seem too excited.

"I can go with you."

"No, stay here," Jaxon snapped. "There's a reason Tobias is going. He won't get distracted by any of the pussy trying to catch his attention."

"Rude," I purred, a smile curving my lips. "But accurate." I fished the cell phone out of my pocket and navigated to my contacts. *Which women to invite over . . .*

"There's another concern." Jax pushed off the wall. I was

surprised he could lean at all with the stick so perfectly lodged in his ass. Sighing, I sank deeper into the seat. "We have a new neighbor. We must not call attention to ourselves. That includes fucking her." Both pairs of eyes fixed on me. "Asher. Put that thing down, you're worse than a child."

I huffed out a breath and crossed my arms. "I don't appreciate you clipping my wings," I muttered sullenly, playing up my disappointment.

They could say what they liked but the human would be mine.

THREE

catalina

IT WAS TOO DARK OUT.

My steps thudded in rhythm with my heart. *Thump. Thump. Thump.* I quickened my pace, trying not to outright break into a sprint.

It was the most dangerous at night. I knew this. The Pale One would pin me down with a shackle-like grip, becoming stiff and unconscious for hours on end. It hadn't taken me long to deduce that it was because of the sunrise. I'd never been able to break free of him even with him out of commission, so I was no match to one that was awake.

I wish I could have afforded ordering a ride to my new place, and come back in the morning to collect my car.

A gust of wind fluttered my hair backwards and I shivered. It was the city, so it had to be safer, right? But with each step I took toward where I'd parked there were less people. It wasn't as bustling as it was earlier. The street looked like a ghost town and the floor was damp from the light drizzle that had fallen before nightfall. Another store shut its lights off and I quickened my pace, my steps slapping against the sidewalk. A block more . . .

My heart rate ramped up as I passed a broken street lamp.

I should have spent the money on the ride.

I knew better. All the research I'd done said vampires didn't go out during daylight, and I'd done *a lot* of research for my books. Writing romance novels about vampires seemed like the opposite thing I should have done with my debilitating fear of them, but the words just spilled out and I soon learned that creating them as sweet, obsessive heroes worked to calm the overwhelming fear I grappled with. Had it developed into some weird as fuck sexual fantasy? Sure had, but it wasn't like I was seeking them out to fuck them.

I was just writing about fucking them.

The tip of my heel wedged into a crevice, and I caught myself before face-planting. Son of a bitch, they better not be scuffed, but I couldn't stop to check.

I was almost to the parking lot. Just a little farther, through the brick lined alley . . .

A heavy thud stopped me in my tracks and I clung to the side of the apartment building. Stillness was key. The possibility of it being vampires was astronomically low, I couldn't be that unlucky, right?

Better safe than sorry. If it wasn't a vampire, then whatever it was would pass by me as if I wasn't there, and as long as I showed no reaction—even if it was a vampire—then they'd think I was a clueless human.

Either way, I could *not* run.

They liked it when you ran. I learned that the hard way and my neck remembered it clearly. I pressed my lips together as my pussy tightened at the possibility of being brought down by fangs.

Not a new thing for me. Fuck.

I'd embraced the perverted mindset I'd developed since it was the only way I got off . . . imagining the Pale One's bite.

But actually doing something with a vampire was a line I refused to cross . . .

Was it really?

Shut the fuck up, brain. Totally not the time.

My jaw clenched as I flattened against the building. Rubbing against the brick would so not be good for the cashmere.

The thud of my pulse against my throat fluttered like hummingbird wings. I inched forward a few steps to round into the alley I had to pass to get to my vehicle. Movement called my attention to the crevice between the buildings. A hiss floated to me and my breathing hitched.

That sound . . . familiar and terrifying.

My heart thundered as my chest reached the pinnacle of tension—lungs squeezing painfully. My hand shook as I buried my fingers into my rose-colored purse. It took a bit of tugging, but I eventually popped my inhaler free. With my thumb, I pushed the cap off and pressed the mouth bit to my lips. Applying pressure to the tip, the medication puffed into my mouth and I inhaled it into my lungs. The tension in my chest eased and I dropped my shoulders as the medicine worked through my body, offering me relief. The ache at my temples subsided.

Stress-induced asthma . . . another little gift the Pale One had left me with—other than life-long trauma and a fucked up sexual kink. Now that I would not pass out, I stuffed the inhaler back inside and gripped the wooden, metal tipped stake and clutched it to my chest.

A soft glow of the lamp over the door illuminated the

spectacle. A man was hunched over another. They grappled, rolled, and twisted. A bald guy got the other one down and his head lowered as he struck.

Vampire.

I needed to run the opposite direction, but I couldn't move my legs.

My stomach tightened and heat spread down my limbs. Fangs . . . blood. I bit my lip to stop my whimper.

It was pure agony. The feeling of my throat being torn, the tug and tear just as hurtful. Agony.

But why did I *crave* it?

A shouted curse tore me free from my thoughts. The bald vampire tore into the man's shoulder. I knew how agonizing that was. Blood sprayed across the cement. He would kill him while I watched.

No.

With my hand around the only weapon I carried, I burst forward, my heels slapping against the concrete.

The vampire turned at the last moment, hissing, and my aim was off, slamming closer to his shoulder than his heart. His eyes slitted and he lashed out, causing me to teeter on my heels and fall to my ass with a yelp. God, this was it, I was done for. I put my hands up to protect my face except he didn't touch me. There was a scuffle, so I peeked between my fingers.

The man that had been flat on the ground was now behind the vampire, pinning him down. He slammed the stake into his heart with ease and jerked it to the side. Blood leaked across his chest in a line.

The vampire froze.

"You Crimson fucker." That was the last thing he shouted

before he slumped. My eyes widened and I gaped, struggling to wrap my head around the deteriorating body.

Stakes really worked. I was still gawking as the bitten man fell to his side, avoiding falling on the rotting vampire. I crawled over to him, leaning over his face. Disheveled hair fell across his eyebrows, the tips grazing his closed eyelids.

The fibers of his dress shirt split where the vampire dragged his fangs. Blood drenched his throat in a gash leading to his shoulder . . . It didn't seem like the vampire tried to feed on him. It looked like he'd tried to maul him.

I blinked and met gray pain-filled eyes. The sharp angles of his face hollowed his features.

"We have to go," I breathed and grabbed his arm. I was what many would call sturdy. Taller than average and bottom heavy, but his height sent me stumbling to the side. Pressing my heel into the concrete, I caught my balance, wincing at the weight and the pinch in my ankle. With my lips tight, I half-dragged, half-guided him to my van. It felt like forever, but the distance was no farther than fifteen yards. "Do you have anyone I can call for you, or do you need to go to the hospital? You feel dangerously cold." Blood stained his face, but the ravaged collar of his sweater covered the actual bite marks.

His lips parted on a heavy, frustrated-sounding exhale.

I gasped and recoiled, but his cool hand lashed out and wrapped around my wrist. Ice spiked through my veins, and I froze in place.

All the blood wasn't what struck me, nope, it was the fangs. He was a vampire. I sucked in a trembling breath, attempting to yank out of his stiff grip. He braced his side up with my van, not giving an inch off my wrist.

"I won't hurt you." His whisper was ragged and accented.

My chest tightened and it became difficult to suck in a breath. Spots danced in front of my eyes. I'd saved a vampire. This was surreal, there was no way fate was this cruel. My hand shook as I dug into my bag and clawed for my inhaler.

I shouldn't have fucking tested lady luck with all that bullshit about "not having *that* bad of luck."

"Girl." The English tone came as if from far away and the world tilted, blurring my sight. As I hit the cement, pain shot through my body, shocking me back to the present. Something cushioned me and my inhaler pressed to my mouth. "How does this work . . ." The vampire was talking to himself.

I inhaled instinctively at the puff and my lungs throbbed as they sucked in the medicine. My blurred sight warbled. Blinking quickly, I couldn't believe the vampire leaned over me, eyebrows furrowed as he took in my features.

The vampire dropped the hand painstakingly holding my inhaler and slumped against my van. Energy worked its way back through my system. *What a shit time to have an attack.* My palms pressed into the ground as I pushed myself to a sitting position, preparing to bounce to my feet and take off. His fingers remained locked around my wrist and no matter how much I tugged, he wouldn't release it.

My gaze dropped to his furrowed dark eyebrows, and I hesitated.

This was a vampire and although I had questionable, physical attractions to the idea of them, it didn't erase their danger. His hair fluttered in the wind as his gaze sharpened, his fangs hinting from between his lips.

His pain-filled eyes . . . the wounded look—hopeless. He had helped me . . .

Too fucking bad. Vampire business was not *my* business, and the last thing my outfit needed was more abuse.

Except he wouldn't loosen his grip.

"They are coming."

Who was coming? More vampires? My gaze dropped to the remnant undead powder smeared on his shoe. One vampire opposed to multiple . . .

My legs moved before my thought finished, and I hooked my arm around his narrow waist and pulled his arm over my shoulders. He wasn't going to let me go, so he was coming with me, and now that I knew stakes killed vampires, my heel would do nicely.

"I-if you bite me. I'll kill you," I spat out in the most aggressive tone I could muster. All bravado, but he didn't know I was happily a wimp.

I had to use every muscle I owned and dug my heels into the ground. Heaving, sweat beaded at my forehead.

"I will not harm you," he slurred and lifted my inhaler. I plucked it from him and stuffed it into my purse.

My purse remained hooked over my shoulder and I reached inside, pressing the button of my key to unlock it. My beat-up van beeped, and I jerked open the creaky back door. There were no back seats, which I was glad for in this instance.

The vampire weaved and fell inside, slumping with his head on the back of the passenger seat headrest. He was out for the count. I huffed, glaring at his large body. This was not the way I expected my first night to go.

Tears pressed against the back of my eyes, and I sucked in a shallow breath.

This sucked ass.

Gripping him around his back, I tugged but was

unsuccessful in budging him, so instead, I nudged and shuffled him until he thumped flat. What was I thinking putting a vampire in my space? They were evil, cruel monsters. They only used. I'd witnessed it firsthand.

After crawling into the back of the minivan, I hooked my hands under his oversized lean torso and pulled. *Okay, finally some progress.* I yanked until I couldn't anymore and then reached over his body to haul his long ass freaking legs into the vehicle to slam the doors shut.

I lowered to the floor, peeking through the window to see if anyone ran after us. With one look at the still vamp, I reached for my heel. I could do this. Killing one should be easy, right?

His head lifted and I froze at his nose grazing my belly and inching near my thigh. I sucked in a breath and pressed my spine into the back of the seat.

The vampire moaned. "You smell good."

The vampire shook his head, squeezing his eyes shut and groaning. That wasn't what concerned me, it was the answering throb at my core wanting more of his praise.

"I apologize." His eyebrows lowered on his forehead.

"You need to leave." I couldn't believe myself; I should be driving my heel into his heart. Or at the very least, propping that door open and kicking him out, but I couldn't move.

I fisted my hands. My brain cells had apparently taken a trip, or more accurately, my questionable sexual appetite had taken the wheel.

His eyes slid shut and he stilled preternaturally. *Was he about to decompose?* That would destroy my flooring. I whimpered and nudged him with my toe, but there was no response.

"Hey," I said, urgency in my tone.

Still nothing.

This was my chance; I could shove him out of the van and go home. I rubbed my palm across my forehead while eyeing the door handle and then the heel in my hand.

He hadn't attacked me . . .

So what? I waited until he got better and asked him for a little fang action? No, that was stupid. I needed to screw my head on straight so I could get back home and write out all these vampire fantasies, because that was what they were—fiction.

I groaned, rubbing my face. No, he hadn't attacked me, and he'd helped me when I was about to pass out. He could have done whatever he wanted as soon as I was unconscious, but he didn't.

My teeth sank into my lower lip.

There was a field close by. I'd drop him there and then he could figure it out, after all, he was a vampire. I chewed my lip as I pushed my fingers through my hair.

His lips were slightly parted and a fang flashed . . . he probably needed blood to replenish his strength or whatever. He hadn't killed me, what if he could tell me some more ways to avoid his kind?

No, no. That was a too-stupid-to-live move. His fangs flashed. My mouth watered and I pressed my knees together. I couldn't help the moisture leaking from my core.

Running my hand over my ponytail, I groaned. *Bad idea*.

But maybe if I gave myself a little taste of the forbidden, I could get over these odd sexual fantasies. It could remind me of how awful being bitten had been while I'd been under the control of that other one.

Oh fuck. I gripped my heel harder and poised it over his chest. I could do this. Killing something never crossed my mind, but it wasn't bad right, he'd turn to dust, I wouldn't have to go and try to hide the body.

Rolling up my sleeves so I didn't get undead dust on them, I lifted the weapon over his heart, eyes squeezed shut. His large hand suddenly lashed out to wrap around my forearm and his mouth pressed to my pulse. Not again. I choked on a cry that cut off as his teeth sank into my skin. Warmth bloomed down my arm and my fingers slackened, the heel thudding on the floor. The vampire's nose twitched, and both his hands lashed around my wrist.

The sharp stab sucked the breath from my body, my skin came alive with electrifying need. My eyelids fluttered as a throb clenched through my core. *What was this?* This wasn't how being bitten had felt. The pulse in my wrist bounced, and my breathing hiccupped as a gush of wetness spread between my legs. This was *wrong.* He was a vampire and they were evil, even if this one had a sinful bite.

I tried to pull away, but he clamped my forearm with both hands, keeping me still. Fear chased away the sudden rush of lust and the hair raised on my arms as I was dragged back to the dark, dank cave where there was only pain.

I was about to die.

The panicked thought ripped me from the dark space.

My lip trembled and I shoved at his face with my free hand, but I may as well have been a feather with how little he budged. His tongue laved the area he'd impaled and then he *sucked.* I gasped as a strike of need blanketed my skin. My nipples pebbled and my eyelids fluttered. Bites didn't feel like this. They hurt. They'd never released a rush of pleasure throughout my body before. It wasn't *supposed* to be how I'd written them in my books.

I whimpered when he sucked again, a low throb building at my clit.

The vampire's eyes remained shut and his hand skimmed down my arm, holding me steady with one hand as his other palmed his erection. The rip of his slacks caused heat to flush to my face as his cock sprang out.

My lips parted at the long thick arousal, and a bead of moisture topped the ridged, veiny cock.

My clit pulsed and I rolled my lips into my mouth. The graze of his fangs shouldn't have me on the verge of combustion. His mouth was extremely soft. My heart raced, but it skipped a beat as his tongue brushed my flesh. This was absolute madness.

"Vampire," I shouted, in a last ditch effort to stop him from making me lose myself, but he didn't even twitch. The brown lashes rested across his sharp cheekbones, he looked around my age, baby face and all.

Licking my lips, I leaned forward and pressed my thumb to his cheekbone since I could not wrap my hand around his jaw with his size, but he didn't release my wrist. He dragged in another pull of my blood, wrenching a moan from my lips.

I couldn't tear my eyes away as he wrapped his fingers around himself and jerked his dick with hard tugs. Once. Twice. The lighting must be playing with me because there was no way it could be that big. A whimper escaped my lips as I squeezed my thighs together.

He was fucking sexy. The mar of concentration to his eyebrow and his slitted eyelids riveted me.

His warm tongue lapped at the punctures in my wrist. My mouth dried and air hissed between my teeth when he used his grip on my arm and pulled, jerking me toward him. I grunted as

I landed on him, our heaving chests pressed together. He gripped me at the back of my neck, sending a rush of wetness to my pussy. Roughly guiding my mouth to his, his tongue speared into my mouth, leaving a copper taste in its wake.

I didn't have time to fixate on that as he lapped the inside of my mouth. Groaning, I sank into him, fusing my lips to his in desperation. His dick dug into my leg, hard and insistent. His fingers pressed into my hips, and he jostled under me, lifting his knee slightly. My legs parted to straddle his thigh.

I gasped at the pressure on my clit and ground down on the hard muscle. Strikes of electricity shivered down my spine, my hips helplessly twitching to grind on him.

His tongue flicked into my mouth and his kiss had me aching for more.

This wasn't right, *he* wasn't human. I fisted my hands and jerked back, and he did the same, both of us panting hard. Inching backward until my spine hit the seat, I dropped my head into my hands, shaking. This was wrong. Vampires were monsters and fangs were supposed to hurt.

The only sound in the vehicle was my breathing. A vice wrapped around my chest.

"I've never fed directly from the vein." His voice was low and ragged. Despite myself, I forced my attention to him. He grimaced, and zipped his still hard cock back in his pants, then dragged himself up. I didn't care for an explanation, it did nothing to rewind time nor did it abate the trembling of my body. How could it have felt so incredibly different from before? "God, you're delicious."

His gaze dropped to where I pressed my palm over the leaking punctures. They were smaller than earlier, which told me they were healing.

"Eyes up here," I squeaked, jerking my arm to my chest. The vampire shook his head, squeezing his eyes tightly and then opening them a little slower.

"My head." He groaned, lifting a palm to his temple.

A screech assaulted my ears and a car careened to a halt beside mine.

"Jax," the vampire said with a frown and swayed, falling to the side. A flash of movement and then my door was wrenched wide.

The guy was taller than the one I'd saved, which I'd thought impossible, and that was the only observation I made as he lunged for me. Scuttling back, I couldn't avoid his hold. He gripped my ankle and dragged me, my leg burned across the rug as he manhandled me until I faced him. No, not again. My pulse sped up and my breathing hitched.

He held me by my shirt bunched tightly in his fists to where the collar dug into the back of my neck. He stared into my eyes.

"What did you do to Tobias?"

I swallowed hard and shook my head as the words stuck inside my throat. It was getting harder to breathe. His grip tightened and I didn't know how I mustered the strength to speak.

"I didn't do anything to him. I was just helping him, I swear," I whimpered. "Please let me go." I stifled my cringe. These creatures brought the weak out of me.

I should have run.

The vampire's brows furrowed and eyes slitted. This one breathed cold aggression.

"Forget what you saw here tonight. Everything." He dropped me on my ass, and I winced, but otherwise stilled as I sucked in a lungful of air. He leaned forward. "Sleep."

I blinked hard, tears gathering as I hugged my knees to my chest. A fist constricted around my lungs in a vice-like grip. I couldn't hold it in anymore. Reaching into my bag with a shaky hand, I desperately clawed at the inhaler and brought it to my lips.

His nostrils flared and he stilled as he watched me, but I didn't have the time to pay attention with my focus on my medication.

I trembled so hard I was surprised the van didn't shake. *What was he doing?* The demonic look on his face—lowered brows, sneering lips . . . *Evil.* My bottom lip trembled as he peered into my face with his intense blue eyes.

"Why isn't it working?" His fist slammed into my door, denting the metal.

"W-what?" I shouted frantically and cringed back. This one would kill me. I wouldn't see Peter any more. This was it.

"Sleep," he hissed, peering into my eyes. He had me so confused, what was happening? I dropped the inhaler back in my bag and hugged it to my chest like I could block him from looking at me.

My lips parted on a gasp and my shakes worsened. I was about to just drop and play possum, but he hoisted me into his arms, banding them around me.

I kicked and screamed, but as hard as I fought, he didn't budge.

catalina

HE TOSSED me into the black car, and I fell face-first into the seats, cheek squishing into the buttery leather. I pushed myself up with my hands, but my wrist bent under me, and I fell to my elbows.

There was a muffled grunt from outside the vehicle and he slid the limp Tobias into the front seat, shoving all his limbs within the confines of the vehicle before slamming the door. He was in the driver seat within moments, the engine revving. I scrambled to yank at the door handle, desperately tugging like it would magically unlock.

I jerked at the sudden acceleration and my head smacked into the back of the seat. A dull thrum at my forehead started and I groaned.

"Try anything and I'll snap your neck." Jax, that was what the other one had called him.

I gasped, meeting his eyes in the rearview mirror. His eyes were fixed on me, unwavering. *How was he driving so well without looking at the road?*

"I'm just buckling myself in," I said hurriedly, yanking the seatbelt. His lips tightened. From the slit of the horizontal mirror, I could only see his set scowl. "Please, don't kill me." The tremble in my voice verged on a wheeze.

I was in deep crap with this. *What had I gotten myself into?* All I wanted was to help someone I believed was being attacked by a vampire, but it was vamp-on-vamp crime. Yeah, the vampire, Tobias, had been gentle, almost courteous; still, this was not a situation I ever wanted to be in. This was why I stuck to myself. Why had I allowed the moment of weakness? I shouldn't have hesitated stabbing my heel into his chest.

I knew vampires were evil. They were all like that *one* hunting me.

His attack had been violent and harsh, his teeth slicing into me without mercy as he gnawed on my throat. There were multiple drags before he tore at my clothing, his blood-scented breath wafting to my nose as he palmed my breast harshly. My attempts at getting away were laughable against his strength. I was no match for the skeletal naked body with patches of hair littering his scalp.

His feeding didn't stop until I was half-dead and then he dragged me away from the isolated street. The cement burning my skin was ingrained in my memory alongside that cave he kept me in. He'd fed on me relentlessly, and for each day that had passed, the cruelty and evil in his red eyes increased.

I picked at the little flesh slightly lifted at my nail beds. Jax took a sharp turn, no longer focused on me.

I didn't know how I'd survived with how much he'd drained from me. Time had become meaningless, running together in that insect-infested cave.

To this day, I couldn't handle the sensation of bugs crawling over me.

Nausea crawled up my throat, and I fisted my hands around the seatbelt pressing into my chest. The memory of how much he broke my body and drained my blood haunted me.

Nausea continued to swirl in my gut as Jax took another sharp turn that caused my temple to smack into the plastic trim. I'd managed to escape that last time and today would be no different. A vice wrapped around my throat. And I would do everything possible to avoid getting sodomized again. I wrapped my trembling hand around the door handle and pulled. Of course, it didn't work.

Tears sheened my eyes and I squeezed my eyes shut.

I'd stared into death that day I'd managed to get away. He'd gone mad with my absence and when he'd found me, he'd clutched me as hard as he could keep me to his body, then pinned me against a building in an alleyway and sank his fangs into my throat, sucking my blood until spots danced in front of my eyes while his cock sank into my ass. I didn't know how long that lasted before he was interrupted by someone who yanked him off me. Flashes of colors was the last image ingrained in my memory before the loss of blood dragged me under and I'd woken to humans around me calling an ambulance.

To this day, I couldn't help but wonder if the man that got him off me was a vampire. After all, a human couldn't have done that. I'd understood many things, the main one being that vampires were monsters. Being within proximity to them raised the hair on my arms, like being near a wild animal.

The engine roared and Jax sped to dangerous levels, winding down the curving roads with enviable smoothness. As if sensing my gaze on him, his jaw ticked and he bared his teeth at me. I yelped, curling back into the seat. This vampire did not like me, and I didn't doubt he'd kill me.

My lungs squeezed, tightening.

So what?

I tensed at the invasive thought. There was nothing magical or exciting about my life since I was always on the run. The only pleasure I ever felt from life was when I spoke to Peter, but he was often in a hurry, dealing with teenage boy stuff. He'd be fine if I was gone, especially with the money he'd receive from my death.

Truth was, I could disappear and there was nobody in my personal life who would care. A knot formed in my throat, and I blinked quickly. Well, maybe my literary agent.

Jax took a turn too hard and my shoulder smashed into the door. I winced. Another bruise to add to the collection.

Tires squealed and he jerked to a stop, making the seatbelt dig into my chest as the move tried to eject me. I scrambled to unbuckle and the clasp clicked in time for my door to jerk open.

Suddenly, I was upside down, being toted with his shoulder pressing into my gut.

My ponytail loosened, my hair swinging as I scrambled to grab onto his back so I could lessen some of the pain.

I was becoming woozier and woozier.

"Stop," I huffed, breathless. "I-I need—" A fucking second. I squeezed my eyelids shut and shook my head to disperse the dots in front of my eyes. I couldn't reach into the purse strapped across my chest since my body flattened it between us.

There was a creak and I found myself looking at a crimson rug for a few beats before he took a turn and it became dark wood floors.

"Go get Tobias, he's passed out in the passenger seat," Jax ordered.

"She has a nice ass," whoever he addressed intoned; the low voice sent a shiver up my spine.

I was lifted and then dumped into the chair. A sharp pain radiated from my wrist where it hit the arm of the seat. I whimpered, holding it to my chest.

"Quiet," he snapped. I jumped, my back flattening against the couch cushion. No wonder it hurt, my wrist bone had smacked into the carved wood jutting to the side of the arm rests.

"That's the woman . . ."

"Not now, Asher. I don't care if she looks like someone you've fucked. Compulsion doesn't work on her." Jax's sharp tone dragged my attention to him.

How had his hair grown . . .? I blinked as my gaze bounced from one to the other. Twins. Except one had long hair that hit his shoulders instead of the short style. The long-haired twin stepped close, head tipped to the side, blue gaze inquisitive and exponentially less aggressive than the other one. A loose, white, unbuttoned shirt flashed his pale skin.

Jax leaned down, his face frighteningly close to mine so the little lines of his pupils were clear for me to see. I struggled to breathe. "Why were you with Tobias?"

My lip trembled, and my eyes kept dropping to his pointy fangs. A muscle in his cheek twitched. He gripped my hair, twisting strands with such strength that it sent agonizing pinpricks through my scalp. "Speak."

"I don't know anything! He was being attacked. I thought he was human, so I took him to my car." The words fell from my lips in a rush.

Jax became preternaturally still and all I could do was sit there as he stared at me. This was it; I could see my death in his eerie blue eyes.

"Fine. You're useless if you know nothing." His hand was suddenly wrapped around my throat. My pulse pounded in my ears, and I wrapped my hands around his wrist, trying to pull free, but it was no use. I used my nails, scratching and tugging desperately as my head became pressurized.

"If you're going to kill her anyway, let me taste her," the long-haired blond, Asher, said.

"Fine, but fucking drain her." Jax released me and I dragged in air. I didn't even have a second to collect myself before the cushion beside me dipped and a gentler hand cupped the side of my head.

"There there, take a breath," he murmured, his lips slightly pursed. "I wish we could have had more time together." He tsked. "Too bad I must kill you. It would have been quite the adventure to fuck a human that can't be compelled." He bopped me on the nose.

He was just as psychotic but he packaged it differently. Before I could even try to beg for my life, his lips brushed my neck and his fangs sank in.

They moved too fast. I was no match. Tears filled my eyes, and I bunched his white shirt, tugging at it weakly. He sucked in a long drag of blood, and just like the last bite, a flame ignited in my gut, spreading like wildfire. I stopped pulling at his shirt and went limp. My head swam with a mix of debilitating fear and lust so strong I clasped his arms, trying to get closer. He dragged in another swallow, pulling a cry from my lips as my core clenched, pulsing needily.

His fangs suddenly yanked out of my throat without

precursor and the heat of his body left my hands. I drooped against the couch.

My hands shook, making it difficult for me to grip my purse strap, and no matter how much I focused, there was no strength in my fingers. He'd messed my neck up and left me floating on the edge of an orgasm. I panted, weakly fumbling with my purse. A hiss lifted the hair on my arms, but as frightened as it made me, I didn't stop trying to unzip my bag. The sound of a scuffle erupted through the room, but I didn't look up as I tried to focus.

"I'm in control now." The rough voice held an undertone of a hiss.

Tobias knelt in front of me, slipping his hand into the purse and pressing the lip of the inhaler to my mouth like he'd done last time. I sucked in and relief loosened my chest.

"*Fuuuuuck*, she's delicious." Asher leaned his elbows on the arm rests, looking down at me like I was some specimen under a microscope. Blood coated his toothy grin. My stomach turned over, but I could do nothing other than struggle to breathe. "She tastes like . . . like . . ." he trailed off, his eyes unfocused.

Tobias pulled the inhaler from my lips, and the back of his finger grazed my cheek. I flinched, swallowing hard as I studied my surroundings.

"You have both lost your minds." The angry twin paced near the entrance.

The wooden floorboards were polished to such perfection that I doubted they'd seen much wear in their lifetime. Two couches faced each other in the middle of the room, an onyx coffee table with the surface made of glass between them. The seat I huddled in gave me a view of the entire room.

There had to be a way to escape. I worried my lip as I sought the latch to the half oval window I sat near. The dark curtains fluttered . . . it must be open. If I tossed myself out, I'd be able to run, but they were vampires. I didn't have a chance of escaping before one of them caught me.

I met Tobias's gaze, and he frowned as if he understood the rioting emotions in my head. His lips parted and he focused on my face, a dent forming between his brows. I avoided his searching eyes.

The inside of the home was Gothic, all dark bars and curving metal. It was beautiful in a spooky way. Like something out of a story book. The chimney, with ornate black-metal framing, was hauntingly beautiful.

A tickle at my neck dragged my hand up. My fingertips slid over my skin, brushing over a stinging wound.

"Let me close that for you," Asher purred. He leaned close, too suddenly.

Panic shocked my strength back to life. I swung the only luxury bag I owned, smacking him across the face. The entire room seemed to still.

Oh shit.

"It was a reflex," I said frantically, hugging my Prada to my chest. I shouldn't have done that to her. The precious baby didn't deserve the last moments of our lives to be spent like this. "Just bury her with me after you kill me," I babbled. "Don't give her to another vampire. As my dying wish, please—"

"I won't let him hurt you," Tobias said, stiff. The promise flowed over my skin. I didn't believe it for a second. "Allow him to heal you." I didn't say anything. What could I do? Say no?

Asher pressed his long finger under my chin and tipped it up, exposing my neck. I squeezed my eyes tightly shut. There was nothing else I could do other than scream. If I couldn't take one vampire, I was practically a newborn fawn to three of them. His wet tongue lashed against my neck . . . once . . . twice. A shiver coasted down to my core and my purse slipped from my grip.

"That's enough," Tobias ordered.

"There, there, all better." Asher's grin flashed fangs. "It was just a nick."

Understatement of the century.

"How do you know about our kind?"

I opened my mouth, but nothing came out, the knot in my throat was too thick. My teeth clicked together, and I took a moment to breathe but my response wasn't fast enough for Jax. He was shoving past Tobias and in front of me in a flash.

"Tell me." He hissed and fisted the back of my hair, yanking my head back with a harsh movement.

I cried out, tears welling. He stared down at me with a deadly look in his eyes.

"Be careful with her," Tobias snapped and pressed his fingertips into Jax's shoulder.

"Looks like Tobias finally wants a pet," Asher said in a too gleeful voice. No. I didn't want to be a pet. My hands shook and I returned my gaze to the English vampire.

"Compulsion doesn't work on her." Jax didn't react, his gaze focused on me as his hold tightened.

Tobias squeezed Jax's wrist, and all I could feel from the action was the tug. Jax narrowed his eyes at him, but Tobias stared back without twitching a muscle.

Jax finally released me, the angry twin hissing as he stepped away with a glower.

"I apologize for him." Tobias crouched in front of me, pressing a hand into the cushion. I focused on the indent in the couch where his hand pressed with neat oval nails, trimmed to precision. A feathering touch brushed my forehead. "Who did this to you?"

My eyes flicked to Jax without a second thought, but I quickly brought them back to my trembling hands. I hadn't meant to look at him.

Tobias straightened in front of me; the back of his torn, bloody knit sweater allowed me a peek at his skin.

I craned my neck and found him glaring, eyes narrowed. It *must* be a requirement to be taller than six three and built like Greek Gods. I couldn't lie to myself, as frightened as I was, their beauty was glaringly obvious.

"When are you going to tell us what happened?" Asher flopped on the couch next to me. The hem of his white button-down rising, his toned abs on full display, and droplets of my blood staining his shirt. His skin was pale and looked silky to the touch.

"You can touch." My gaze snapped to him at his low words. His hand splayed on his stomach, and he lifted his shirt inch by inch, raising it to expose more of the leanly-packed muscle.

Jax's open hand smacked him across the forehead.

"Fuck you, Jaxon," Asher hissed.

"We don't have time for your shit," Jax snapped at his twin.

Tobias motioned for my attention, taking it away from the bickering vampires and held out a hand. I stared at it, then up into his patient eyes. He'd treated me with care, but I wasn't foolish enough to think I actually had a say, so I placed my fingers in his. They gently constricted around mine. Vampires weren't supposed to be this gentle.

Asher clicked his tongue. The surprised sound dragging my

attention to him. He straightened from his slouch, staring at Tobias. "Did you just smile?"

Tobias's lips flattened and he met my gaze.

"I can't get a read on her."

"Impossible!" I startled at Jax's shout. Tobias's eyes shut briefly, and he released me as he turned, angling himself in front of me. Jax must overreact often. The short temper, the quick assumptions . . . anger issues was written all over this man, er, vampire. "If you would have remained at full strength and fed as you're supposed to, you never would have landed us in this situation with a mutant human."

"And don't forget *delicious*," Asher chimed in.

Tilting my head so I could see around Tobias, I noted the flush creeping up Jax's neck.

"Breathe, brother, if you don't simmer down, we'll have to have another blood run." Asher smirked, obviously enjoying poking at him. "And like you said, we can't be going out too much, considering everything going on and with Ren gone—"

"Shut it," Jax roared. The hair on my arms lifted and I pushed off the seat as I slinked behind Tobias. His back tightened against my palm. My thumb slipped into the ripped hole in his soft sweater and pressed gently onto his spine. A tremble coasted up his back, and I swallowed hard as I snatched my hand back.

"We must kill her."

"Jax, calm yourself." Tobias's deep voice vibrated over my skin.

"She's just a human." Jax *really* didn't want me around. *Fucking dick.*

I sucked in a breath when Asher elbowed Tobias out of the way. His glittering blue eyes seemed much deeper up close. An inquisitive, mocking expression marred his face as he peered down at me and lifted his hand to cup my cheek.

I sucked in a breath and Tobias hissed, but it did nothing to stop him as Asher rubbed my lower lip with the pad of his thumb.

"Lovely, just as I thought you'd be," he purred. What?

His pupils expanded, engulfing his eyes with near darkness. He breathed me in and my body reacted to his nearness, nipples pebbling. It was too hot in here, but I didn't fan my face like I wanted. Instead, I stilled like I was near a predator, because that was what he was, and I had a feeling he'd like it if I ran.

One of his hands slipped to the dip in my waist, but he didn't stop there, and with each inch he lowered, my heart thundered louder in my ears. My skin prickled with awareness and his grazing touch left a fire in its wake. My body was betraying me. It didn't get this hot unless I was near designer stuff. I sank my fingernails into my palm. *They* were not sweet like the vampires in my books. If I repeated it to myself enough, it may sink in.

But why were they just as seductive?

"Enough." Tobias shoved Asher by his shoulder, and Asher tilted his head back, laughing.

"Don't like what's going through my mind, Ancient One?"

Tobias said nothing as he stared back. What did he mean by "going through my mind?"

"Can you read minds?" The question slipped out before I could stop it.

The brothers were different kinds of dangerous. It was a good thing I'd just taken a pump of my medicine because it was holding my lungs over even as my pulse skyrocketed.

Tobias's brows lifted at my question. "Not yours."

So, some vampires read minds then. Jax had mentioned something earlier about compulsion, and I'd read enough to understand what that was, yet he said that didn't work on me. My attention jumped from Jax's stiff face to Tobias's concerned one to Asher's curious one. I needed to say something, I had to muster up the courage so my voice didn't shake.

"I already knew about your kind," I muttered. "I've known for years. Do you think that's why it doesn't work?"

"How did you know about us?" Jax crowded me. My gaze ping-ponged as I switched from face to face. They were all within touching distance, towering over me like statues. "Are you owned? Who do you belong to?" The rapid-fire questions forced me back until the back of my knees pressed against the edge of the couch. I was already shaking my head, only understanding about half of what he was saying. "Who sent you to spy on us?" His leaned into my face, so close that my ass dropped onto the couch. I grunted upon landing, leaning away until I couldn't. His palms slapped on the furniture, his arms corralling me and his body blocking my view.

"N-no one sent me." I lifted my hands in front of me and waved them in a calm-down motion.

His sweet breath fluttered the hairs that had escaped my ponytail. I gritted my teeth and forced my eyes to meet his. The pupils expanded for a different reason than Asher's had and the hair on my arms lifted. Jax's hands slammed into the cushions, and his thumbs pressing into my thighs as he leaned over me, face an inch from mine—using his body to intimidate me. Looking into my eyes like he could see into my soul. He was the dangerous one. I wiggled my bare toes and fixed my eyes on his nose.

"Just kill me if that's what you're going to do." Tears

helplessly gathered in my eyes and the vampire blurred into a large blob hovering over me.

"No one is killing you, Pet," Asher's disembodied voice murmured from somewhere behind him. He was so similar, yet so different to his twin.

Jax shoved off the couch and scoffed, disgusted.

catalina

ASHER SLINKED over and ran his hand down my arm. It was strange seeing such a concerned expression on a face that had glared at me so fervently. Miraculously, some tension fell away under his reassurance. Now that I had a moment to think, I couldn't help but be grateful they hadn't slapped me around or locked me in a cave.

Expecting the bare minimum, Catalina.

I was messed up in the head.

"Humans are never immune to compulsion. How are you blocking us?" My reservations melted away, and I struggled to wrap my head around what slipped from his seductive bow lips.

"What are you talking about?" I croaked.

Asher lowered to his knees and placed his elbows on the edge of my seat, setting his chin on his fisted hands. "So, tell me, how are you doing it?"

I huddled closer to the arm rest, shaking my head. "I don't know what you're talking about."

The smile he directed at me never wavered.

"My brother is so incredibly suspicious of you." He paused,

leaned forward, and stretched his fingers in my direction, caressing my chin and along my neck. His canine teeth were already pointed, so I watched, enraptured as those two fangs extended from his gums, lengthening past his blunt teeth. He brought his fingers back up and dragged them down the side of my neck.

"Please don't." I breathed hard as my hands became clammy. Not again.

"It won't hurt, Pet. I'll make sure you like it." Tears made him blur in my sight, and there was a sigh. My body wanted to simultaneously curl and open up. Vampires were terrifying, but somehow, the fangs . . . I shuddered and images of snarling vampire at my neck filled my head and I squeezed my eyes shut. Tears streamed past as I struggled to breathe. I would suffocate if I didn't get myself together.

His long fingers gripped my shaking hand and my eyes popped open at the soft squeeze. Asher's lips pressed together tightly.

"Breathe, Pet. *I* won't force you again," he tacked on, but after emphasizing the 'I' in the sentence, I didn't feel too great about it. The tips of his fangs poked from his smile, even with them retracted, they remained pointy.

"She's human," Tobias announced curtly.

"How are you so sure?" Jax crossed his arms.

"As delicious as she is, she doesn't smell like any supernatural creature—and in my long life, I've encountered any that could exist." Tobias's curt response startled the twins and their expressions looked creepily alike. The corner of their bow lips slightly turned down and brows furrowed with a dent between them. Asher released my hand with a final pat and stood to face the other two. I stared down at my tingling fingers, rubbing the pads together. His touch wasn't repellant . . . nor was Tobias's. It was nothing like the one who hurt me.

"I agree, but she tastes—" Asher paused, and a shiver moved his shoulders. "Heavenly." They spoke about me like I wasn't present.

I rubbed my neck. Although I didn't trust these vampires, I needed to calm myself before I gave myself another anxiety attack that triggered my asthma. After all, the worst they could do was kill me . . . okay, false, they could torture or rape me before they killed me, but at this point there was nothing I could do. I was in their lair in who-knew-where.

"I still think we should kill her." It didn't seem like Jax was going to let go of that, but fortunately, Tobias waved that away, like he was used to his over-the-top suggestions.

"No, we'll not hurt her." His English accent sharp as he snapped the words.

"I agree," Asher added. "*Broder, sluta prata om att döda henne.*" It sounded like a Germanic language, but for the life of me, I couldn't pinpoint which one.

That was the slight tilted accent in the twins. It was obvious in Jax, but Asher seemed to have suppressed it. Jax still glared at me.

"How is it that I saved his life,"—I poked a finger toward Tobias—"and you're pissed at me?"

I met Jax's eyes as they slitted. I swallowed hard but didn't regret the question. They'd already intimidated me. I sniffed and tipped my nose up with false bravado.

"See what you've done? She thinks she can start asking questions."

"Let her speak her mind." My eyes rounded on Tobias. Well, then.

"I expect this bullshit from Asher. His obsession with pussy doesn't leave much room for consideration in which way he'd argue for, but you, Tobias? You've never shown interest in anything, least of all a woman."

Tobias's jaw ticked.

"She saved me from Calliope's progeny. *The least* I can do is speak for her since you won't allow her a moment. Humans are sensitive."

"She saved your life because you've been weakening from not feeding. And give it a rest with the blood bags. Drinking directly from the vein will hold you longer. Let me get someone here to feed you," Asher interjected, straightening the hem of his shirt.

Tobias's teeth clicked together. "No one comes here, Asher, don't start with your mind games. As you well know, I haven't been drinking as many of the bags, because we need to ensure we have enough."

"So considerate. Must be the priest in you." Jax smirked.

Tobias's nostrils flared.

"Oooo, it's getting juicy." Asher crammed his large body beside me on the love seat. It was a tight fit with his huge body invading my personal space. He wiggled his leg beneath mine so my thigh was half on him. I gawked as he maneuvered me with ease.

"What are you doing?" I wheezed, tugging my purse into my lap and hugging it to my chest.

"Don't worry, Pet." He stroked my arm, dragging his warm fingers down the flesh in gentle caresses. My attempt to jerk away was met with resistance and he forced my arm back down. I didn't get to continue arguing, because the other two continued their argument.

"It's not about giving, it's about decency. I also must chase after Asher to make sure he doesn't do something idiotic while you stay here sulking, trying to find Ren's whereabouts."

My back was as straight as a board, but it didn't take long to relax under Asher's soft petting, and soon, I leaned into him as exhaustion weighed on my limbs.

"Tobias is—was—a priest in the sixteen hundreds. His moral compass sadly remains intact." His breath tickled my ear and I shivered, releasing an unintentional laugh. My shoulders tightened and he chuckled but said nothing. Something hard pressed into my leg and it took me a few seconds to work out that it was his cock. I sucked in a breath, heat flushing over my face. It really shouldn't have intrigued me as much as it did. I cleared my throat, my fingers flexing around my purse strap.

Warmth bloomed in my belly, spreading and inching low, near my core. My toes curled. Asher's hand tensed on my arm, and I groaned at the pressure between my legs. If I moved a smidge to the side to straddle him, it would relieve some of the pressure.

Jaw clenching, my body tensed. No way was I getting turned on by an evil *vampire* right now. I refocused on the argument. It had faded to the background with the pleasure flushing through my nerve endings, but I was done with the petty sniping back and forth. What boiled my blood more was that Jax was hitting low blows, while Tobias was trying to find a logical way to get him to calm down. "The human needs to give us answers—"

"Okay," I shouted and shoved off Asher's lap before his wandering hand reached my inner thigh. When all eyes rounded in my direction, I cleared my throat and shuffled from foot to foot. "I knew about vampires because I've met one before."

Jax crossed arms, making them bulge intimidatingly. "That's it? That's all you're going to say. No explanation? Was he your lover? Were you his pet? What?"

I rolled my lips into my mouth.

"I can make you talk." Jax's threat flushed through my brain and shot off warning bells. A boulder settled on my chest. I didn't have the luxury of choice.

"I wasn't with him willingly."

Asher released a half-rumbled hiss. "And he released you?"

"He likely didn't know she is resistant to compulsion," Jax snapped.

"Wait a minute, she's *immune* to vampire abilities," Asher said like it was a revelation, which it clearly wasn't. Jax uncrossed his arms and moved a step in my direction. They stared at me like I had a dick growing out of my head. Tobias smoothed his torn sweater down his chest.

"That means she can get close to them to figure out where Ren is. They'll think they compelled the memory from her, but she'll be able to tell us everything she hears." The interest in Jax's eyes scared me more than anything else. The twins seemed to speak on the same wavelength.

I licked my lips at the sudden interest glinting in my direction. They wanted me to get close to "them?" *Oh no.*

"I-I'm not getting involved with more vampires." My fingers clenched as I wrapped my arms around my torso, shielding myself.

Jax's eyebrow lifted and his lip twitched up in a sneer. The judgment in his expression hit my pride because although I may look a little disheveled, I wasn't *that* fucked up. The twins exchanged a look and it caused my stomach to dip. Freaky blankness entered their eyes—almost glazed. A chill skittered down my spine.

"What do you desire?" Jax tacked on. Head twitching predatorily to the side. "Money?"

Unbelievable. Did I have needy written all over my face or something? I clenched my hand to hide the tremble.

Okay, yeah, it wouldn't hurt to have more funds, or to build up my savings, but not in exchange for working with vampires. My mouth opened and closed but I was already shaking my head. I wasn't to the point of desperation that I was okay with being exposed to vampires for a longer period of time. Being with them was already enough for me, any more and I may have a heart attack from the panic. I didn't know what they wanted me to do, but it sounded like I would be surrounded by them and no thank you.

"No," I said forcefully. *Fuck no.* They were stronger than me and outnumbered me. Force wasn't out of the equation and I understood that, but if they ended up forcing me into it, there was nothing I could do.

Jax's jaw twitched and he shrugged. "So she chooses death."

I gasped, my heart rate spiking.

"Jax," Tobias intoned.

"What? Do you want to let her go even though she knows of our existence? Our laws exist to ensure shit like this doesn't happen."

Vampire laws about their existence? That would make sense. I couldn't imagine the hysteria if people knew about them.

"We need to keep her here until we decide."

Tobias inclined his head.

I inhaled sharply and looked at the ex-priest. His eyelid

twitched like he felt me looking at him, but he didn't face me. I'd never given much thought to vampires other than they were evil, but they had extensive pasts. They'd witnessed so many historical events.

"There's no need. You can let her return home." I was really starting to like Asher. Relief lifted the corners of my lips. One of them had some compassion.

"After all, she lives right next door."

I blinked at him. I lived where?

"I jacked off to her earlier." My mouth dropped at the easy way Asher admitted it. "That's what I was trying to tell you earlier before you so rudely interrupted. She's our new neighbor."

I rushed to the window and pulled the curtain to the side. The scratch of the metal rings lifted the hair on the back of my neck.

Even from the first floor of the house, it was more elevated since it was on an incline. The slanted roof of my home stared back at me from a small distance away. A huge leap over and you'd be on my house.

"You okay, neighbor?" I slowly craned my neck, nose almost grazing against Asher's. *Did he need to stand so close?*

"I'm going to go," I rushed out, hugging my Prada as I shoved past his looming form. Half of me expected to be stopped but no one did. It was a good thing, or I might have had a breakdown.

"Don't try to run from us, human, or you won't like it when we catch up to you." Jax's sharp words swirled in my head, stacking on to my dizziness.

The door was heavy, and I struggled to get it open. The

chandelier lighting the entrance spilled into the darkness, and I left the front door open to guide my way.

I tripped descending the massive amount of stairs but caught myself in the last second. Fortunately, since that stumble down was steep. I reached the base with moisture beaded on my forehead, plastering the hairs to my skin. A burst of noise broke through my ragged breathing, and I yelped, cringing away from the gate. Black wings flapped with fervor, and I clutched my chest. A bat. A fucking bat. It disappeared into the night, and I staggered forward. The gate clanged as I shoved it shut behind me.

There were yards between their home and mine. *Yards*.

This was not good. I'd been trying to run away from vampires but instead, I'd moved in next to a group of them. They didn't chain me up or stop me, but it wouldn't last long. They were vampires, it was in their makeup to harm others.

The worst part was, I was stuck. There were currently no funds in my account to run.

I could try to sell my handful of luxury items I'd managed to collect over the years . . . but they were outdated and not in the cool vintage way—their resell value was nonexistent.

My hand wouldn't stop shaking on the doorknob, making it difficult to open my front door. As my adrenaline wavered, lightheadedness surged forward, making my movements sluggish. I felt so weak . . . and aroused.

SIX

"YOU NEED to approach humans with much more finesse, *dumhuvud*." Irritation seeped into Asher's tone, and I scoffed. I'd leave that to him. I didn't have time for that bullshit, and I'd learned force resulted in many more answers than trying to cajole them out of someone.

"We can't just let her go," I snapped.

"For once, you're both right." Tobias scratched his fingers through his scalp. "Jaxon, she can't be compelled. I can't read her mind. And unless we kill her—"

"We can't kill her," Asher said so quickly, his words ran together. "Her taste . . ." he shuddered. "It needs to be savored."

"Besides that, she can be useful. But a human we cannot control is playing with fire. She can leave while we're undisposed." Tobias's gaze unfocused as it did when he got lost in thought. It happened to him more than any of the others. Asher called it his 'ancient gazing'.

Asher plopped on the settee, crossing his ankle over the other. "No need to worry about that." Asher waved his hand in the air like he was batting the words away. "She doesn't have a landline, *annnnnd*." He plucked a device from his pocket. "I snagged it from her purse." A cell phone dangled from his fingertips.

"When exactly did you discover her lack of landline?" Tobias said slowly . . . patiently. I could understand the need to smack my brother. An urge he likely fought with every carefully spoken word. "I believe you were ordered to stay away from the human."

"I've just been watching her," Asher pouted. "It's only her living there. We don't have to kill her. We can play with her a little while she helps us, can't we? A willing human is much more entertaining than a screaming, crying, vomiting one we have chained up in a room somewhere." Tobias's eyebrow raised. "It's not like she has a car to go off in. And look." He waved a phone in the air. "She can't call someone."

Tobias turned to me. "What do you think we should do?"

"I think we should kill her."

Tobias tapped his chin, gaze unfocused.

"I am in agreement with Asher." The win made my brother preen like an idiot. "I'll call Talia to send over a human to watch the house to ensure she doesn't leave." Tobias began walking down the hall, his steps echoing from the high ceilings. I'd been out-voted, again. Fucking shit.

"I'll keep an eye on her until nightfall," I snapped. Humans were, in essence, lazy . . . and stupid, so she'd doubtfully make any successful escape. A concept that should comfort, but her presence irked me, and I wanted to extinguish the tempting smell of her skin. Of course, the inconsiderate human had left the door wide open. I sneered and slammed it behind me.

A shiver coasted down my spine as my body shrunk and shifted, morphing into a cat. I hated this fucking form. When I was like this, I felt too vulnerable, but I had no choice if I wanted to keep an eye on her, and cats were as inconspicuous as they came unless I wanted to morph into an insect, but fuck that. I had lines and that was one of them.

I padded over the grass and loped downhill, slipping between the vine-infested bars of the gate. It was a tight squeeze, but I wiggled through. I slipped between the hedge and the brick gate, so I'd be harder to spot. That was the difficult part of my morphs, whatever animal I chose was always the same color as my hair—sandy blond, which made slinking around as a cat difficult.

Standing on my back legs, I clawed the gate and sheathed them into the wood to assist in my balance.

I was only watching her because she was a danger to us. Even without a car or a cell phone. There were new-age gadgets I didn't keep up with and they hadn't considered the possibility of that. Who knew what sort of trouble she could get up to, but the other fuckers didn't seem to care.

Bounding onto an outstretched tree branch, I crouched, keeping my belly low.

If Ren were here, he would have had the same train of thought as me. He probably would have snapped her long tan neck instead of beating around the bush like the other two.

Tobias was behaving out of character. But it was probably his fucking morals, and considering she'd saved his ass, it likely had more to do with that.

I hopped to another branch, peeking through the windows. She flitted around the bedroom, organizing the last of her belongings. She seemed to have an obsession with pink.

Her ass wiggled as she smoothed the blanket over the mattress and fluffed the pillows. Finished with her bedding, she moved to the kitchen and set on pulling dishware from a paper bag and only filling in one pantry. She wasn't behaving the way I expected of her after she'd run out. I'd thought to find her curled in the corner of the room, rocking back and forth.

Watching her move from room to room was tiring. It was a good thing we had someone come to the house to clean it once a week, I wouldn't want to go through this. I'd hated doing this when I was a human and as soon as I was able, I paid someone to keep everything in my home tidy, especially since Asher was a slob.

The girl moved again . . . the girl, we never asked her name.

I'd never cared to get an invitation into this house, but being up close would have been much better than trying to keep up with her erratic movements.

I lost sight of her and when she didn't stride back into the bedroom, I stretched my limbs to hop off the tree. The wood of the fence rasped against my paws as I followed the path of the boards surrounding the house. My ears twitched. She wasn't in the kitchen. I rounded another corner to the next window and came to a stuttering halt. My stop was so quick, I lost my footing. My claws dug into the wood as I struggled to regain my balance.

The girl was in the tub, ecstasy on her expression as she tilted her head back, her midnight hair spilling over the lip. My claws flexed into the wood, gouging indents into it. Her hair was beautiful . . . I wanted it splayed across my chest.

She plucked a loofah from the side counter and lathered it up. Her long arms flexing as she scrubbed it across her shoulders. Straightening, her full breasts peeked out from the water, brown nipples pebbled. She took her time stroking it across her breasts, caressing the hard nipples. Her lips parted and she shifted, sending a ripple through the bathwater. Her fingers splayed over her skin as they slid under the water.

A purr rumbled from my chest. I lowered against the wood, my paws flexing into the fence. I was undoubtedly turned on.

Why was she making me react this way? It wasn't like I hadn't seen women fuck themselves or being fucked before, but I longed to sink my fangs into her skin and fuck her as I held her face into the mattress.

Hooking my claws into the tree hanging over the window, I climbed higher to get a bird's eye view into the bathtub. Her lips parted as she delved into her pussy and caressed her clit with her thumb. So fucking sexy. Her pointer digit slipped into her core and she thrust it in and out.

I stepped forward and lost my hold. I flipped and turned in the air before landing on my paws. *Fuck.*

My nails embedded into the wood as I scrambled up, I wanted to watch her face as she came. The parting of her lips, the arching of her back . . .

As soon as I was at the top, I found her fingers floating in the water instead of deep in her cunt.

I missed it.

I hissed, forgetting that I was morphed. She pulled the drain and reached for a towel to wrap her body as she stepped on a different towel she'd laid on the ground.

Strange female human. Unexpected . . .

Next time I'd watch her as she came.

She exited the bathroom in a set of shorts and a strappy shirt with frills at the edges. I rushed to get to the other side so I could continue watching her in time to see her collapse on the mattress. She swayed and dropped to her back, unconscious. Her chest continued moving up and down rhythmically.

Asher must have taken more blood than she could handle. He usually had a better gauge of that.

She left the light on in the room. If she would be a tool for us to use, sating my lust on her could be something to consider.

After all, I hadn't craved another body in decades . . . since *Imogen*.

catalina

TREMBLING FROM LUST AND FEAR, *I gingerly felt my raw, bleeding throat. My body was giving in even as it craved. The rancid scent in the cave burned my nose and I blinked, trying to make out more than just rocks and shadows in the cave.*

I hated the darkness.

His heavy weight shifted, large, boney fingers flexing around my thigh. My heart slammed against my chest.

He would kill me soon—drain me dry. Pressure settled on my lungs, and I struggled to draw in breaths.

I shot up in bed, clasping my chest as my other hand scrambled at the nightstand, hunting for my medicine. My fingertips grazed it and relief drooped my shoulders as I put it to my mouth. *Puff.*

A throb started at my temples. The encounter with the vampires were making my attacks more frequent. I hadn't had to use my inhaler this much in months, which checked out considering it was stress induced. The sun hung low in the sky. Last night, I'd paced around, cleaned, mulled over how to come up with the money to leave, but after my bath, my eyelids had grown increasingly heavy. I'd meant to sit for a second, but I'd slept through the entire day. I looked to the thrashed bedsheets, seeking out my cell phone. But the spot remained empty.

I couldn't find it at all, not just now. I'd turned my things upside down, but it was nowhere to be seen . . . it likely fell out in my van miles away from here. And I couldn't use my laptop because there was no WIFI.

I had no way to get out of here since my car was still in the parking lot and I'd had no way to call for a ride, even if I *could* afford the expense. I scrubbed my fingertips through my hair.

I felt helpless and tears pushed to the surface. The vampires would likely kill me, and I'd leave Peter behind, but I didn't want to disappear on him without a word. Not again.

When that vampire took me and I was gone for a little more than a month, Peter had to fend for himself. He got himself to and from school, fed himself. All of it. When I'd gotten back from the hospital, he'd told me it was because he didn't want to go into child protective services—he didn't want to be taken from me.

My heart throbbed at the memory of his young tear-filled eyes. I'd kept him with me for a few months as I kept on moving, but eventually I'd recognized how I was hurting him more than anything. And I'd wanted him away from me if the vampire or *any* vampire ever caught up to me. Looked like my instincts were right.

So I'd sent him to boarding school in Mexico despite his pleas not to. I'd figured, since we had some extended family over there, he could always fall on them if something happened. If anything, my brother was taken care of if I died.

They couldn't find out about him. I would rather die than have them get their evil hands on him.

I groaned and scrubbed my face. Enough melancholy, time to figure out how to run from these fanged monsters.

Shuffling out of the bedroom, I went directly to the Keurig and smacked it on. I'd set everything up last night so that was all I had to do in the morning. I'd learned it was my best bet in waking up, since I was *not* a morning person. Not even a little bit.

Using the pads of my fingers, I drummed on the counter as the brown liquid sputtered into the mug. The curtain hanging before the window fluttered, exposing my phone on the sill. I hurried to grab it. It hadn't been there yesterday . . . or had it? I frowned, wracking my brain. I was pretty sure I'd looked, but then again, it had been dark because of the lack of lightbulbs.

Now I felt like I was gaslighting myself.

My coffee machine beeped to tell me it was done, and I wrapped my palm around the warmth of the mug and shivered at the heat. It felt good in the chilly weather. Opening the front door, I studied the area. It was quiet and empty. I stepped out onto the porch, breathing in the crisp late evening air. There was nothing better than this and once the coffee kicked in, I would figure out my game plan. With their threat hanging over my head, I didn't want to chance them catching me, so I had to be one hundred percent sure I could disappear without a trace.

Birds were the only sound as my eyes slid closed and I inhaled deeply. A desk set up out here would be perfect for evening writing sessions. At least that was what I would have done if I hadn't moved in next to a bunch of vampires.

Turning, I frowned at the envelope in the mailbox. It must have been delivered while I slept.

I plucked the envelope from the box, read the sender address, and groaned. The boarding house worked quickly. Didn't even give me a week to settle in, as soon as they'd gotten my new address, they sent over next quarter's bill. I stuck my phone in my armpit and using my nail, I ripped it open while balancing my coffee.

My eyes rounded, my hand holding the mug growing limp. I didn't hear the crash of ceramic with wood as brown liquid sprayed across the porch. Another tuition raise?

I whimpered, leaning against the wall and sliding down until my butt hit the slats of the porch. A chill crept into the bottom of my cheeks at the lack of coverage from my shorts.

My phone vibrated and I lifted it to my ear without looking at the caller.

"Hello."

"Hey." Peter sounded winded and there was an edge to his voice. Something was wrong.

"Why are you whispering?" Silence and then he cleared his throat. "*Peterrrr . . .*"

"My cell phone was taken away."

"What happened?" I curled my toes within my slippers—very much on edge. He was lucky he wasn't in front of me because I'd be dragging him by the ear to get him to spit it out.

"Nothing," he whispered and cleared his throat. "Catty, I fucked up." The dejected tone wrenched into my heart.

"Peter, what happened?"

"Um . . ."

"Peter," I repeated and even though my voice sounded normal, my eyes watered.

"Fine," he breathed in my ear and he went silent. "Catty."

He paused. "I'm so sorry. I can get a job and help pay—" Dread tightened my stomach.

"What happened?"

"I should have known better . . . I'm so sorry, Cat."

"You're freaking me out here."

"I took a car out for a joy ride." I snorted an incredulous laugh, but quickly stilled it. I pressed my lips between my teeth. It better not be what I thought he was insinuating.

"I crashed it." He shouldn't have done it, but at least he was safe— "Into the side of the administration building."

Worry swelled to life.

"Are you injured?" I said, rushed.

"Nothing happened to me, but . . ." He hesitated. "They're sending you a bill."

I thumped my head on the wall.

I said nothing, instead squeezed my eyes closed. This was no good. My headache worsened to a category five level.

"I'll deal with it," I said stiffly. What else could I say?

"I'm sorry." The frustration seeped from his tone. "I can get a job to help pay—"

"No," I snapped. I blew a raspberry. "I will handle it, Peter. What were you thinking?" He inhaled sharply and I could feel another revelation coming.

"It was stupid, I was trying to impress this girl." A girl. My little brother had an entire life he was building over there . . . without me. I struggled to swallow.

"I'll handle it, but I have to go. I need to figure some things out." Clicking the call off in the middle of what he was saying, I navigated to my emails and opened the one from his school. I was already gritting my teeth before I read it.

They had wasted no time sending me the bill, whoever had drafted this email must have sent it during the night.

But sixty thousand dollars?

That was more than my next book advance that was scheduled to deposit in four months. I whimpered as I typed my response informing them I would have their money by their deadline when all I wanted to do was call and go off about the charges. But it would be a waste of time, the school had been such a peach and sent attachments of *everything*. Peter fucked up, and I had to fix it or he'd get kicked out.

I needed to get a hold of my agent, Erin, to ask about getting my advance sooner.

So much for getting a new anything. I thumped my head again and dropped the phone in my lap.

Fur tickled my leg and I sucked in a startled breath. Looking down at the largest, strangest colored cat I'd ever seen rubbing against my leg. It released a vibrating meow and pressed the front of its head to my leg, rubbing hard.

It was dark blond—a coloring I'd never seen. Her piercing blue eyes met mine and her tail flicked. She looked like a Maine Coon.

I lifted my hand and hovered it near her face to make sure she was okay with me touching, and when she did nothing, I touched my fingertips to the back of her neck. She arched and grumbled, stepping toward me and rubbing against my side.

I dragged my nails through her fur and she climbed in my lap. She seemed docile, so I pressed my fingers under her little joints and tested lifting her. When she didn't freak out, I held her over my face, checking her genitals just to make sure.

A boy. He hissed and lashed out, claws raking across my

arm. I gasped, and dropped him as carefully as I could. Blood dripped down to my elbow.

"Okay, okay, my bad," I murmured. He didn't have a collar, but he seemed clean and healthy.

It happened often that families left cats behind because of moves, and I wondered if this was one of those instances. I ran my fingers gently over his body. Everything seemed intact.

I removed my touch lest he slice into my arm again. He grumbled throatily.

"You hungry?" His bottom flattened to the ground, tail lashing out behind him as his incredibly blue eyes peered back at me, framed by blond little lashes.

"Let me get you some turkey." I padded inside, slippers shuffling across the uneven floor.

A meow stopped me in my tracks, and I looked over at the entrance where I'd left the door open where he'd waited, looking directly at me. So cute, it was like he was waiting for an invitation.

"You want to come with me?" The cat meowed as if answering. "You're a smart one," I cooed and crouched. "Come here." He hopped over the entrance, tail swishing as he pressed into my fingers.

I laughed at the desperate way he asked for head scratches.

"Are you touch-deprived, little guy?" I hummed and gave into his demands. "Let's go get some food."

Fortunately, the prior renters had left their stove and refrigerator. I'd had little time to get food, but the ice chest I carried on my drive held all the makings for a sandwich. Pulling out a plate, I set it on the counter and cut up some thick turkey.

Crouching, I placed it in front of him, but he hissed at it.

"Is this not good enough for you?" I grinned, scratching the top of his head. I snatched my vibrating cell phone and answered.

"Catalina? It's Elsa, from St. Helena's Animal Shelter."

"Good morning."

There was a brief pause on the other end and then she cleared her throat. Was this more bad news? I wanted to groan, but I stifled it since I was on the phone.

"I'm sorry, we're having a few issues with the volunteer scheduling. We won't be needing you until next week."

This worked in my favor, considering I may be long gone by then.

"No worries, see you next week." I finished, though I'd heard the click while I was mid-sentence.

I squeezed my eyelids shut, slamming the phone down on the counter, then sucked in a breath and lifted it, making sure I hadn't broken it. There was no way I could afford another expensive phone right now. Fortunately, it was fine, so I *gently* set it aside and pressed my palms onto the surface. Blood tickled my arm, and I grabbed a napkin to absorb it. I hissed at the touch of the paper towel grazing the scratches.

My volunteering was the only way I left the house and experienced a little socialization, but at this moment, it would have been a distraction since contacting my agent was at the top of my to-do list. The throbbing had worsened, and it was slowly spreading down my neck. Nausea swirled in my stomach, and I pressed my fisted hands to my eye sockets. Hopefully, Erin could get me my advance a sooner.

If that didn't happen, I was screwed. I needed to come up with sixty thousand dollars, next quarter's tuition, and living expenses. Even if I obtained a second job, there was no way I'd come up with that, it'd take me a decade. God, why was I freaking about this, it was highly probable I would be dead soon.

Swiping to Erin's information, I called her. It rang once and her voice crackled through.

"There's my favorite paranormal romance writer," she announced, forcefully cheerful. "What can I do for her?"

"Is it possible to get my advance sooner?" I didn't bother beating around the bush. She had many clients and was always doing something. The line went quiet.

"Sorry, Catalina, there's nothing I can do. The publisher has you scheduled in four months."

The edges of the cell dug into my hand, and I puffed a breath out and the hair framing my face fluttered around my cheeks.

I was shit out of luck.

"Hey babe, I'll call you later, I'm dealing with an interview emergency." The line went dead, and I drooped, the lip of the counter digging into my side as I lowered to the floor. I'd spent hours cleaning yesterday, so the floor sparkled. I dazed on the linoleum flooring and it blurred in my sight.

What do you want, money?

That vampire mentioned he'd pay me if I helped them, but with what?

I scoffed and shook my head, blinking the tears away . . . I couldn't believe I considered this.

"They would have already killed me if they wanted," I mumbled. "I mean, they know where I live, so they could have snapped my neck last night, right, kitty?"

The cat meowed like he was agreeing.

It was a bad idea to get tangled up with the soulless creatures. Being near them would only serve to remind me of the torment the red-eyed Pale One put me through. Although . . . I didn't think they would just let me go now that they found out I couldn't fall under their weird mind control. I shivered, rubbing my arms.

"Do I even have a choice?" The cat tilted his head and pressed his front paws into my thigh, sinking his claws into my skin. I winced, and avoided the claws. "I'm gonna do it." I couldn't believe I was pumping myself up to a cat. "I *have* to do it."

I didn't even know what 'it' was, but I didn't think I had the option to be selective.

Nervous energy pricked my skin and I rubbed my arms.

"Why haven't they come to drag me out of my house yet?" I sucked on my lower lip.

The cat rubbed against my calf.

Earlier, I'd said it couldn't be worse, and now I reaped the consequences. I'd successfully jinxed myself. I had no choice but to turn to the vampires.

catalina

NO OTHER CHOICE. The phrase repeated like a mantra with every step I took toward their home.

The knot in my throat had expanded by a ton, weighing each step down. The structure of the house blocked the moon from shining over me and no matter how far I tipped my head back, I couldn't see the roof. Even the cat must have been intimidated because he'd disappeared as soon as I headed this way.

The gate creaked from a gust of wind, and I took it as my cue to nudge the latch open. The hem of my shirt snagged on a thorny vine wrapped around the bars. *Shit.* I fiddled with the cloth, unhooked it from the sharp greenery, and brushed the pad of my thumb over the tear, then smoothed it down.

I didn't know if the inhabitants would be awake, but I'd knock once and if there was no answer, I'd leave and return later. Simple as that.

After two flights of about fifteen stairs each, I halted with one heel on the step before ascending the last couple that led to the dark slabbed door. The ornate wood on each side bulged out to a tip at the top.

Without a doubt in my mind, I knew there was no turning back after I walked through there. I exhaled sharply and my teeth clicked together. Everything would be fine. Even if this got me killed, it wouldn't be the worst. I was paying out the ass for life insurance and Peter's name was on the document. I pressed my lips together.

It was wrong of me to think that way, but I was just so fucking tired of being positive.

Squeezing my hands into fists, I exhaled sharply, nose flaring.

I shook my head.

There was a way out of my financial issues, and I was taking it by the horns.

The knocker was a bat hanging upside down, its ominous black eyes staring back at me from the stone. I reached for it and held it distended.

No choice.

Then freaking knock!

"Are you just going to hang around out here, Pet?"

I jumped, releasing a mixture of a squeal and a yelp as I let go of the knocker and the thud resonated as hard as my thundering heart. My heel slipped out from under me and my arms windmilled, but before I went tumbling down the stairs, the twin with the longer hair—Asher—wrapped his arm around my waist, clutching me tightly to him.

His body was warm and the grip he had on me fastened me to his muscled chest. I blinked up at the laughing blue eyes.

"Catalina," I wheezed. "My name."

The corner of his eyes crinkled with his smirk. He was too close and smelled sweet, like vanilla. I inhaled deeply. It was addicting.

Something hardened into my hip and I yanked back, putting distance between us.

My face heated.

"Are you always horny?"

"Only for you," he murmured, leaning over to get in my face, so close that our noses almost touched.

I valiantly attempted to contain my nervous laugh. His lips quirked and his finger tapped my nose, cutting me off.

"That's the first time I've ever been laughed at. I was expecting more of a swoon."

My nose scrunched as he stared at me expectantly. I licked my lips and took a deep breath. Approaching them was my choice, I couldn't wimp out now.

"Vampires aren't really my thing, but thanks."

He blinked at me and the corners of his lips twitched as he tilted his head.

I shuffled my feet and cleared my throat. Why was he staring at me so intently?

"Come in." He stepped past me, the door creaking after him before he turned back and held out his hand.

The hand—pale, long, and obnoxiously big—hovered in the air, waiting for mine.

I was putting my life in their palms, without reserve, and I would make sure I did a good job, whatever it was they asked of me, while I sought a way to escape safely . . . if at all.

His hand was slightly hot when I gripped it and stepped into the dark house.

"I wasn't sure if you slept during the day." Lie. The Pale One always passed out on top of me and even though we were deep inside a cave, I connected the dots.

"We do." He didn't try to lie to me.

"But you were just outside." I blinked to aid my eyes in getting used to the lack of lighting.

"Direct sunlight will incinerate us, *if* we manage to stay awake." His arm hooked over my shoulders, and I tensed up. This vampire either had no sense of personal space, or he didn't give a shit. I bet it was a mix of both.

As long as he kept his fangs away from me, then I would be fine. Fangs had proven to be a weakness and I couldn't let my mind be muddled from the truth of what monsters vampires were. Last night in the bathtub had proven how much my mental state had been compromised. I refused to think of the lapse in judgement, and I'd stopped with a mix of disgust and lust before I got off.

Asher grinned and my gaze dropped to the pointy canines. His smile widened, and I looked into his sparkling eyes.

"What brings you back, Pet?" His dark blond eyebrow winged up. "Miss me already?"

I elbowed him lightly, trying to get him to release me, but it was like ramming into marble. Wincing, I rubbed the tender spot.

"What did you all mean about me helping?"

Both his eyebrows lifted high, and a piece of hair flopping near his eye flirted with it.

"Asher. Don't tell me you've brought another woman to the manor at a time like this." A curt English accent called out. I could practically hear the sneer in Tobias's tone. His voice became closer as I craned my neck toward where it echoed from. From here, I could see straight up the long staircase to the platform of the second floor.

"What makes you think I've brought a woman?" Asher shouted back, a smirk gracing his lips.

"The stomping. Does she have weights on her feet to be making such a racket—" Tobias's words cut off when he saw me from where he stood at the banister.

My lips flattened before I forced a smile to stretch. I was pretty sure a blush creeped up my entire face.

I waved with my fingers in an awkward little move, and Asher's hand pressed to my spine, guiding me into the hallway. If I kept looking at Tobias, I would break my neck, so I cleared my throat and faced forward.

Asher's side brushed mine, arm fastened around me. His boundaries were nonexistent and it put me on edge, causing my teeth to grind. I inched to the left, but he followed, not detaching.

"What has you so intrigued by the offer?" He asked it so casually. A vampire, being casual.

Telling him I wanted money straight out seemed weird, but I saw no other way to phrase it. I was about to spit it out and lay it all out in the open, but Jax's voice echoed into the hallway before I could get a word out.

"She wants money."

I pressed my lips together as Asher guided me into an open kitchen. Polished dark granite glinted across every surface, including the island near the stove. Tall seats lined this side of the island, the back of the chairs tall, metal cylinders. To the right of the room stretched a huge refrigerator where Jax leaned on the open door, in search of something. All I could see of Jax was his lower half since his head was in the fridge. *Vampires ate?*

My gaze dropped to what was in his hand as the fridge slammed shut. It was a plastic bag with red liquid sloshing inside.

Oh.

Jax's expression remained flat as he met my eyes and ran his tongue over his front teeth. The sharp incisors elongated and he pierced the plastic bag, sucking as he squeezed.

My stomach soured at the sight. Blood wasn't usually a big deal, it was more the fangs that freaked me out. He didn't move those blue eyes off me as he drank, and his Adam's apple bobbing with each swallow. A trickle of blood slipped from the corner of his mouth and his tongue lashed out to swipe it, flashing bloody teeth.

"Right? You need money?"

How did he know that?

"How . . .?"

"There are only a handful of things that coax flawed humans. One is money." The dispassionate way he said it flushed embarrassment through me, and I rubbed the back of my neck. "You know there was no way we'd let you go, so you're biding your time. Playing two sides of a coin. You get some money as you work for us, and you bide your time to figure out how to run away."

It was my turn for my throat to bob. I smoothed my expression.

"Ignore him, he was dropped on his face when we were children. It damaged the speaking skills." Asher rubbed his hand down my arm. Like yesterday, it relaxed my tense shoulders. I exhaled at the warm friction.

"Yes, I want to help in—"

"You mean, you'll work."

Jax made things sound dirty and wrong. My eyes lowered to the ground, fixing on the frayed hem of the dark jeans near his boots as my temper lashed out.

"You didn't let me finish. Yes, I want to help in exchange for payment—seventy thousand." Asher's eyebrow twitched.

"Why do you need the money?"

Jax's abrupt question shouldn't have taken me off guard. God, I felt like a mouse being taunted by a cat.

"My debts." I never spoke about my brother. *Never*. It would put him in danger.

Jax snorted and tossed the blood bag into the trash overflowing with others just like it.

"Are you sure? It'll be dangerous." Tobias leaned against the entrance way, watching me with gray eyes. "We can't ensure that you'll survive." I bit back my scoff. I wouldn't survive either way, so why was he acting like I had a choice.

"Are you trying to scare her off?" Jax snapped.

"Yes," he responded crisply. From what, why did they even need me?

His gaze didn't waver from mine, and there was nothing I could tell from his expression. His emotions were veiled behind the calm, put-together mask.

I nodded slowly. It didn't matter why they needed me because they were paying me the money. The baggage that came with vampires was something I'd already accepted as soon as I'd climbed their steps. Involving myself with vampires lead in one direction. Death . . . unless I ran. I understood that.

"There is one more thing I must *humbly* request," the

mischievous twin announced. "Since your services will be paid for." He waved his fingers toward the ceiling.

I frowned at Asher as he clasped his hands in front of him, smiling so wide his pointed teeth were on full display. My stomach lurched at the excited look in his eyes. So, this was what it was like selling your soul to evil.

I really should have asked for more money.

catalina

"WE GET to bite you whenever we want," Asher finally said. I opened my mouth, heart thundering in my ears. "Without killing you, of course."

I blinked quickly. *Well, it's a good thing he mentioned not killing me.* The sarcastic thought faded with thoughts of biting . . .

I shivered, stomach churning with discomfort and something I didn't want to face.

"That's a bit unreasonable," Tobias lashed out.

"She's skittish around us and that doesn't exactly scream vampire-lover," Asher drawled. "Pet. You're jumpy and I don't see you surviving around vampires long enough to get what we need if you don't learn how to curb it. You have to act like you want to be around our kind, that you crave our bite."

That wasn't too far from the truth. I wetted my lower lip, trying to wrap my head around his words. It was true; vampires put me on edge—in too many ways, and what he insinuated was that I would be around many of them while doing whatever it was they had planned.

"Exposure therapy. What better way to make you relaxed than to bite you until you're used to it?"

"He has a point," Jax mused. Sounded like a load of bullshit to me.

Asher invaded in my space, and grazed his nose against my ear.

My mouth dried, eyes widening.

"See, Pet, you tighten up like a clam."

"No," Tobias snapped, shoving off the wood and stepping to my other side. The crippling effect vampires had on me was a detriment. If I managed to not tense or freeze up, and the vampire ever came after me, I might be able to slam a stake into his chest just as I'd seen Tobias do to the one that attacked him.

"Let's leave it to a vote, then."

"Asher—"

"What?" He blinked innocently. "I vote yes, Jax already voiced his thoughts. This is for Ren, so I'm sure he agrees. What was that?" He cupped his hand behind his ear. "Bastien is in agreement too which means you're outvoted."

So they decided on things by voting. As interesting as it was seeing their little interaction, I weighed the pros and cons internally. Yes, it would help my phobia, but it meant getting close and personal with them. Also, there was a Ren and a Bastien? I knew Ren was the one I was helping them find, but this was the first I'd heard of Bastien.

"But of course, none of that matters without you," Asher purred, slipping his arms around me and peering down at me. I craned my neck to look into his eyes, offput by his touchiness.

"I-I don't know . . ." Anything vamp related freaked me out, but it had more to do with the fact that I'd loved when Tobias sank his teeth into my wrist and Asher bit my neck. I didn't want to face the ugly truth of my addiction. I'd much rather just keep writing about it, thank you very much.

My morals were so screwed.

"Consider this just a training of sorts, a physiological test in effort to help you." Asher pursed his lips, waiting.

There wasn't a doubt in my mind he was doing this purely for selfish reasons and pure self-interest but it kind of made sense. Plus, if what they were going to have me do was be around a lot of vampires, the thought of freezing up surrounded scared the shit out of me.

"And what am I going to have to do?" My voice held an underlying tremble.

"Hm, just a little bit of this, a little bit of that. We'll explain more later." Asher flexed his hands against me. I was really doing this.

I nodded slowly . . . helplessly. I licked my lips, squeezing my nails into my palm.

"Then we have an agreement," Asher announced, stepping away from me and clasping his hands in front of him. "I'll order her some suitable clothing and shoes since the places she's checking out have requirements." He crossed his arms, rubbing his lower lip with his thumb.

"Jax, we'll need you in a few days, she seems the most scared of you. I'll introduce her to my bite today."

I sucked in a breath. "Now? You want to get started this second?"

"Come around in a few hours, I favor *hunting* during the witching hour." A shiver coasted down my spine. Asher clapped once, a grin on his lips. "I'll start planning our fun."

His palm pressed into my back and he nudged me. I

mechanically left the kitchen and my movements almost hurt with how stiff they were.

Tobias followed me to the door. The hollow thump of my steps echoed with each beat of my heart.

"Are you sure about this?" There seemed to be genuine concern inflecting his tone.

"No." But I didn't have much of a choice.

As I climbed the steps, I side-eyed the crow perched a-top a windowsill. Everything about this place screamed spooky. I rubbed my arms. This was it, there was no turning back. I'd wallowed in bed, wracking my brain for the couple of hours before coming back, but no matter what way I tried to think of it, I was in this, so I'd dressed in a simple green sundress exposing my neck. Hopefully, with a willing participant, he'd be a clean eater because getting blood out of clothes was close to impossible. My stomach lurched and I pressed my hand over the bulge of my inhaler in my dress pocket. The door swung open as soon as I stepped forward.

"I've been waiting for you, Pet."

A chill swept over my arms, lifting goose bumps as I stepped inside, my dress fluttering around my ankles. It *felt* empty in here. It was odd.

"Is anyone else here?"

Asher hooked his arm around my waist and the door creaked shut.

"They went to fetch blood and talk to someone that may have information on Ren." Again, mention of Ren. They seemed especially concerned by his absence. I tapped my fingers against my thigh in a quick rhythm.

"So what are we doing?" I slipped out of his grip, moving toward the black leather couch. I hoisted myself onto the cushion and plopped down.

My feet hung from the couch and I frowned down at the space between my flat ballerina shoes and the floor. They must have been custom made to fit these vampire giants.

Asher's gaze weighed heavily on my face, and I sank my teeth into my lower lip. His blue eyes swirled, heat in their depths.

"Do you have your inhaler?" I dropped my chin. "Be sure you have quick access to it."

Okay, that put me on edge. What *games* were going down today? "You're making me nervous." His teeth flashed with a grin. God, this was not going to be good.

"I thought we could start out with a little round of hide and seek." His lips tipped up. "I want to see how much you can stifle that fear of yours. If you keep your fear in line, I won't be able to find you. But if I sense you." His fingers grazed my throat. I flinched and his smile widened. "I get a treat."

"I-I don't know if this is the smartest course of action." I cleared my throat. So, he would basically hunt me down, and I had to go hide somewhere and try not to fear him finding me? Yeah, it sounded impossible. A game he expected, no, *wanted* me to fail.

"Would you like to back out?" He tilted his head, and I wet my lips.

"Don't act like I have a choice," I croaked.

Asher grinned again and placed his hands at his knees as he bent near my face. His nose hovered over mine and his sweet scent wafted to me. I cleared my throat again and wiggled into the couch. He shouldn't smell so good.

"Your fear makes my mouth water." I sucked in a breath, spine straightening. I backed up, cringing into the couch, but he followed, pressing the tip of his upturned nose into mine. "Vampires sense things in many ways." His nose caressed my cheek. "The quickening of your heart rate is a dead giveaway."

"Y-you can hear my heart race?"

The corner of his lips twitched. "More like I see it pounding in your throat . . . we are very attuned to blood, and the scent racing through your veins emphasizes with your racing heart . . . with your fright."

He dropped to his knees and was still taller than me in this position.

"Human bodies have an immediate reaction to fear, and oftentimes, many can't distinguish the difference with other urges. Like when you're wet and needy." He purred and the low pulse of my clit throbbed in answer. I squeezed my legs together, not wanting him to sense *that*. His eyes widened, drawing his head back in a jerk. Asher's eyes slitted and he breathed in deep, hands flexing into the cushion of the couch, corralling me with his arms. A groan slipped free from his lips.

My face must be as red as a fire engine. I wanted to plead and beg that he wasn't sensing my lust toward him, but I very much doubted he'd believe a word I said. Part of my brain railed at me, telling me how wrong it was for me to be excited, but the other part didn't give two shits. He was hot, no, he was damn sexy. Every flirtatious touch, smirk, and expression was meant for seduction.

"To some, your reactions could simply seem like fear." He grinned so wide I could see, the thankfully retracted, incisors.

I swallowed hard.

"So you only *scent things* when I'm turned on or scared?"

"*Mmhmm,*" he rasped, fingers diving into the couch near my thighs. He shook his head hard and backed up, leaning on his fists.

"When hunting, the primitive side of a vampire takes over and it's difficult to pull out of that mainframe."

"And is this what hide-and-seek will be? Hunting me?" It didn't seem the brightest, especially since we were alone.

"It's not an issue for me. I've never lost control." He waved his hand in the air as if physically brushing my worries away. "You will not die today." I blinked at him. He spoke about killing so callously, and I took a moment to soak that in. It was a hint at his inhuman nature, and I didn't like it, but there was no turning back. I'd made a decision and I could only stick to it.

"Okay," I said, nodding slowly as I slid off the couch to land on my feet. "I'll hide, but no using vampire speed." He tilted his head eerily. A fear-riddled shiver ran down my neck.

"You have thirty seconds."

Shit. I quickened my pace, jogging around the corner of the entrance. I chewed on my lip, debating which direction to go.

TEN

catalina

"TWENTY-FIVE SECONDS." I pounded up the stairs, using the banister to aid my way. My feet slapping on the ground echoed off the walls, raising my pulse with the frantic beat. Stopping on the second floor was my best bet otherwise he'd catch me quickly since I was nowhere near as fast as him. It split into two directions, left and right.

I worked to even my breathing and rushed to the third door down the right hall, slipping inside as stealthily as I could. The door snicked shut and engulfed me in the dark room. Squinting, I tried to make out as much as I could. There was a bed, and a chair thing near the window where a sliver of moonlight came through the curtains.

I rushed directly past the large bed and to the massive wooden unit against the left of the wall. I pulled it open as swiftly and quietly as possible. Slipping within the various clothing, I climbed into the wardrobe and enclosed myself.

A sweet scent wafted up from the clothing and I slapped away a silk shirt from my face and straightened it in front of me to block me from sight in case he opened it.

It smelled a lot like Asher. I involuntarily inhaled another lungful. No wonder it was so easy for him to attract women. He was not only beautiful, verging on pretty, he smelled like a damn dream.

The air in here felt a little sparse. I pulled out my inhaler and puffed between my lips. A muffled resonating slam echoed, and I froze, holding my breath. My hand shook as I slowly lowered my hands, pressing them against the cool surface on either side of me, being careful to ensure my inhaler didn't click against the wood. All of this was a sham. These vampires played me like a toy, and I could do nothing but go along with it. I squeezed my hand so hard the plastic of my medicine dug into my palm.

A beat later and the doors from the wardrobe were snatched open and light flooded into the space. Blood red eyes glinted back at me and I screamed, cringing back like I wasn't trapped in the wardrobe. It was just like the one that took me. The demonic glow took over the blue of his iris.

His palms thumped on either side of my neck and I froze, swallowing hard. Asher seemed unrecognizable as he looked down at me. His head bent and he pressed his nose into my throat, his warm breath puffing over my skin.

Was this how I died?

A hiss escaped, lifting the hair on my arms. His nails scraped the back of the wardrobe as he dragged his hands down. I knew the tip of the nail had become pointy and claw-like, similar to the Pale One that had taken me. I'd deducted the saliva in vampires had a healing quality since I wasn't scarred by all the punctures the other one made on my body.

I squeezed my lids tightly as his wet tongue prodded the

fluttering pulse in my neck. His sweet scent wafted to my nose and a mix of emotions clenched my stomach. I went limp, breathing coming faster as he rasped his fangs across my throat. Panic squeezed my chest. I wanted to run, but I couldn't move.

Maybe this had been his plan the entire time.

His palm slid down my arm. My stomach tightened when he moved lower and lower until he flattened his palm against my core.

Jolting, I puffed out a breath, practically panting. The fear morphed, but didn't fade, instead it heightened the tension in my body. My mouth watered and my nipples grew sensitive, and with each breath, they rasped across my bra.

Asher grazed his teeth against my throat again, applying pressure. This time, I arched my neck, needing more. My hips wiggled, grinding my throbbing pussy into his demanding hand.

He hissed and licked my neck again, wrapping his hand around my thigh. His long finger settled into the crevice where my thigh bent, while his thumb pressing into my clit. The rest of his fingers dug into my waist. I whimpered, twitching from the pressure he applied on my sensitive bud. My dress bunched under his touch.

There was a pinch at my neck, and I tensed for a moment and then he sank his fangs deep into my carotid. Asher sucked, and the drag tugged at my clit.

A moan ripped from my throat and Asher echoed it, his palm sliding down to shove against me.

So, so good. I'd attempted to shield my brain from the pleasure, from the craving. But with my body responding so quickly, I faced my reality. I wanted the fangs in me, I ached for the sting all over my body. That desire battled with the fear ingrained within my memories.

He sucked again and I forced myself harder against him, bunching my fingers in the front of his linen shirt. His mouth suctioned at my neck and his tongue laved near the entrance wounds.

His fingers delved under my dress, curving and searching. The waistband of my panties tightened. *Rip.* His claw, short enough they didn't do much but add more sensation with their rough edges, grazed the sensitive skin near my slit, and I whimpered. Then his cool fingers slipped over the bud. I gasped, arching toward the rolling sensation of his fingertip.

Asher lifted his head and I panted, staring into red eyes that seeped hunger. His other hand lifted off the surface near my head and he curved his claw into the collar of my outfit. With a quick jerk downward, he tore through my shirt and bra to expose my breasts. The dress gaped open, hanging off my shoulders, and I arched my back as his teeth sank into the skin near my pert nipple.

I screamed, tossing my head back as he sucked. The orgasm rippled through my body, cascading tremors down my spine as his fingers practically vibrated against my pussy. He was so fast. I shook, riding out the wave and twitching as he continued running over my wet folds. The sensitivity reached a painful level, but he didn't relent. His fangs retracted from my skin, and I looked down at him hovering over the swell of my rapidly rising breasts. My eyes attached to his long incisors, blood dripped off them and splattered on my skin. He stared at his bite marks as if in a trance. Asher ran his tongue over his reddened lower lip and a shudder rolled through his frame.

It was the most erotic image I'd ever seen. His finger slipped down my wet core and delved inside my core. I gasped, my eyelashes fluttering from the onslaught of pleasure.

My sexual experiences consisted of when the Pale One raped me. After that, I held no desire for anything physical and I'd tried. Had this been because my brain had turned my desires into forbidden cravings?

I couldn't delve into my messed up psychology because no part of my imagination or moments of touching myself compared to Asher's fingers and fangs.

His tongue glided over his incisor and his hair fluttered over his shoulder as he lowered to lave the blood dripping from my breast. His warm tongue smoothed across my skin and I whimpered as he cleaned it away, my body twitching with his swipes. He easily continued the pace of his fingers sheathed in my pussy.

Asher slowed the speed of his fingers, and shallowly dipped them in me, while his thumb smeared my wetness over my clit. He repeated the slow motion, and heat spread throughout my belly. His claws rasped my folds. Oh my fucking God. The level of pleasure should be criminal.

He suckled my nipple, heightening my need and then nibbled up to my neck and sank his teeth in again.

"Asher," I gasped.

His cock nudged my bare leg, hips thrusting. I slipped my legs wider and tugged him tightly to me, so my thighs corralled his wide hips.

I arched my neck and slipped my fingers through his hair as he fed.

This. This sensation. *Ache.* Was what I'd been craving for too long. The foreign craving I'd tried to deny.

Heat swept over my skin, and I became short of breath. My

legs tensed at his side, drawing up at the encroaching release. Asher's arms wrapped around my back, fingers digging into my spine as he drew me as close to him as humanly possible. The position forced his covered cock to thrust over my aching pussy while his hands slid to my hips.

Desperation marred each touch and movement. I couldn't get enough of him.

A whine swelled in my throat as I arched to rub myself against his thickness.

Even within his slacks, he felt huge. If he was freed, I couldn't imagine his size.

Lust crashed through my senses and I whimpered, the heat at the apex of my thighs reaching levels it never had before. I was heavy and needy. The hollowness begged for something to fill me. It was wrong, but in this moment, I didn't care it was a vampire helplessly thrusting between my legs.

His teeth retracted from my neck without sucking then he slammed them back into me, triggering my release. Heat flushed through my pussy, throbbing and achingly good. It spread through my core and expanded through every sense. My legs hooked around his hips and I ground against him.

He felt sinfully right in my arms. My pulse fluttered in my throat, beating like bird's wings.

Asher groaned as he drank from my neck, and his furious thrusting lost rhythm as he stilled, whimpering into my throat as he sucked hard.

The tension leaked from his body and his panting chest matched mine. His teeth slipped from my neck and he lowered to his knees as I leaned against the bunched up clothing. A few strands of his long hair escaped the leather thong tying his hair back.

His forehead pressed into my belly, shoulders lifting in quick pants. I tugged at the strands of hair and he rolled his head to the side so his cheek rested against my thigh. The blond lashes languished across the crest of his cheeks before they fluttered open.

On the other side of coming, reality sank in. I stopped petting him and my grip turned limp. *How could I?* Warmth blazed on my face and traveled down my neck. I tried swallowing the knot at my throat. Shame nipped at my heels and I gritted my molars. Vampires were evil and here I was with one between my legs.

Asher stood, blue eyes not leaving mine. For once, they weren't sparkling. He reached over my shoulder and I tensed, but he ignored my reaction, pulling out a fresh pair of sweats.

With jerking movements, he unbuttoned his slacks and tugged the zipper. The cock that sprung out was still hard and pointing in my direction. The tip of his dick glinted with slightly red cum that covered the barb piercings gracing his shaft. He tossed the slacks aside and slipped on the fresh pair. His dick's outline was clear for me to see, and I pressed my legs together.

Did he have to put on gray sweats?

Flattening my lips, I tried to focus on something else so the low throbbing at my clit could disperse. Asher clasped my face and pressed his lips to my nose. I blinked into his eyes.

"Delightful, human," he rasped, releasing me and striding out of the room.

My lips parted and I gawked after him. *Well.* I needed to get moving, except my limbs weighed a hundred pounds. Liquid tickled my neck and my dress was torn. After a night like this, I needed self-care. A rose scented salt bath, a shopping spree, I didn't know, just *something* to distract my frantic mind.

Exhaling shakily, I slumped back. What the fuck was wrong with me? Screwing around with a vampire shouldn't have happened. I'd avoided them for so long, how could I be so weak?

Tobias stepped into the room and I startled. His lips formed a thin line. My hand trembled as I tried covering myself, but my movements were sluggish.

Tobias tugged a blanket off the seat near the window and strode over to me, wrapping me up in it.

"Thank you," I muttered.

His jaw tightened. I couldn't get a read on his thoughts.

I stared at the tip of my shoes hanging over the lip of the wardrobe. His sigh was the only precursor before his arms swept me up. I gasped and wiggled in the hold, my heart racing.

"M-my inhaler." I coughed and he balanced me with one arm and placed the inhaler on my chest. Since he held me tightly, the blanket pinned my arms to my sides.

Tobias clutched me tighter as he exited the room and strode down the hall, cradling me against his wide chest. I was too tired to do anything, so I rested my head on his shoulder. Here I was draped against a vampire, not freaking out. My years of running felt pointless, yet at the same time had culminated to this conclusion. Had I run because some deep dark piece of my soul had known I held such perverse desires? I sighed. My writing proclivities didn't help me out on denying that.

He went a few doors down, to the first one down this hall, and shoved the door open with the tip of his shoe. Not bothering with the light, he moved across the room through the second threshold that opened to a lavish marble bathroom. He balanced me in one arm and turned the water on. The spout sputtered to life and began filling the round tub.

"Are you okay?"

I blinked quickly, trying to find a way to respond.

"I don't know," I admitted. The experience with Asher was altering and I wanted to run, which I would be doing if I could move. "I-I need to bathe."

Tobias set me on my feet and tugged the blanket off me, tossing it into the corner, so he could help slide my clothing off. My face heated but I needed the help, regardless of how embarrassing it was to have him touch me with such ease. I covered my breasts as he lifted me and lowered me into the filling tub. A tremble coursed through my limbs and a knot swelled in my throat.

I should tell him to leave me alone, but the words refused to come out.

He crouched in front of me, running the tip of his finger over my cheek and I stilled, holding my breath. There had been nothing aggressive in his touch, but that didn't mean he couldn't kill me with a twitch of his pinky.

Squirting some soap into a loofah, he worked it onto my skin. Tobias's brows remained furrowed, the pensive expression unwavering as he worked the rough material over my shoulders with gentle swipes. The way he dragged it over my flesh was impersonal and efficient.

"He's never lost control."

So Asher wasn't lying about that. I'd imagined he'd used it as an excuse to get my guard lowered. After all, morality and vampires were concepts that didn't coexist. I stayed quiet, trying to swallow my emotions. The encounter played back in my head, warming my entire body with embarrassment. I'd acted crazy and horny.

There had been no reservations in me and I hadn't cared. I simply wanted. And the catalyst was Asher's bite.

I wanted to get as far as I could get away from here, but I couldn't. I needed the vampire's money. My stomach lurched and I struggled to swallow.

Tobias swept the loofah over my breast, and goose bumps lifted across my arms. My nipples were sensitive, and the slow swipes Tobias did across my flesh weren't helping. Tobias's jaw worked and his throat bobbed.

"His eyes were red." Like the Pale One. I wiggled my toes trying to get movement back; water reached the middle of the tub.

"When we become red-eyed, our conscience is gone. We are true monsters like that, he had no reservations in holding back."

"Oh," I whispered. Tobias finished rinsing me down and left the room to fetch me some clothing. I flexed my hands and movement came more easily to me. Getting out of here was my only goal so I pushed out of the water and it sluiced down my skin. A white towel rested on the metal holder and I plucked it to quickly dry myself and then wrapped it around my body, securing it over my breasts.

Waiting for Tobias wasn't an option. I had to get out of here —now. I skulked to the door, and peeked out, then padded across the wood floors. No one was there so I rushed down the stairs, half-staggering from dizziness. Each of my steps sounded excruciatingly loud to my ears, but it served to spur me on faster.

The front entrance swung behind me as I booked it to my house; without shoes and wrapped in a towel.

There was no way what just happened was real. It had to be some manifestation I'd conjured from my darkest fantasies, but the soreness in my throat told another story. It was horrifying and wrong . . .

And why did I want more of it?

catalina

THE FOLLOWING afternoon I woke up after a restless night of sleep. I showered, worked on my computer for my scheduled hours, then spent the rest of the day slothing around, feeling guilty, scrolling my phone, and acting like I wasn't peeking at the door every other hour. There was no way I anticipated seeing a vampire. None at all. It was pure madness.

Yet, the sex dream that had torn me out of sleep shouted otherwise. I rubbed my fist against my temple. Maybe I should just embrace my little vampire kink. That was all it was, some psychological reaction to the traumatizing time I'd spent in that disgusting cave. The fangs . . . I shivered.

The cat meowed on my lap, purring and rubbing his face into my boob. Soon after twilight came, the cat appeared and was inseparable from me. I had to draw the line when he followed me to the bathroom, though. Yeah, it was an animal, but I got skeeved out when he stared at me with his eerie blue gaze.

"It's a good show, huh, Binx," I mumbled, raising the volume. It wasn't an original name, but eh, I liked it, especially since he seemed to hate it. His little nails were partially out, so he pricked my legs. My nose scrunched at the sting.

My phone dinged and I lifted it, hoping for . . . I didn't even know what, but it was just an email about the debt. There. *That* was my reason for my anticipation—paying the money I owed.

"I suppose I should get ready to head over." My neck rested against the back of the individual used couch I'd found and paid for with the last of my funds before I'd arrived at this God-forsaken town. It had taken a hell of a lot of effort to get it into my house, but at least the people who'd sold it had been willing to drop it off.

My alarm rang, notifying me I had about thirty minutes to get ready. I tapped the notification off and puffed out my cheeks, rubbing my face. Heat spread in my belly like a trigger and I groaned as the unbidden image of Asher came to my mind. The sexy smirk . . . the flirting touches . . . the ravenous touches like he wanted me more than anything. I shook my head, pressing on my temples with both hands.

It was just because I was touch-deprived and had a twisted vampire kink that should have remained in my fantasies.

I should get therapy to work through it not write about it, or else I'd end up dead and drained if I continued down the route I was on, but what would I tell a therapist? I was trapped in a cave by a vampire who feasted on me repeatedly for days and ended up developing a craving?

Nudging Binx to the side, I scooted off the couch. He wasn't a fan of being picked up, he grumbled so much I was surprised he didn't speak.

I donned a cute midi skirt with tights under and platform wedges. Yeah, it was chilly and gloomy outside, but looking cute mattered, especially if death could come at any point. Over my dead body would I die in some ratty outfit. Still, I'd selected a simple top in case it ended up torn or blood stained.

Shaking out my styled hair, I left the house, the door clicking shut behind me. I strode off the porch and slowed to a stop . . . my van sat in my driveway as if nothing had happened, as if it were always there. Which vampire had brought it back to my house? I'd heard absolutely no one drive up and that freaked me out more than anything. I rushed to the driver's side and peered through the window to find my car keys sitting on the seat.

They'd given me a way to escape. I worried my lip. Were they testing me? I rubbed my bare arms.

Binx stared at me steadily from the porch, like he could look into my soul, his tail flicking behind him. I released a steady breath. I'd already made my choice.

A loose rock crunched under my heel as I took a sharp turn toward the manor. Asher was in there . . . My heart rate picked up, the thud deep and increasing. The way his hips ground on my core, rubbing and dominating me, was seared into my brain. I pressed my lips together and patted the inhaler I'd tucked into my skirt pocket. I was fine. Everything would be fine.

My pep talk didn't stop my stomach from squeezing when I approached the manor. My fist raised but before it came down, the door swung open to Asher with his lips curved slyly. Brisk air caressed my cheek from the air conditioner.

He grinned down at me, his pearly white teeth flashing, and he gripped my arm, tugging me inside.

"Hey," I squeaked, at the swift manhandling. His arm curved around my waist, and he pulled me to his lips while lifting me. I left the ground as he straightened, keeping me attached to him. My lips parted on a gasp and his tongue flicked into my mouth.

Every inch of me froze up. It was a crime for it to feel so shattering, but what was his deal? This was too quick to—he wasn't human. Right.

On his second prodding flick, my shoulders relaxed like he'd put a spell on my body and I groaned into his mouth, giving into to the kiss.

This wasn't so bad . . . it was good. So good. Teases were nothing to him. I could tell in the ease he touched me that flirting was second nature, but I couldn't help the shivers he caused.

The hard prod of his cock dug into me and I whimpered, my legs automatically lifted to the sides of his hips, my reaction instinctive. His fingers dug into my thighs where my skirt had risen up as he clasped me tightly to him, bunching the sheer nylon tights.

Asher angled his head, licking my tongue. Warmth bloomed at the apex of my thighs, and I tipped my hips toward him as if my body had a mind of its own.

When his mouth detached from mine, my head tipped back, exposing my throat. Lips grazed along my chin and he pressed butterfly kisses to my neck.

Shivers coasted to my pussy and I ground against him harder.

"Oh," I moaned.

"Is this the training you mentioned, Asher?" Tobias drawled crisply.

I yelped and shoved his shoulders. Asher released me and my arms windmilled without his secure grip. I squeezed my eyes tightly, waiting for my back to slam into the ground. Hard biceps slipped under my thighs and behind my neck. It wasn't anywhere near as hard as it would have been had I fallen to the ground.

Panting, I gawked at Tobias as his grip loosened. I wiggled until I slipped off his lap and onto the ground. When he'd caught me, he'd dropped to his knees. That had been a close call to a sprained tail bone.

Asher crouched beside me.

"Must you be so careless," Tobias snapped, and his chest vibrated against my back.

Asher ignored him and clasped my face within his palms. His blue eyes were wide and his eyebrows furrowed.

"It was your fault for being so abrupt," Asher snapped. "Are you all right, Pet?" His thumb grazed my lower lip and the softened line of his mouth tightened my chest.

I sniffed exaggeratedly and brushed nonexistent dust off my knees. My movement pressed me more against Tobias and his breath halted.

Asher tilted his head questioningly.

"You're lucky my skirt didn't tear. It's limited edition." False bravado was all I had. Shooting to my feet, I avoided their grips as I straightened my shirt, blushing hard. I'd enjoyed being between them more than I wanted to admit. Tobias didn't meet my eyes as he stood and strode down the hall without comment.

"Did the priest have a hard-on?" Asher's shock seeped into my senses.

Licking my lips, I met his eyes and rage flashed to the surface so briefly I could have imagined it. He bounced to his feet and stepped up to me, forcing me back until I was corralled by his body.

"Good thing I caught you first." His breath brushed across

my lips. "Nothing has ever pulled an erection from Chastity Belt."

I mouthed his last phrase, wrapping my head around them.

"Oh," I whispered, the warmth that had bloomed spread at his words. I couldn't tear my attention from his warm bowlike lips. They perpetually tipped up at the corners, the seductive smile exploding butterflies through my chest. I swayed back and flattened against the wall.

"I ordered some things for you that will arrive too late for the first location we must take you, but there are a few outfits upstairs that may fit you. I was pulling them out when I saw you making your way over."

"Were you waiting for me?" I teased, but I slammed my mouth quickly shut. Where had that tone come from?

The line of his shoulders stiffened briefly as he became preternaturally still. Then his lips spread into a smirk, his scoff sounded forced and he waved an elegant hand in the air.

"As if I'd wait for anyone," Asher said, turning on his heel, the loafers scuffing across the tile as he ascended the stairs. I wrinkled my nose at the swift retreat. "You can wait in the parlor."

The swift steps widened as he rounded the staircase, and I shuffled foot to foot, a little lost at the reaction. Vampires were too confusing. Much more than I had anticipated. There were facets to them that weren't simply evil. Tobias's patience had shown me this. The one truth I had to admit was that they could have snapped my neck two times over.

I rolled my shoulders as the remaining tension leaked out of me and I slowly entered the living room. It was the same location I'd first been dragged into when Jax stole me away from my van.

The arm of the couch dug into my side as I leaned against it. I tapped my foot as I waited for Asher to return, a giddiness expanding my chest. His touches were electrifying. I hungered for the feel of his fingers grazing my neck, or his palm splayed on my thigh. I licked my lips and shook myself out of it as Asher rounded the corner of the entrance, hugging a pile of gray tulle to his chest. Oh no, the dress was going to be hideous.

Asher smiled at me over the fabric and the pressure in my body bloomed and heated. I blinked. I eyed Asher's cutely upturned nose. Sexy and a vampire? I was asking for trouble.

"Put this on so I can get a look at you."

Asher dropped the dress onto the couch and I stretched it out.

It was . . . gaudy. But I took the material and smoothed it down. The old fashioned fabric was raspy. The sort of thing that was all the rage in the eighteen hundreds.

I gripped the bottom of my shirt and paused, looking over at Asher with a frown.

"Turn around."

His head tilted slightly to the side and his eyebrow raised. It was worth asking. Sighing, I lifted my shirt, trying to act as nonchalant as possible, like flames weren't licking down to my chest. Lust blazed in his searching eyes and I nervously licked my lips. Asher's fangs sprang out and his jaw bunched, but he didn't make a move toward me as I set my wedges to the side. Holding eye contact, I slowly rolled my tights down to my feet.

My fingers prickled with excitement and my movements slowed. I craved the look in his eyes. His gaze lifted to my face. I'd never behaved so wantonly, but I didn't care to stop.

Shuddering, he exhaled and turned his back. "If I keep

looking at you, I will devour you and we won't get what we need done."

My heart skipped a beat as I finished undressing. I rubbed the goose bumps on my arm and swallowed hard. I was kind of addicted to this new heathen side of me. All the desires and needs I hadn't been able to satisfy raged forward and it felt freeing. As train-wreck coded as it all was, I didn't want to stop.

Pushing out my cheek with my tongue, I snapped out of my thoughts involving his body on mine and pulled the dress over my head. I sputtered when the rough fabric scraped my lip. *Grr. Damn thing.*

I ran my hands down the scrunched side of the dress. The back gaped and my breasts pushed over the lip of the dress.

I reached behind me and attempted to pull the buttons together . . . but it wouldn't. I bit my lip and my boobs popped out farther with each breath. *God dammit!*

Who the hell did this belong to anyway, a damn toy?

I curled my toes. What to do? Okay, if I got it off and refused to put it on, he'd probably wonder why I was being difficult all of the sudden. But who cared . . .

Too late. Asher turned and met my gaze.

"Er, it doesn't fit." My face blistered with heat.

Asher was clocked in on my bra-covered breasts pressed together even more because of the tight fit. "Hm, what was that?" He blinked quickly and I crossed my forearms over my chest.

I gripped the top of the dress, jerking it up with little wiggles. His eyes flared and he was suddenly before me. I gasped, taking a step back, but his hand at my spine caged me.

"You delectable human." His nose grazed across the column of my neck. "*Du är en oöverträffad frestelse.*"

"Asher?" I breathed and it sounded too close to a moan. I wasn't sure if I was begging him to bite me or not. I didn't have to wonder for long. His fangs speared my throat, and both of his arms lashed around me, holding me tightly to his chest. Moaning, I clawed my fingers into his sides, sinking them into the hard muscle. Pleasure zapped to my clit, flaring lust to a boiling point. Asher sucked my blood with a long, hard tug, his fingers spasming in my back. After another tingling drag, he shuddered, his grip nearing painful. He lashed his tongue across the punctures.

My arms fell back, limp as noodles. He loomed over me until my spine curved in his palm and all I could see was his chiseled features hovering over my face, overpowering my senses. My breasts moved up and down with quick pumps from my breathing. His blood-stained smile sent shivers down my spine—but not in a fearful way.

I was sick.

He grazed his nose down my neck until he hovered over the swell of my breast. I held my breath. Asher's pupils dilated and he closed his eyes, breathing in an audible gust of air. In a burst of motion, he struck his elongated teeth into me. My skin easily submitted to the sharp incisors. They cut in like a knife to butter. The initial sting faded with the swell of ecstasy. I whimpered, my toes curled, and my head fell back. The tips of his shoulder length hair caressed my skin.

"Asher," a bellow sounded from far off. I jerked against him, and he lifted his head, spitting curses in his language. His tongue smoothed over the leaking puncture wounds in my chest, the same way he'd done to my neck. I fascinatedly watched them heal.

He clicked his tongue in his mouth with irritation marring his face.

"I will return," he responded tightly, reluctantly releasing me, and turned on his heels. The front of his slacks tented with his more-than-generous-sized dick.

He exited the living room and I watched him with my head tilted and a stupid smile on my lips. I needed to snap out of it. Straightening, I smoothed my palms on the skirt and shook my head. Honestly, I was glad the ugly thing didn't fit. I reached for the back of the zipper to loosen the small bit I'd managed to get up so I could get it off the rest of the way. In the middle of a full body wiggle, a hiss floated to my ears.

Rounding toward the noise, I wilted at the rage-filled expression on Jax's face. He stormed in my direction, his face molted red. I stumbled back a step and then straightened my spine. Jax leaned near my ear. The hair on my neck lifted and I hugged myself. He could lash out at me at any moment and end me easily. I tipped my chin and angled my head to the side.

"If you're going to bite me, hurry up." It was pure bravado since I trembled, but I was sick of fearing.

He stilled over me, his lips grazing my neck as his hand harshly grabbed my arm. There was nothing gentle about his grip, but it served to enflame my achiness. I licked my lips, squeezing my thighs together to assuage the need, and the tulle rustled with my movement.

At the brush of his nose, I sucked in a breath, withholding a moan.

"You're perilously close to becoming a blood-whore." The hissed words felt like a physical blow. He suddenly shoved me away from him and my legs tangled with fabric as I fell to the ground in a pile. Choking on my breath, my chest stung. I met his eyes with mine, my lip wobbling. I wish he couldn't see how deeply he'd gotten to me. The evil prick likely felt good about it too.

I scooted back and reached my trembling hand into the pocket of my skirt hanging off the couch. Was that what was happening to me? He stated 'blood-whore' like it was a title. Breathing in from the lip of my inhaler, I looked up as soon as the pressure loosened. *Why hadn't he left yet?*

His nostrils flared as he looked me in the eyes.

"I deposited the money into your account." With those ominous words, he turned on his heels as Asher entered.

"H-how did you get my account information?" I rasped, but he ignored me.

"Jax, have you come to join us in preparing our little human?"

"Don't put her in those clothes again." Jax paused at the threshold. "They don't belong on her."

Asher's jaw tightened and he shook his head at his brother's retreating back. The rage-filled way Jax spat the words out held more fury than he'd ever directed at me, and I didn't think he could hate me more than he already did.

"What did he mean, Asher?" I rasped, straightening on my feet. A dull throb pierced my ankle. "Whose clothing is this?"

"Nothing for you to worry about, Pet." His smile was stiff as he ran his hands down my arms.

I frowned, studying his expression as I shimmied the dress down another inch. "I don't think it's too much of a hassle to get my questions answered since one of you will end up offing me."

His eyebrows raised. "We never mentioned killing you."

"You all think very little of human intelligence for creatures that used to be one."

"I believe we've underestimated you." His lips quirked. "You do not let your fear cloud you."

"So please, give me the grace of answering my questions." I had nothing left to lose in facing him like this, but the way he looked at me, aware and intrigued, gave me the impression that I surprised him.

He hummed. "A woman we used to share . . . She was the one that brought all of us together."

My stomach soured and I squeezed the material.

This belonged to that person. It suddenly felt so wrong wearing it. I yanked the dress off my body before stepping out of it. Lifting it, I handed it to Asher with my arm pressed over my bra covered breasts.

They used to *share* someone?

"You used to share one woman?" I was simultaneously fascinated and envious.

"Yes." His smile slipped and became blank. I had no idea what caused his shift but I had a damn good guess. Had he loved her? That uncomfortable tightening started up at my chest and I forced my attention to dressing myself.

"Where is she?" I tacked on, trying to be as nonchalant as possible.

"Dead, Pet."

There was still tension in my throat, but I valiantly tried to shove it off.

"I-I'm sorry." My apology tilted up at the end as if it were a question.

"It's not a problem, for me at least." His smile widened. I didn't have time to nitpick at those words because he continued. "It looks like I can't take you today, but I express-ordered you a few outfits. They should be here tomorrow."

"Ah, okay." My voice sounded pitifully small. Asher stared into the distance, his gaze unfocused. I rushed to finish dressing while he was distracted. "How did she die?"

The corners of his lips twitched, and he turned his attention fully on me.

"You fret too much about matters that don't concern you, Pet." Asher lifted a finger to my lips. The featuring touch fluttered through my chest and I swallowed hard.

The recollection of his teeth sinking into me shot flutters through my belly and I cleared my throat and dropped onto the couch.

My teeth clicked together. No more shaming myself.

"We'll continue this another day, Pet."

I couldn't help but feel disappointment, it was because of the dead vampire—I was sure of it.

Tobias entered. "Already done?"

"Yes, tell her the plan." He looked to the frowning English vamp.

Asher paused at the entrance as Tobias settled on the cushion beside me. His eyes flashed, but whatever was there quickly disappeared. Looked like I could clear a room quickly. I swallowed the bitterness growing in my throat.

I lifted my gaze to meet Tobias's. The corner of his eyes wrinkled, and his throat bobbed. I frowned at the tension lining his face and he squeezed his eyes closed. He expelled a slow sigh.

The harsh set of his lips indicated pain. Ending up closer to him on the couch, I grazed my fingertips across his cheek. His eyes flashed open and he jerked away from my touch. I clenched my lifted hand and stared at it in astonishment. Touching them so openly and thoughtlessly wasn't like me. A sickness bloomed inside me and caused me to behave this way. That could be the only explanation.

"Tobias." His brow lifted questioningly. "What's a blood-whore?"

"Well . . ."

"Please," I choked out, almost desperate for an answer. Could it be why I behaved the way I had?

"A human that becomes addicted to vampire bites."

My eyes rounded. I didn't want to be a blood-whore, but was that what was wrong with me? I loved being bit. I ached for it, like a kink. I didn't need it to survive, but would I eventually be there? My heart slammed against my ribcage.

"It's an addiction stronger than any human drug you can think of. Obsession is a large mark of blood-whores. They're willing to do anything just for a bite."

My shoulders lowered. Fuck. This sounded just like me.

"I can't do this anymore. I want out," I croaked. The words came without thought and my lips felt numb.

Tobias stared at me.

"No, Catalina." The steady way he looked at me held no hesitation. Even the vampire that other vampires believed had a moral code no longer made a show of acting like I had a say.

What had I gotten myself into?

"There are ways to combat becoming a blood-whore." He straightened, angling his head back. I clenched my fingers so hard they dug into my palm. "Don't allow the same vampire to feed for more than a fortnight."

"So I can't be a blood-whore right now?" Even as I said the words, I knew the question was useless.

"It is too soon." My body drooped. Little did he know. The

thought of losing myself to obsession soured my stomach. A mindless blood-whore at the whim of vampires was last on my list. Two weeks. They could only bite me for two weeks . . . but the Pale One had fed on me for much longer. If I had the potential to be a blood-whore, it would have already happened, so what's to say that was not why my little 'kink' had manifested.

"Is there any other way to 'combat it'?"

"If a vampire offers you their blood, but no vampire will willingly share blood with another. It creates a temporary bond with a slew of side effects."

And . . . never mind.

"Oh." The ground felt unsteady even though I was sitting. "I have to go."

He caught my wrist. "Do not attempt to leave this city or we will have to lock you up here."

"Why—" I blinked rapidly, wrapping my head around the situation I'd gotten myself in.

"We will know. You will be watched day and night."

He almost seemed regretful uttering the threat. His thumb caressed the top of my hand. The little touches inflamed my need and I yanked away, shooting to my feet. I turned my back on his gray searching eyes and rushed out of there.

TWELVE

SHE'D ADDICTED me and I'd only tasted her once. Drinking her blood felt like sunlight caressing my skin. I shouldn't have been able to recall the sensation when it had been centuries since I was human.

The sweet taste spreading on my tongue, rushing through my system, like lightning sending electrical pulses through my psyche. My cock stiffened; the sensation foreign. I'd felt desire for blood and feeding, but never had a woman's body tempted me as Catalina's did. Having her under me as I fed on her . . . Lord forgive me, but I hungered for her.

I tapped my thigh, waiting for her run-down van to exit the drive thru.

I didn't understand human's obsession with caffeinated drinks, or their need to have one daily, they behaved as if they had to live off it. There was a store every other block of some chain or another hosting the same product, nonsense I couldn't wrap my head around. The thoughts I'd heard from humans craving the substance reeked of addiction.

Catalina rolled out of the drive-through—another luxury

humans took for granted. Everything was terrifyingly easy for humankind, and they didn't understand true suffering. The horrors of war, plagues . . .

I snapped back to the present, revving out of my parking spot to follow before she was out of sight. I followed a distance behind until she pulled into a large, wide building with red blinking lights at the front.

Though fearful, she picked herself up each time she'd been slammed down.

Humanity was the Lord's creation while I was an abomination, something dark and sinful that should have never been, so I'd abstained from feeding directly from humans once I became a monster, feeding from animals and then blood banks when they surfaced. Until the curvaceous human appeared and saved me. I watched said human disappear through the swinging glass door of the building.

Knowing other's thoughts, forced me to be more conscious of their emotional state. Reading human minds were easier than reading the minds of other vampires which always seemed shrouded in a layer of fog. Furthermore, any emotion humans felt at a powerful level leaked into my conscious. I understood the emotion from an outsider perspective, even if I couldn't feel it as they did. When thinking back on human memories, they remained behind a hazy curtain. Present, but not fully formed. Little details faded, like smells, tastes—

You two always get on me, *but no, when you want to stalk the human, it's fine.*

I narrowed my eyes at the door.

The voice was—

"What you doin'," Asher slipped into my vehicle and slammed the door shut.

"How did you get here?" He hadn't driven up.

Asher's seat creaked as he scooted it flat so he reclined and he hooked his arms behind his head.

"Compelled some human." Asher smirked. "What, you didn't see me following you because you were so honed in on the pretty little ass?"

I stiffened, offended. "How dare you—"

"I feel like we're bonding with this whole stalking thing." Asher's grin widened.

"This is not stalking," I snapped. "I volunteered to keep an eye on her."

"Let's stop the bull, we can have our hired humans, or one of my progeny could have watched her if we truly wanted eyes on her."

"Nonsense." I left it at that, not bothering to try to make sense of it all. We'd kept our relocation silent to all under our coven. Neither them nor the humans could know where we'd relocated. Jax sent them the girl's location virtually with strict instructions to notify us of her every move, and if the time came where she attempted to leave within a twenty-mile radius from this address, then she would be detained until we collected her, yet she hadn't tried to flee.

The front door opening dragged our attention to Catalina as she sped to her car, peeking around her. She popped the door open and bent inside, reaching for something I couldn't see.

"I want to fuck her." He groaned, rubbing his crotch.

I eyed him. "Tone down your vulgarity." He only lifted an eyebrow. Catalina retreated from the vehicle with a bag swinging in her hand.

"Whatever you say," Asher scoffed. "So, has Calliope contacted you to complain about you offing her child?"

"No." And I was as surprised as he looked. It lent itself to our theory that she had Ren. In any other instance, she would do whatever possible to be as much of an annoyance as she could.

Calliope likely played her little games . . . I counted on this because if it were another, more volatile enemy making a move by taking Ren, he may not be alive.

We could not storm into her territory without her being able to call a hearing, turning all vampires against us. Many would gladly take the chance.

It would be a bloodbath from both sides and humans would be the collateral.

Toe the fine line. Play the long game. We would prevail but we had to take care when moving the pieces.

catalina

FORTUNATELY, the 24-hour animal shelter asked me to come in on short notice to fill in during the evening shift, giving me the perfect excuse to avoid the turbulent shit going on in my head. Mainly, the fact that I was being 'watched day and night', whatever that meant. I believed it even though I vigilantly kept an eye out for anyone following me, but to no success. On my drive over to the shelter, I'd squeezed the steering wheel in a death grip and my shoulders hadn't relaxed since I arrived. I tapped my fingers on the front desk surface, my mind staying on the havoc causing vampires. Plural. Something about Tobias and Asher pulled me into their rotation and fantasies spawned in my brain at an alarming rate. Especially after the mention of sharing a woman. My fixation felt wrong, but right at the same time. At my increasing fascination, I could only conclude I'd become a blood-whore.

These emotions were a complete shift from the fear that normally haunted me. Indigestion burned in my throat, so I took a swig of the water.

No more mulling. I'd been thinking about what kind of

woman she had been to inspire them sharing her, and I couldn't wrap my head around it as much as I tried. What was so special about *her*? Wait a moment. Plastic crackled under the pressure of my hand.

I was jealous. *Absolutely* not. There was no need to be jealous of someone else—especially a dead *vampire* woman.

"Cat!" I jumped at the shout, straightening in the chair so quickly that it rolled back.

The urging tone told me Leroy was hailing me down, not randomly calling out at a cat. I'd already requested they simply use my full name, but it hadn't stuck. I followed Leroy's voice through the door to the end of the hall. He grunted as a Shepard mix jerked between his legs. He swiftly got a hold on him again, but I stayed on edge to catch the dog if he tried making a run for it.

Sweat beaded on Leroy's forehead.

"Can you switch out his food while I take him on a walk?"

"Sure." I skirted the edge of the hall, but the pup was too busy barking at nothing. I'd only been asked to man the front desk in case we received calls, but I'd already had to help around a little here and there with the animals.

I swiftly switched out the food as the barking faded. After a swift inspection, I left the cage slightly ajar and made my way back to the front.

The door dividing the office from the holding stalls snicked shut. I propped my fists on my hips to survey the neat desk, there wasn't any more I could clean up. As a volunteer, I didn't have much of a say with anything other than organization, so I'd been making the most of twiddling my thumbs up here. A touch on my neck had me whirling, but there was no one in here. I rubbed my neck. The draft in here . . .

"Catalina." I stumbled back frantically looking side to side.

A palm pressed over my mouth, cutting off my scream. My chest heaved when I saw nothing in front of me. I stumbled back, almost tripping before something that felt an awful lot like a palm, pressed on my spine.

"Hi, Pet." I could hear the humor in Asher's tone. My eyes rounded. "Don't freak out . . . more than you have."

Asher was here. Invisible. I backed up until I was up against the wall, searching in front of me but could see absolutely nothing.

"How?" I hissed, still sweeping my gaze around, hoping to see something, anything, a ripple in the air, but no.

"It's my ability." I could practically hear his shrug. Hands coasted to my wrists and he pressed them into the wall at my back. I bit back a moan.

"Are you okay, Catalina?" George rushed into the lobby. He was the shift manager and the one to call me in to help . . . he was also a little handsy.

All he could see was me, plastered to the wall, with my arms flat as I panted. I jerked my hands free and flattened them to my side. Stepping forward, I swung my hand, trying to shoo Asher away inconspicuously. My fingers smacked *something* and the breath from a soft grunt brushed my ear and my face heated.

"Yes, sorry, I just needed a second." I cleared my throat.

George scratched his neck, nodding quickly.

I yanked on the door to the office, but he cleared his throat. "Cat."

A soft hiss near my ear made a tremble coast up my spine and I licked my lips.

"Could you come to my office please?" Seemed like a rhetorical question, because he brushed past me and pulled open the door for me to trail after him. I carefully stepped forward, not wanting to slam into an invisible vampire.

Once inside, I approached George where he leaned on his desk, legs out and affable smile on his lips. I'd put him at a few years older than me. I kept a few feet away from him in case he started getting too touchy as he'd been with every interaction I'd had with him, and there hadn't been many.

"How are you holdin' up?" He smiled, but somehow it didn't reach his eyes, or maybe I just couldn't tell because they'd dropped to my boobs.

"Good," I said, trying a polite smile. With Asher unseen and hovering near, I was too on edge to be more talkative.

"Good, good. Seeing as you're new around these parts, I'll take you out to dinner this weekend to thank you for all the help." He straightened from his slouch. In that one step he took, I could reach my arm out and touch him with my fingertips.

Whatever I was about to say got stuck in my throat when a firm grip flattened on my belly. Fingers dug into me as if Asher wrapped a hand around my waist. The harsh touch softened as he trailed down to my thigh. It was light and teasing. Another hand lightly cupped one of my breasts.

My teeth clicked together.

I worked on keeping my attention on George.

"I . . ." Asher caressed my mound, the tip of his fingers dragging across the front of my pussy. The slow rub against my clit shot electricity through my body.

I sucked in my cheeks and crossed my arms over my chest, dislodging the teasing nipple touches.

"Are you okay?" George's eyebrows furrowed.

"Yep," I squeaked.

"I'll be sure to treat you to a good meal," George continued, stepping close enough to invade my personal bubble.

Blunted teeth grazed across the side of my neck and a soft whimper slipped free.

George reached out to touch me, probably to squeeze my shoulder as he'd already done, but this time, he didn't make contact. His hand froze mid-air and a sudden, ear-splitting crack rent the air and his face contorted in agony.

"George?"

He whimpered, sweat beading. I connected the dots. "Asher, no," I gasped, throwing my hands up in the general area I could only imagine he stood. As my palms connected with a torso, he appeared. George released a choked scream that cut off as Asher twisted his arm with the barest of movements. Another ear-splitting crack of bones cut him off.

I hugged myself to Asher's raised arm, but even with all the weight I used to try to get him to let George go, he didn't budge. His expression remained affable, but the lowered eyebrows and ticking jawline hinted at his irritation.

"Stop, please," I begged, clinging onto his arm. "Please."

Asher's tongue lashed across his lower lip and his pupils had expanded. Evil stared back at me. There was no care, no emotion, a lack of . . . everything humane in those blue eyes.

"Just for you, Pet," he dragged George higher, closer to his face. "You fell and broke your arm. You do not remember the last few minutes. You never had a conversation with Catalina nor have you ever seen me. Leave my sight." He released George who staggered backwards then flicked his hand up as if shooing a fly away.

George stiffly walked out, hugging his arm to his chest, gaze unfocused and dazed.

"Why would you do that?" I choked out, breathing hard, hugging myself as I backed away from him. Asher blinked at me, mouth twitching up at the corners.

"Silly, Pet. I protect what is mine." The low words rang in a matter-of-fact tone.

Protect? He would protect me . . . a knot of emotion swelled in my throat . . . I'd never been protected by anyone. His words settled over me like a blanket and I hated how good it felt.

Asher stepped to me and I put up a hand up to halt him since my brain hadn't stopped whirling. All the strange emotional reactions were swamping me.

"Wait," I mumbled. He forcefully shoved me back, so my ass dug into the desk. The rough shove quickened my heart rate to the point that my throat tightened. He easily maneuvered me, forcing my back to him until his front was flush to my spine.

I couldn't push any words out as instinct to escape kicked in. The room seemed to get smaller, like the walls were creaking closer to smash me under them. Run. Run. My pounding heart echoed the word through my veins.

An arm lashed around my chest while the other hand unbuttoned my jeans and slipped into my panties. His warm hand grazed my belly on its slide downward.

"Shh, Pet. It's just me. Your friendly neighborhood vampire, here to pillage your wet pussy."

I choked out a laugh, caught off guard.

"That's a bit of a stretch, no?" I said with the last of the air struggling in my chest. He hummed and it skittered shivers down my spine. Blazing heat throbbed through my core, and my thighs spasmed to close and apply more pressure between my legs.

Searching fingers grazed my clit and moved past it with a rough rub before sliding into my pussy.

"Pet is so wet for me," he purred, pleased. I hated that he was so right. His fingers had to be drenched, but I couldn't stop wanting him.

I sucked in a harsh breath and desire consumed my paralysis. I sank back into him, wanting this . . . wanting everything he offered. My panicked heartbeat calmed under his gentle coaxing.

My body just gave in to him. I slumped, resting the back of my head against his torso.

"This is his office," I panted, enjoying this too much to shove him off. I rubbed against the bulge nudging my ass. "Someone is going to walk in."

His long fingers pressed into my clit, rolling softly. I whimpered and arched against his palm with my eyelids fluttering. A dull ringing echoed through the closed door and I gasped, straightening to pull away, but he resisted. It was no use. Panting, I slumped against him, cradled, so *close*. Maybe being a blood-whore wasn't too bad . . .

"Vampire," I moaned low. "If I don't answer the phone, someone else will come." And I didn't want anyone else facing them. I'd be the one to blame for bringing evil to their door. After a moment of hesitation, his grip loosened, and I extricated myself to exit the office space.

A low chuckle followed me as I stiffly walked back to the front desk. I needed to get a hold of myself. I slapped my palm on the desk surface and gripped the pen. It creaked in my palm.

An invisible, hyper-sexual vampire almost killed my boss,

and I was all a-flutter over him. I scoffed, shaking my head down at a blank notepad. The pen tip dug into the paper, and I forced my fingers to relax. The phone had stopped ringing, which was fortunate because if I'd answered, I would have been panting.

Helping here was supposed to keep me away from my mercurial neighbors, but if Asher hovered around, that would defeat the purpose.

A poke in the middle of my back made me jerk to the side and the pen skidded across the desk. A big black mark scratched across the page. I whirled to no one there. I could imagine the smirk he had though.

Annoying vampire kept pressing my buttons. He was lucky I wasn't stabbing this pen into his eye. I scowled at the empty air behind me and dropped into the rolling chair. Fingertips grazed my shoulder, pressing into the tight muscle.

"How long are you hanging around?" I tried to not move my lips with the query.

"Whenever you're ready I'll hitch a ride with you."

I scoffed. "Have you dismissed whoever you had 'keeping an eye one me'?"

"It's for your safety." Whatever he was selling, I wasn't buying. Honestly, I doubt he believed it himself with the humor seeped in his voice. 'Friendly neighborhood vampire' my left toe. This was all about control and keeping me under their thumb.

The ridiculousness of the situation shot me into a laughing fit. This was not my life right now.

There was no light at the end of the tunnel though. They needed me to help them find their vampire friend. That descriptor sounded off. Did vampires even *have* friends?

"Tell me about Ren," I burst out, sounding slightly crazed.

His hand settled on my neck, thumbs pressed into my muscles again, and I melted into the seat as he kneaded. I bit back my whimper. He was so confusing. On one side, he seemed flippant and almost considerate, but on the other was the vampire that had forced me to the desk to shove his fingers into my pussy.

"Ren is a bit of a dick—"

"Like Jax?"

Asher chuckled. "A different way than Jax. Ren is calculated, you'd think he'd learn with all those centuries under him . . ." He clicked his tongue disapprovingly

"Centuries. . ." My lips felt numb. "How old is he?"

"He was turned in the mid seventeen hundreds at thirty-five."

"*Holy shit*—" I coughed into my fist. Right. Vampires—Immortality and all that jazz. "And the rest of you?"

"Tobias and Bastien are the oldest." Tobias looked to be around my age, twenty-six, but Asher mentioned Tobias being a priest in the sixteenth century.

"Tobias looks young." I said it more to myself than to him.

"He was turned while he was younger." Well, that made sense. "Jax and I are the youngest born seventeen-eighty-two and turned when we were thirty-one." Those were a lot of ancient numbers. He'd also mentioned another name.

"Who is Bastien?"

"You don't need to worry about him."

"There's a lot of people I don't need to worry about, huh," I muttered.

I read between the lines he was skirting. Like he told me to not worry about the woman they were with too. "Why are you answering all my questions? Because I won't live long or because I'll be a blood-whore?"

"Who taught you this phrase?" His fingers twitched against my shoulder. I hated how his voice conveyed he didn't take anything I said seriously.

"Unless that's been your plan all along." I said through gritted teeth. Well, jokes on him, I was already a blood-whore.

His ministrations paused for a beat before resuming. "Would it be such a bad thing to be my blood-whore?" Every cell in my body froze. I couldn't breathe anymore.

The rubbing on my shoulders paused again. "Just playing with you, Pet." He chuckled and his sweet breath brushed against my cheek. "I will keep you nice and safe." There was that vow again that made my entire body clench with longing. His sweet breath caressed my ear, enflaming lust through my senses. "After all, I want to savor fucking you."

"Oh." It came out as a breathy sigh. His lips pressed into my cheek. I couldn't trust what he said as much as I ached to, so I would continue with planning my escape from this vampire infested town.

catalina

WE'D ARRIVED at their manor moments ago and I'd gone directly to the living room couch and sank into it. The cushion dipped as Asher settled next to me, tossing his arm around my shoulders, and my heart rate picked up with his careless touch. He didn't know how it affected me, but if he kept it up, he would scent it.

I cleared my throat and focused on unsexy things like . . . crying children . . . outhouses . . .

If I got all this 'bite-me-horniness' out of my system, when I escaped, and *I would escape*, I could live the rest of my life with that desire satiated. Because I wanted it more than I'd wanted anything for myself in a long time. I must face my addiction. Fear, confusion, and lust started from the Pale One and I'd never wanted to face it . . .

"Vampires are arrogant, prideful creatures. At the core of it we like to play." He twined my long, loose hair within his fingers. "When you're at the lounge, don't look at any above the neck. That's an immediate way to draw attention to yourself. You're not there to be curious, you're there to serve."

That was disgusting. Fear swelled and nausea soured my stomach. He said it so callously.

"Vampires can have varying personalities, but never forget we are instinctual and there is one thing we can't live without—blood. A submissive personality is the best default." He pinched my chin. "You're a smart girl, use that intelligence and don't say or do anything rash." He flashed his distended fangs and my breath hitched. "Your pupils dilated." His smile widened. "You're not flinching at the sight of my fangs. When someone bites you, just let them get it over with."

I licked my lips. At the beginning, I'd understood this was a probability, but I'd thought . . . after he . . .

"You're okay with someone else biting me?" I thoughtlessly asked, eyeing him from under my lashes. He blinked slow, his golden eyelashes cresting at his cheekbones before meeting my gaze, almost as if he had to process my words.

"Why wouldn't I be okay with another biting you?"

Red flashed in his iris but he closed his eyes and when he opened them again, it had disappeared.

Did he still go out and bite others? Irrational jealousy spiked through my veins.

I pushed that away. *It wasn't my business.* Wasn't like I was his girlfriend. *Did vampires even do bite-monogamy? Bite-ogamy?* Likely not since the end result was an addiction. These 'blood-whore' thoughts were getting on my nerves.

Stop. I didn't *want* to be a vampire's girlfriend. What the fuck was wrong with me and these ridiculous intrusions?

"What if they try to do more?" If biting and screwing went hand in hand every time with Asher, where would that leave me while I had no one I could hide behind?

"You mean fuck?"

I nodded hard, mostly to hide the blush on my cheeks. I felt so inept and inexperienced.

"If you're feeling it, go for it." He traced a shape into the arm of the sofa, keeping his gaze on me.

"Go with it?" My spine tensed.

"Bodies aren't meant to be for only one person." So not only was bite-ogamy not a thing, neither was monogamy. A possessive swell had lifted its head inside me, but there was nothing I could do about it.

"And if I'm not feeling it?" I struggled getting the words out.

He just stared at me.

"Oh." I tried stifling the fact that my stomach soured. "Where will I go?"

"We're sending you into one of Calliope's private lounges. We want you to get as close to her as possible to see if she mentions Ren."

"Why do you think she has him?" My question forced him to pause and he raked his gaze down my body and back up to my face.

"The only person Ren may give in and fuck after a decade is close to Calliope."

"A decade?" I gasped. Jeez.

"You're shocked at *that*?" Asher scoffed. "The others three are worse." Three, as in Jax, Bastien, and Tobias?

I cocked my head questioningly, but he didn't elaborate.

"But you?"

"I don't have some odd obsession with Imog—her memory like my brother." He was about to say Imogen's name. I licked my lips as jealousy burned my stomach. So the others loved her still. "I stayed around because I refuse to leave Jax. It might have been best I did, thinking back to that bit—"

He stopped mid curse and shook his head, anger bleeding away as he turned his attention to me.

"Don't wo—"

"Worry about it," I finished his sentence, rolling my eyes.

"Did you just sass me?" I tensed even though I could tell he thought it was funny.

"Absolutely not," I muttered, clearing my throat. He stared at my mouth with sharp focus. I nervously wet my lips. His body twitched and he suddenly lunged at my mouth. He swallowed my shocked scream, coaxing my lips open. Silky lips pressed into mine insistently, battering down my defenses.

My tongue flicked out to meet his. His fingers dug into my waist and he hoisted me onto his lap. My legs spread to accommodate his thighs, and even though I was flexible, there was a pinch with how much bigger he was. The good thing was his thick swelled cock pushed against me at the perfect spot.

I tipped my hips forward rubbing against him harder. My body no longer belonged to me.

Asher's fangs extended and I groaned into his mouth, trying my best to not prick myself as I tongued him. The sharp edge scraped my lower lip and I groaned again.

A stinging prick opened on my flesh and Asher's fingers twitched, his entire body stiffening as his hips jerked up into my core. His hum turned guttural, and the grip tightened painfully.

"More," he groaned into my mouth, hips bucking up as he sucked on my lip.

Good thing I'd taken a hit of my inhaler before this because he effortlessly stole my breath. His hands slipped under my blouse and into the hem of my slacks. With a quick jerk, they tore down my leg. He yanked them to the side and shucked them, leaving me in my panties until they were also destroyed by Asher.

He pressed them to his nose, inhaling deeply. My face heated. *That was so hot.*

Slickness pooled where I rubbed myself against his pants. His finger pressed into my clit. A whimper escaped me at the gentle rub.

"Harder," I mumbled.

"*Fuck*," he rasped but it sounded more like a promise. I reached down and jerked the buttons open. His cock sprang out, and I almost choked on my saliva. The long—incredibly freaking long—cock was adorned with a gold ladder piercing that extended to the base.

I blinked at it, but my core throbbed.

His finger curved into my slick entrance, sliding in and out in a slow rhythm. A moan crawled up my throat. I helplessly twisted my hips, seeking to be filled.

Asher braced his hand at my hip, lifting me so the tip of his cock teased my folds. He slammed me down while simultaneously thrusting up. A yelp slipped from my mouth and I tensed. I could feel every inch inside me, and I couldn't breathe. I squeezed my eyes shut as tears sprang to life.

"Catalina," he whispered, cupping his hand at my neck. I peeked at him from under my lashes. His eyes were wide as he looked into mine. He could tell he was the first inside my pussy.

His eyes flared and red swirled with the blue before taking it over. Sharp fingernails stabbed into my ass as he gripped my hips firmly and with ease, he lifted me and slammed me back down on his cock.

A scream ripped from my throat, and I cinched my eyes

tightly shut. Without mercy he forced me to fuck him even though I had no time to get used to his length. Each slam of his cock caused him to stab my cervix.

"Asher," I whimpered, half in pain and half in pleasure. Agony struck with every forceful movement, but then why did I like it so much? Tears trickled from the corner of my eyes as the evil, lust ridden gaze watched them slide down. A cruel smile curved the corners of his sinful lips, but he did not cease. My pain seemed to please him. "It hurts."

"Take me." He hissed low and smiled with his fangs extended. Leaning forward, his fangs sliced into my neck, sending suction to my clit. He moaned against my throat and the rub of his piercings scraped against my insides, raising the sensitivity with each stroke. It hurt too much. I couldn't take it. Tears full on leaked down my cheeks, but he didn't cease. "Fuck," he spat lifting from my neck and jerked up hard, sucking the air from my lungs in the best way. He did it again and again. The angle of his thrust had him hitting my clit and I whimpered. Blood dripped from the corners of his parted mouth.

A sudden orgasm spiked through my pussy, causing me to grip at him with jarring squeezes. More intense than any I'd ever given myself. It was uncontrollable and unstoppable. Tingles spread across my skin and my channel clutched him with the incoming inevitability. He moaned, head tossing back and sending his hair around his face as his mouth opened on a cry. With each spasm of his cock, his hips slammed up, bouncing me on his cock and dragging out the electricity, my pussy milking every last drop.

I could no longer hold myself up and I slumped on his chest. Liquid continued leaking from my pussy and as the swell of the orgasm faded, the agony of his cock in my channel settled in.

I twitched, and quickly froze, hissing in agony. I'd never experienced such a foreign pleasurable pain.

Asher's lips tightened and his hands smoothed down my sides, dipping to play with my slick clit. My pussy pulsed and shot another slice of agony to my depths. Crying out, I wrapped my hand around his wrist. He lifted his half-lidded blue gaze to mine. One of his hands lifted to my shirt and with a jerk, he tore it off.

"Such pretty brown nipples," he murmured into my skin. His praise made my body clench around his pierced cock and I whimpered again, but I no longer knew if it was from pain or pleasure. It melded together in a pot of utter lust.

Asher captured one of my nipples and rolled his tongue over it, playfully nipping it. I moaned, yanking his hair. He hissed as I arched, forcing him deeper inside me, taking the slight pinch with it.

"I'm going to have you again, Pet." He wrapped his arms around my midsection and twisted me so my back dropped onto the couch cushion. The movement caused his cock to slip out of my pussy. I felt every single piercing rub against my inside. I winced, shying away from his hold, but he forced my legs open.

I gasped and pressed my hands over myself, my face warming so much it burned.

"But before I fuck you, I need to heal you a bit."

My eyebrows furrowed, but he shifted so his knees pressed on the ground and his head hovered over my dripping heat. I pushed to my arms to see him inspecting my glinting, shaved pussy. Blood mingled in the liquid coating me and I gasped, but before I could say anything, his head dipped. His warm tongue speared inside my core and I yelped, falling back. Swirling his tongue, he thrust inside me and around me, licking everything up with long lavish laps.

My thighs trembled and kept trying to close, but he kept them in place. Even that hiked my lust. Being held down by a vampire was my nightmare . . . but why did it feel so delicious?

"My Pet," he groaned and the vibration of his voice shot me into another orgasm. His tongue didn't relent as he pressed it against my trembling clit.

He climbed up my body and fastened his mouth around my nipple. He suckled me, teeth grazing my breast. I gripped this hair again and arched as his fangs speared the soft flesh. I whimpered as my legs shook. He hummed, taking more and more from me, but I didn't fucking care—it felt too good.

Panting, I pushed to my elbows and stared down at the blood dripping down my breast, painting my skin. It made me unimaginably hot. Asher lifted his head and steadily stared at me as his tongue lashed across the wounds and the blood stream cut off from his saliva.

I dropped on my back, floating in ecstasy as I tried to put the scattered pieces of my mind back together.

We lay there for a while, his fingers moving across my nipple in gentle circles.

Goose bumps pebbled my flesh and I wiggled my hips. How was it possible I was ready for another round?

A yawn made my eyes water.

"You need to rest." He chuckled in my ear. "Don't worry. I'll please you again." That really should have sent me running but I wanted this. It would only be for a bit longer. I could enjoy it until then, right?

He pulled his shirt off and carefully pulled it over my head so it fell around me. Lifting me into his arms, he curved me close to his wide chest. He walked upstairs and then a soft bed was under me. Asher pulled the blankets over my shoulders.

"Rest," he ordered. "You should have told me you were not experienced." He pressed his soft lips into my neck and grazed along my chin. I arched closer to him, and he took me into his arms. I lulled, following his directive as I was dragged into a restful sleep. A type of sleep I'd never had since I couldn't turn my brain off. But my body agreed with my mind at this moment and they were on a damn cloud.

The world faded away, and my limbs became weightless.

My eyelids fluttered and I *sank* . . .

Prying my eyes open, I gasped and found myself surrounded by pitch black—and standing. I blinked down at my feet. Black tile stretched across all edges, seemingly endless. *Was I dreaming?*

A hiss dragged my attention up and all I could see were the red eyes watching me within the dark space. They practically glowed.

A shiver coasted down my back. I hated the dark.

"Who are you?" I muttered, backing up. Everything seemed to stretch, but my back flattened against a wall, blocking me from escape.

Was it the Pale One? Was he back to take me? I whimpered and stumbled away from the wall but slammed into another surface. It may have seemed like it was never-ending, but it was a cage. I slid to the ground, shaking as I hugged myself while the eyes continued to stare at me. They didn't blink as they watched me until everything faded from my mind.

asher

I PRESSED my lips to Catalina's cheek and felt her smile. She lowered her head, clearing her throat. Pet was shy. Her reactions didn't fail to enthrall me. Everything she did pulled me, and I couldn't stop touching her. It was an addiction I didn't want to be rid of. Her skin was silky smooth, and I wanted to curl into her body forever, which was a tall order, considering my immortality.

We'd slept well through the morning. It was close to sunset when she shot up like a bullet. I could tell because my limbs felt weighed down, but I'd managed to be aware of my surroundings. Any moment now, the automatic window panels to block out the sun during the day would begin to rise. Her knee dug into my side and I squinted to find her staring at me. The rapid thumps of her heart calmed down. It warmed my dead heart in a way it never had been. Pet was an anxious bundle, and she was usually so good at attempting to mask her fear. She made me feel things I didn't know how to describe but all I wanted was to wrap her in my arms.

A temporary thing, I was sure. I'd never experienced desire

anywhere near this level, but sex was sex. Even good fucking sex. I'd fuck myself out of this odd obsession soon. I'd already allowed her more liberties than I'd ever allowed a human. She'd slept beside me while I was utterly vulnerable.

Today would be a step forward in the search for Ren. She would enter Calliope's den. I didn't think the pretty human was prepared, but we had no choice. Coaching her a bit more about how she should behave in the lounge should have been priority last night instead of fucking her, but I hadn't been able to help it.

My gaze dropped to her bronze neck and my cock tented the silk sheet. She already had me hard and primed for her, *den lilla katten*.

In my long existence, her blood was the closest thing to heavenly I'd ever encountered. I understood Tobias's uncharacteristic draw to her. The way we were wrapped up in her was because of her delicious blood.

Biting her was an unmatched experience, she embraced it and loved it. Not in a way a blood-whore sought it out, or one of those fear-filled humans that always had to get their minds wiped by the end. She was different and my fangs ached to sink into her at all moments of the day. Even now I itched to sink them into her when I'd fed too much last night already.

I'd never lost myself the way I did with her. Never come in my fucking slacks that way either. Then she made me come twice in her slick cunt. Her little pussy squeezing me tightly. I was the first cock in her.

The memory sent a shudder down my spine. Even as a whore, I'd never been with a virgin. I wasn't fixated on how many lovers my women had, nor had I ever cared. But a strange billowing in my chest when I sheathed my dick in her wasn't something I could ignore and I'd lost control.

But it was only because it was her.

Then there was my reaction to our conversation before we fucked. An odd knot in my gut had been present since then. Another vampire biting her . . . fucking her . . . had nothing to do with *me*. As I could—would do the same. Unbound and free.

The knot tightened in my chest. It became easier to move as the weight lessened. I stretched my arms up and set them under my head. Catalina finally relaxed next to me in bed, slipping close to my side. Every time she was close it reminded me of the sunlight beaming on my skin. I struggled to grab onto the memory with each year further from my vampire birth. Or like the comforting heat from a fireplace.

"The clothing should be here today. I chose some outfits for you that will grab the attention of the vampire you're going to seduce into taking you to the back." Saying the words made me angry. I forced my fangs back in.

Catalina hummed and nudged her nose against my neck. My cock and throat tightened at the sweet movement.

My cock twitched and my fangs distended.

"Are you sure you're okay to go in there?" *Where was this coming from?* There was no choice. Yet, I couldn't stop the question.

Cat lowered guards I didn't even know I had.

I gripped her hip and she smiled up at me, the shy tilt of her mouth drawing me in. Pressing my lips to hers, I swiftly moved back when my fangs ached with the need to bury them in her. *If I drain her dry, I will not be able to savor her.*

"Is there something specific I should be listening for?" I flexed my hand into her hair.

"Mentions of Ren. Or Crimson." The corner of her lips tipped down.

The doorbell rang, it was an annoying echo at the back of my head. Catalina did not react. She'd not heard it.

"Asher." I ignored Tobias's roar. It wasn't rare that he was pissed about something or other.

My eyelids slid shut. Right. I'd scheduled these take-out orders weekly so I could sneak some human blood straight from the source. Perfect time to get a feeding.

"Come with me, Pet." I pushed to standing and held my hand out to help her up. She frowned, obviously leery about following me, but she slipped her hand in mine.

Her long legs peeked from the shirt I'd given her and the honey color of her skin caused my cock to spasm. Her hips swayed with every step and my fingers twitched to grip them. If I fucked her, I wouldn't stop from feeding. I gritted my molars, accidentally nicking my lip. Newbie move. I left my door open and Catalina quietly followed me down the stairs, sending me a confused look.

Tobias glared at me and all I could see of Cat was her head tilting to the side and her long lush hair rustled down her back like an onyx waterfall.

A girl slightly younger than Cat stood at the threshold, her eyes wide on Tobias. Fascination sparkled in their depths, and it only deepened when she turned in my direction.

"Delivery for Asher Crimson," she breathed, lifting the bag of cardamom buns I'd ordered. She licked her lips, her eyes trailing down my naked chest. Since the girl was here, I may as well top up so I didn't have to feed on Catalina today before we headed out. I couldn't have her passing out before then.

"Come here, sweets," I purred. The girl blinked at me and her eyes unfocused. She moved forward, toward me, and stopped a foot away. She seemed vaguely familiar; she must be from the last time I'd had a delivery.

"Sweets." I gripped her arms as she slid her hands up my chest. Catalina sucked in an audible breath.

"I-I'll go wait in the kitchen," Cat stammered and left the foyer. I'd hoped she'd wait for me. I frowned at her retreating back; spine straight as a pole.

Tobias shoulder checked me as he stepped past me. *What was his problem?*

My attention was dragged away from where Cat disappeared by the flexing hand on my shoulder. "Ah, sweets, tilt your head to the side a bit." She immediately did as I ordered, and her eyes slid shut as her breathing elevated.

Compulsion didn't work on Cat like it did on other humans. *What was wrong with her that she could withstand it?*

Why was I thinking of Catalina before feeding? My meal deserved my full attention.

Lowering my head, I paused near her neck. The scent of her skin made my nose wrinkle. There wasn't necessarily anything wrong with her smell, but it was overwhelmingly off, like it didn't suit my taste.

It wasn't the liquid sunlight I'd been surrounded by for the last few days.

I pursed my lips and gripped her wrist to my mouth, forcing my reluctant fangs out. The tip grazed the thin line of her skin. The paper-thin flesh housed blue veins running down her arm.

Nothing like Catalina's. Her scent not only attracted

vampires, but humans as well. Like that filthy human at the shelter.

The knot tightened painfully. Aggression lashed at my insides. I clenched my hands until blood dripped from my palms.

What was this emotion?

The girl whimpered in pain. I loosened my grip as she jerked away with pain marring her expression. Gouges graced her arm. Ten of them, all from my fingers.

"No noise." I tsked.

Lifting my fingers, I licked my bloodied fingertips. I grimaced. That was disgusting compared to the delicacy of Catalina's blood.

I sighed and tipped the girl's face up, peering into the pained eyes.

"Forget everything that happened as soon as the door opened. You made your delivery and on your way out, caught your arms on a jagged gate." She nodded and turned on her heel, closing the door behind her. I didn't bother healing the slices in her wrist.

My loafers shuffled over the carpet leading to the living room where Catalina waited for me. A grin tugged at the corners of my lips. I was only away from her for a split moment, but I wanted back in her presence.

She perched at the edge of the diner seat, her arms crossed as she looked at her tapping foot engulfed in one pair of my slippers.

"All done?" The question sounded light and even. Her gaze didn't sparkle with that happiness she'd had while nuzzling into my chest. *Was she getting sick?*

I pressed my palm to her forehead and it was rather hot.

"You're coming down with something." Panic squeezed my chest and the dead heart in my chest tightened. I knelt in front of her, peering into her eyes to look for any cloudiness. My prior training rushed to the forefront, something I'd never turned to.

My thumb pressed into her wrist to time her heart rate. It was accelerated but there were no other irregularities.

Her shoulders seemed especially tight and there was a little indent between her brows. I leaned over and smoothed it with my finger. Her brown eyes met mine, tension bracketing her mouth. She leaned away from me.

"Are you nauseous?"

Her eyes flitted to the side and she nodded tightly.

"We're going to the lounge soon, but if you continue not to feel well, we'll postpone it."

Cat cleared her throat and nodded tightly.

"I'm sure I'll be fine, but I should go wait at home until you're ready to leave."

"Stay here, I'll watch over you." I trailed a finger up her leg. A shiver trembled her hand but she jerked her leg away from my touch, smiling tightly. My brows furrowed. What was wrong with her?

She shook her head.

There seemed to be *anger* to the line of her flattened lips.

I pinched her chin and peered into her eyes, but she refused to meet them.

"Are you unwell?"

Her chin tipped in a jerky head shake, and she *finally* looked at me. It wasn't easy to read what she was thinking, but the irritation practically shouted from her gaze. I couldn't understand where the swirling anger came from. Catalina's temper had hinted out before, but she'd never released it, like right now.

"What's wrong, Catalina?" I murmured, my mouth hovering over hers.

"Nothing." She yanked her chin out of my grip, and my fingers curled at her absence. "I'll see you later. I have to feed my cat and clean my bed."

I trailed after her as she made her way down the hall, my shirt grazing her thighs. She didn't even retrieve her clothing or shoes.

The door slammed after her pretty little ass and I frowned.

catalina

ADJUSTING the sports bra around my torso, I dipped to clutch Asher's shirt where I'd dropped it before showering.

"Idiot vampire," I snapped at the inanimate object. I tipped my head back. The emotions rioted in my chest, and I was angry. *How could he bite someone else? Why did it hurt?*

Bunching the linen cloth, I tossed it to the corner of the room and dropped into my bed with a huff.

It was around seven in the evening. I'd slept a long damn time in Asher's comfy room, a room I was sure hosted many women. I rubbed my face and groaned.

If Asher was okay with biting her, what was to say he wouldn't sleep with her? In so many words, he said he didn't do monogamy. Binx's front paws pressed into my arm and he peered at me. It was so eerie. His claws extended and pricked my arm. I yanked my arm away from the demon cat. *Just add to the agony, Binx.*

I could be cool about this, after all, he was only my first lover, kind of . . . I bit my lip recalling his delicious, pierced dick. But it wasn't like I was actively trying to not be with others, it just worked out that way with the lack of opportunities and being on the run.

My ass had been taken, by force, and that was the extent of my experience. I puffed my hair out away from my cheek.

"I'm internally rambling, Binx."

He meowed and climbed on my chest and tucked his paws beneath his chest. He was heavier than he seemed, but the weight was comfortable.

My eyelids drooped, growing heavier. The nightmare from yesterday teased the edge of my thoughts . . . Those eyes . . .

My eyelids sprang open and I sucked in a breath, shooting straight up. I was back in that dark space. The cool surface of the tile pressed into my thighs and I shot to my feet. These nightmares were surreal. How did I recall this when I was awake?

Was this lucid dreaming?

A thud brought my attention to the left and I fisted my hands, stepping back from the heavy red gaze. The figure suddenly burst forward with speed too quick for my eyes to catch. I squeezed my eyelids together as a grip slammed me against the wall.

Just a nightmare. Just a nightmare.

The hair escaping from my ponytail tickled my cheek. The strand waving back and forth from the harsh breathing coming from the thing grabbing me. By his rough palms, I could tell he was male. The large pawing hands engulfed my arms. I kept my eyes closed, breathing slowly. It couldn't be the Pale One because the massive body felt too muscular. It wasn't the skeletal monster that had profoundly scarred me.

My heart pounded against my chest, ready to burst. I gritted my teeth. This was a dream, this wouldn't hurt me, I needed to defeat my fear.

Lifting my head, I glared into the face peering down at me. This close, I made out that his hair was white and long and the shoulders were a wide shadow, larger than I'd ever seen. He didn't move, just continued watching me eerily.

I wiggled in his grip, but he didn't loosen it and snarled.

Squeezing my eyelids shut, I imagined myself back in my room, waking up next to Binx. The thin skin of my eyelids turned yellow and they fluttered open.

I was in my room, the light came from the lamp beside the bed, but somehow, the white-haired beast of a man was still with me, pinning me against the wall. I angled my head to the side but didn't see Binx, and my bed was made. My mattress was no longer on the ground, instead, the room was beautifully furnished with a caramel bedframe of my dreams—literally. Now that I was getting a good look around, I noted the fuzzy filter surrounding everything.

I craned my neck to get a look at his face.

I took a deep breath.

The sharp angles of his face created an indent to his cheeks, chiseled and abrupt. His thick brows were dark, a contrast to the white hair. The vampire tilted his head to the side, red eyes devouring my face. His attention dropped to my neck and his fangs sprang out. The scrape of his palm slid down the wall as he dipped toward my neck and nestled his nose in the crevice. My heart pounded, but I remained still. As odd as this all was, it was a dream.

He suddenly struck, teeth burying into my neck so hard it burned. I screamed and he continued gnawing into me. I could feel it as if I were awake. This was like some sick version of sleep paralysis.

The dragging sucks burned, but it felt off, like there was a sheet of wax paper between us.

"No," I shouted, slapping his shoulder.

He growled against my throat, and I slapped him again. The teeth retracted from my neck with a wet slurp.

I put my palm up, facing him. He glowered, blood dripping down his chin and staining his teeth. The big vampire inched forward, and I instinctively flattened my palm against his chest, breathing hard. The hard muscle was silky and smooth, the bronze skin matching mine. The vampire jerked, startled as he looked down at my hand against him. His wideness made me feel smaller than I'd ever felt, and Asher already dwarfed me in height.

Poking my other finger near his face, I cleared my throat. "No." His brows furrowed so hard I was positive he didn't understand. The odd blank eyes didn't tell me much. My eyes flicked to the side, and I clocked the door.

Even if this was a dream, there was a level of reality. I gave into the urge to take off at a sprint but didn't get far. Running face-first into his chest, I grunted as the sting radiated. He roughly grabbed my arms and tossed me on the bed. I bounced with a scream and his heavy body settled over my back, his teeth slamming into my shoulder.

I sucked in a shaky breath and shook as he sucked. The odd sensation causing a pulsing at my core. I could feel his body pinning me and his teeth in me, considering the height differences.

I rolled my hips up, trying to buck him, but he thrust down, his hard cock digging into the cleft of my ass.

Was this some vampire fantasy I'd conjured? That idea enhanced when a gush of wetness spread between my legs. I liked his domination.

I groaned and tipped my head back, grinding up as my heart battered against my ribs. Panting, I continued to grind, but he seemed lost in biting me. His teeth extracted and he slid them into another spot. Each stab of his incisors added to the gathering wetness.

Nails pierced my arm and I shot up in bed, panting. I scrambled for my inhaler, sucking in medication. Able to breathe, I hugged Binx to my chest.

"Thank you for waking me up," I rasped and patted my neck, but there was no bite.

That dream felt so real.

The memory faded along the edges, and I couldn't get a full grip on it. I groaned, rubbing my forehead. Binx grumbled on my chest. I stayed up for as long as I could, trying to find shapes within the popcorn ceiling. This must be some weird side effect from Asher biting me, it was bringing nightmares to the forefront.

Though, why would I not conjure the creep that initially starved me and instead some wide-shouldered hunk. *Beats me.*

asher

I TOOK a slight detour before we headed to Saphire Lounge in a few hours. He'd touched her and I couldn't let it go. His lust seeped from his pores and it infected my veins like poison. How dare he touch her? Leaning against the brick wall, I watched him exit the large building.

I'd been sure to put the large parking lot lamps out of commission and scour the area for any cameras to destroy them. George, the human male, held his arm to his chest, talking on the phone about going to the emergency room now that his shift was over. Blah, blah, blah. His whining grated on my ears.

I'd shared lovers of all shapes, sizes, genders. I'd partaken in orgies, and I'd never felt this overwhelming urge to murder for a mere touch. I left the pesky killing to Jax, Ren, or Bastien, when he was of sound mind—as sound as the big fuck could be.

Catalina had done this to me.

He arrived at his car a few feet away from me and set his phone on the top of his car as he fished for his car keys. I pushed off the wall and his eyes swung to me.

"Do you always touch what doesn't belong to you?"

His expression crumpled in confusion.

"Who are you?"

I grinned, making sure my teeth were on full display. His scowl froze when I pushed my fangs free.

I took another step closer and he backed up, starting to breathe harder. The whites of his eyes became startlingly obvious.

"Don't move," I said pushing my will upon him. His body stiffened from the order and his eyes flicked side to side. "Remember."

He jolted and tears flooded his eyes. Weak, little weaselly human.

"P-please, don't hurt me."

I pouted. In a sudden move, I lunged and gripped the back of his hair, leaning down so he had a clear view of my teeth. I tightened my grip on him until strands ripped in my fingers.

Torturing for anything other than sexual reasons hadn't ever attracted me, but I could see the allure.

"Please—" I tightened my grip and his words choked off.

"Please, please," I mocked, pouting. "Such beautiful cries of pain." I shivered. "While you're dead, cold, and six feet under, I'll be sliding my cock inside Catalina's sweet, succulent petals." I grinned.

His eyes widened. He touched my Pet and now look how he ended up. I tsked, shaking my head.

catalina

BINX JUMPED off the couch and his long tail swished as he disappeared into the house. The doorbell rang and I grunted as I extricated myself from my couch. It creaked as it bounced from my weight leaving it.

Asher stood at the entrance with his arms at his back. The silk cream shirt fell over his muscled shoulders, the indents of his muscles hinting through the thin material. I squeezed the doorknob. He was so fine it was criminal.

"Hello, Pet." The smile directed at me struck me stupid for a beat, but I shook myself free of the lusting cobwebs.

"Are you going to invite me in?"

My lips parted, the words about to slip free, but I snapped them together.

"Is that a myth or do you *have* to be invited?"

"Regrettably, that bit is not a myth. Has something to do with energies." His brow lifted, waiting for me to wave him in. My face heated thinking about him seeing my place. It wasn't even furnished. After seeing their elaborate house, I wasn't putting myself through that embarrassment. I cleared my throat and hugged my chest.

"I'd rather keep my house vamp free," I mumbled.

Asher frowned, but it didn't last long.

"We leave soon. But you know that right, since I told you to return." My cheeks heated at the accusing tone.

"Uh, a thing I'm watching got really good." It was a lame excuse, but I'd rather die than admit to him I didn't want to see him while I was feeling so raw and sensitive. These emotions were new and I didn't like it, especially since I could hide none of them.

I'd attempted to work through them, telling myself he was a vampire and drinking blood was how he survived. It meant nothing sexual necessarily—lie. The entire act was seeped with seduction.

I couldn't help recalling how good his bites felt and that meant the innocent, unknowing human would feel the same way . . . and the way he called her "sweets" raked my insides. I studied his features, taking in the impassive smirk that always seemed to curve his lips. Specks of red on his sleeve caught my attention.

"Is that blood?" My eyes widened.

"Would you look at that," he clicked his tongue disapprovingly and brushed at the spot, fixating on it. I puffed out my cheeks, shaking my head. I couldn't bring myself to ask.

"Let me put my shoes on." I left the door open and scurried away. It was a good thing I showered earlier. I shoved my shoes on, pocketed my inhaler, and emptied Binx's water bowl. He never drank out of it, instead, he seemed to take perverse pleasure from spilling it.

As soon as I stepped out, Asher swept me close to his chest, pressing his lips to my cheek. I instinctively cringed, the pressure in my chest tight. I cleared my throat and tried offering a smile, but I wasn't sure if it looked too much like a grimace.

"Are you all right, Pet?" His palm pressed to my forehead.

"I'm okay." I gripped his arm.

He leaned close, invading my space and his nose wiggled slightly.

"Have you been around Jax?"

"Uh, no." I hadn't even seen the guy since he got all pissy about the dress Asher made me put on.

Asher hummed, distracted. The wrought iron gate creaked in the cool wind and the crow resting on one of the metal bars, twisted its head as it observed us. The breeze fluttered my hair around my shoulders, and I rubbed my arms for warmth.

I puffed my cheeks out, focusing on the steps as I ascended. Arms swept me up and I blinked at Asher. He briskly and quickly got us to the top. My hair whipped around my head and settled on my shoulders as I scrambled to hold onto him.

Cool air washed over my arms as he entered the manor.

I peeked at him from the corner of my eye. He was quiet, less teasing. Introspective almost. His bow lips pressed softly together, and I wet my lower lip, valiantly trying to keep my thoughts PG.

"Here we are, Pet." He dropped my legs, bending so my feet flattened on the ground. I blinked at the packages stacked across the couches.

"What's all that?"

"Stuff I ordered for you," he responded, smiling. He gripped my shoulders and I gawked up at him. His head lowered and he met my lips with a disarming kiss.

His wet tongue brushed against mine and I moaned,

sucking it. The tip of my tongue flicked across his fang. My eyes flung open.

"Is something the matter?" Asher's eyes softened, looking into mine inquisitively. A chunk of his blond hair fell forward in front of his blue eye, and it did something bad to my insides. I was okay with his soap box, right? We weren't tied together. If I kept telling myself that, maybe I would be okay with it.

I jerked my head in a hard nod and slid my fingers through his hair, pulling him back to me. Squeezing myself to him, tight and desperate—a hold he mimicked—he straightened and my feet dangled as he clasped me tightly to his chest while our tongues played with each other. I groaned, twisting my head to the side so he could—

He nipped my lip, and I gasped as he tongued the wound. His arms clenched as if trying to fuse us together and his sucking on my lip became more insistent.

"We're running out of time," Tobias snapped, and I jerked my head back, but Asher clenched me tighter. "Asher."

Asher lifted from my mouth, leaving me raw and wanting. I caught a red hue to Asher's irises before he closed them tight. Tobias released the back of Asher's hair where he'd used it to jerk him off me.

"Killjoy," Asher panted, eyes still bright with lust and then he lowered me. I wobbled, gripping his arm to steady myself.

I turned my attention to Tobias. His lips were set in a straight line.

Before I could greet him, Asher gripped my shoulders and turned me toward the couch. A long magenta dress rested across the back, and with each step I took forward, the jewels beading the bodice glinted. My hand hovered over the fabric, similar to the shirt Asher wore. It seemed airy and too expensive to touch. I didn't want to ruin it.

"It's for tonight." Well, that gave me all the permission I needed to lift it. It slid across my fingertips, so buttery and silky I wanted to rub my face against it. Asher gripped the hem of my shirt.

My eyes widened, pressing a palm to his wrists before he exposed me, and peeked at Tobias.

"Don't worry about him, nothing tempts the priest." I frowned. I begged to differ. I thought back to the feel of his cock shoving against me when we were in my van on the day I met him.

I shook my head and handed Asher the dress to remove my clothing myself. If he took my clothes off, it would turn sexual and that's probably the route I should stay away from.

Unbuttoning my jeans, I shoved them down. My face warmed at the non-matching set of bra and panties. At least they were both around the same realm of nude.

Asher's attention fixed on my ass, his look smoldering. His tongue poked the inside of his cheek causing it to distend.

"If I don't leave, I'll fuck you and we don't have time for all the delicious things I want to do to you," he rasped. "I'm going to fetch Jax." Asher trailed his fingers down my naked spine. "I'll be back, Pet."

He'd already disappeared by the time I pulled the dress up my legs. The material strained at my thighs and over my hips. I puffed my cheeks out at the squeeze. It was nowhere near as bad a fit as the dress that belonged to their past love. Ignoring the odd pang, I shucked my bra, pressing the dress hem to my breasts tightly. Asher would have to carry my inhaler. Hopefully I managed not to get an attack so I didn't have to use it. After all, that was why I'd been around Asher 'training' so much, so I didn't freak out so easily. I reached behind me, straining to grip the little clasp midway up my back.

A finger grazed my back, and I tensed. The touch was electrifying and gentle. The zip slipped up the rest of the way with a loud noise, and I remained frozen as Tobias's presence radiated into my back. I swallowed hard and turned, finding him close. Lifting my chin to meet his expressionless gray eyes, he leaned down to stare directly into my face and my lips parted. His hair was sexily mussed while remaining stylish.

"You're a sweet girl, Catalina," Tobias murmured, his lips grazing my hair at my temple. "Don't expect anything from vampires."

He inhaled sharply, grazing my ear. A shiver coasted up my back and I blinked, my heart rate picking up pace.

The slight tilt of his aristocratic nose drew my attention and those lashes that rested against the crest of his cheeks whenever he blinked heightened the desire.

"Beautiful." I sucked in a deep breath at his murmur. Tobias straightened and caressed my cheek.

I took a nervous step away, face blistering. I was attempting to wrap my head around his words, but he was scrambling my thoughts with his nearness. Asher made it very clear that Tobias wasn't one to be interested in things sexually, but jeez, he was alluring. Tobias's hands grazed my bare shoulders as he collected my long hair and pulled it to my back. His fingertips grazed the ends of it near my waist. A shiver coasted down my spine. I slowly turned with my breath held.

He suddenly stiffened and slipped his hands in his pockets.

"They're on their way down." Asher's steps were clipped

against the floor, but he halted when he looked at me, eyes slightly widening. "Gorgeous. Just as always."

My smile evaporated when I noted the cut on his temple. Blood dripped down his cheek and I inched forward, alarmed. My legs tangled with the dress, so I bunched and lifted it.

"Asher," I murmured, lifting my hand that he caught and pressed a kiss to the palm.

"Jax and I had a slight disagreement, nothing to worry yourself over." I frowned at Asher. His eyes were alive with anger, practically spitting fire, but he covered it with a sly smile. I curled my fingers in my fist and blinked quickly. What was I doing worrying about a *vampire*?

A towel slapped him across the face, and I dragged my attention over to Jax. I gritted my teeth at the scowling jerk, directing my self-hatred at him.

I slit my eyes, but he hadn't even looked at me.

"I'll fetch your heels from my room, Pet."

"I'll pull the Benz around."

I blinked as they disappeared. *They were leaving me alone with the vampire that had anger issues?*

My teeth clicked and I couldn't help taking a few steps back when he moved my way. His lip curved with disgust.

"I'm not going to eat you, girl."

"Could have fooled me," I muttered, and he narrowed his eyes, so I pressed my lips together. I still couldn't get over the differences in personalities between the twins.

He approached me until I was backed near the couch, pulse pounding in my throat.

Jax dropped in front of me and slipped his fingers through the slit of the dress. He gripped and lifted my calf so my foot perched against the couch, splaying everything. A blush scalded my face while I struggled to regain my balance.

"Hey, *hey*." I shoved at his shoulders but he didn't budge as he slid fabric up my leg. His nails scraped across my thigh and then a strap flattened, tightening near the apex of my thighs. He'd pulled a sort of garter up my leg.

I sucked in a breath when one of his digits rubbed the sensitive spots near the growing heat. My chest heaved as I looked down at his twitching jaw. The strap's tension around my upper thigh was snug. His palms flattened at my leg, the tip of his left fingers grazing my lower ass cheek. I wobbled again and gripped his head for purchase. The short strands of hair were hardly long enough to peek through on the other side of my splayed fingers.

Jax's touch became light and his fingers grazed my thighs as he inhaled sharply. As he stood, his grip slid up my side and his other hand clinched my waist.

His body was packed with the same lean muscle as Asher, though he was slightly larger.

"Jax," I said, not knowing what to do and not wanting to pull away. Though he put the fear of vampires in me, my body wanted to go supple against his. The fear bloomed into something else and a pull at my core sucked the air from my lungs. His nostrils flared, gaze becoming like ice chips.

"You disgust me, human," he whispered near my face. My lips parted as I gawked up at him.

Steps sounded and he shoved off me with one last icy look, and I landed on the couch butt-first. I licked my lips, trying to catch my breath. My panties were drenched by that look in his eyes . . . and the way he grabbed me. I shivered and lifted my gaze to his glaring one. Asher narrowed his eyes at his brother and shoulder checked him as he passed, lowering in front of me.

He lifted a pair of black heels and plucked the price tag, dropping it on the ground. The cool leather slid onto my foot and Asher set my heel on his knee so he could buckle the strap.

"Don't put yourself in unnecessary situations. We'll be outside the entire time even though we're going in different vehicles," Jax spoke succinctly, staring me down. "Per *their* insistence," he sneered. "I rigged the button on the strap attached to your leg. Hold it down for five seconds if you're in danger. But only as a last, final, all-hope-is-lost resort."

"Is it like that alert thing when elderly people fall?" I muttered as I lifted my skirt over my knee to take a look at the thin strap and the flat button attached that was set on my outer thigh.

"What?"

"Nevermind," I muttered at his snapped response. So grouchy.

Asher looped the strap to the other shoe and held his hand out for me, but I brushed him away, navigating the six-inch heels easily. I recognized Prada like the back of my hand. The satin pumps were dreamy.

Jax stepped near, looking at his brother over my shoulder. If Jax stepped a foot closer, he'd be flush against my side. A shiver worked its way up my back.

My heart thundered at the thought.

If Jax and Asher tasted me . . .

I licked my lips and clenched my fists.

Jax narrowed his eyes, nose flaring.

God, he definitely knew I was flushing for not-so-innocent reasons.

Asher's brows lifted, staring at my rapidly rising chest. A smirk lifted his lips and he softly hummed, eyes flashing.

"Uh, can you take this?" I muttered, holding out my inhaler. A smirk lifted his lips and he chuckled.

"Of course, Pet." Asher lowered his head, staring into my eyes. "I'll do all those naughty things you want me to do to you as soon as we get back." The purr caused another gush of need between my legs.

I was left gawking after him as his shoulders shook. He was laughing at me. I pinched the bridge of my nose and rushed after his retreating form, trying to ignore the sensitivity between my legs.

catalina

"BE CAUTIOUS," Asher said near my ear as he squeezed my hip. Well thanks, if I didn't already have my heart in my throat, that would have done it. One of my heels sank between the crevice of the sidewalk and I grimaced. I was thankful that Asher was quick to right my wobble or the beauties could have ended up irreparably damaged. *Come on, Catalina, you were much better in heels than this.* I couldn't let my anxiety get the best of me while in these, they were too precious.

Asher guided me thorough the entrance of a lonely looking building. Other than a few stragglers, there was no one loitering outside. We'd traveled miles until we reached an area downtown, further into the middle where all the bars and nightlife were located. It was much further than any area I'd driven to around my new city. Once inside, the pristine, granite floors led down the hall to a man standing before an oversized black door with fancy red trim. I gawked fascinatedly at the various paintings lining the walls. Different scenes of women in compromising positions, draped in silk or sheer material.

"Crimson." The man standing at the door said as we

stepped up to him, attention on Asher who paused, a charming smile spreading on his lips. "Haven't seen you around in a while."

"Binet," Asher responded jovially. "Always a pleasure."

My toes curled as I shuffled from heel to heel. Asher patted the guy's arm and waved me ahead of him. There was no obvious indication the guy was a vampire other than how his gaze dropped to my neck. Skirts fluttering around my legs, I moved past him with distance between us. On the plus side, my heart only slightly jumped. I could do this.

"Welcome to Saphire Lounge." Binet's tone skittered up my spine.

My heels sounded especially loud in the secondary hall. The noise bounced off the cement ground and there was nothing to look at in the long dark hallway.

"Is Crimson your last name?"

Asher hummed. "It's what our coven is known as, but my given last name is Magnusson." His magical tongue wet his lower lip and he peered at me from the corner of his eyes. "I'm known in these circles well."

"So, you're saying you're a party boy."

Asher frowned. "You lost me, Pet."

I scoffed, smirking. I wasn't sure if he was purposefully acting like he didn't know what I was talking about, or if he truly didn't understand the terminology.

We reached the end, but instead of pulling the silver latch, Asher turned and crowded me. I licked my lips as I stared up at him, eyes wide.

His palm pressed flat next to my head and I blinked up at him as his breath caressed my lips.

"I do not have say in this region, so don't get tangled up in something you shouldn't."

I nodded tightly, breathing hard. The arousal simmering since the manor rushed forward in a wave. Asher leaned forward and nipped the tip of my nose. Oxygen squeezed out of my lungs at the soft look in his eyes.

There was no way he'd be interested in anyone else while he looked at me like this. At least for now, I wanted him to be mine.

"You're going to mess up my foundation," I breathed. He'd provided me with the makeup on the drive over and I'd done the best I could with the jolted steering. Asher was a distracted driver.

"I know you don't believe in monogamy, but—" I started, high pitched, but then the door creaked open, interrupting me. I pressed my lips together. I was relieved because it meant I could put off potentially being rejected.

Asher frowned down at me, but said nothing as he wove his arm behind my back and tugged me through the door. Two men strode past, and Asher guided me through the threshold.

Soft music pumped from the speakers, low enough for conversation to flow.

The low leather couches sporadically placed were filled with people. At first glance it was difficult to tell which were vampires and which were human, until you looked closer, the vampires seemed to let their fang freak flag fly.

That couple in the corner weren't making out, it was a vampire feeding and the guy being fed on *really* enjoyed it by the tent in his pants.

A human manned the bar, and he served blood red mixed drinks, complete with the salt topping the rims.

"Asher," a voice called out. I dragged my attention to the two women approaching. Asher's grip tightened around my waist.

"Make sure you head to the bar, he's the one with the pullover collared shirt. I'll keep my attention on you the entire time." I stifled the shiver prodding my skin at his whisper grazing my ear.

The women stood in front of us, but I could have been making a whole spectacle of myself and I wouldn't have existed since their full attention was on Asher. He stepped away from me, leaving me bereft and cold. I attempted to hide the strain tightening my face when the two girls pressed into his sides, hands at his chest as they stared up at him.

My lips flattened and my stomach ached. It was a good thing I hadn't gotten the words out earlier; I would have made a fool of myself.

Asher's hands hung over their shoulders.

"Sweets," he purred. "Long time no see."

The girls grinned.

Sure, his attention would remain on me. I scoffed and fluffed my hair to nip the crawling sensation skirting up my neck.

Even though he'd warned me, I'd foolishly hoped that he would at least not be with another, or bite another so soon after we'd been together. He was my first fucking experience after all, but that was obviously a tall order. Asher leaned to say something into one of their ears, his nose near her neck. I swiftly turned my back before I did something embarrassing.

The urge to smack him tingled my palm and I fisted my hand. I was not a violent person, so the desire threw me for a loop. Looked like one major difference in creating the fictional vampire world in my novels was that the ones I created were faithful.

My heels clicked as I navigated to the bar, and fortunately, no one tried to get bite-y with me.

I set my elbows on the counter next to the preppy-looking vampire and squeezed my eyelids tightly. I needed a moment, but with closed eyes, I couldn't help but see the image of Asher leaning over that woman. It soured my stomach.

I fully understood it wasn't my business who he bit or slept with, but it stung. Caring was the epitome of stupid—surrounding myself with vampires must have incited some sort of psychological breakdown.

I puffed out my cheeks.

"Just take a little more," a feminine voice said from my other side. She squished herself against the male vampire leaning back with his elbows on the bar top. Her neck was riddled with scars, bite marks from vampires feeding on her.

He stared over the woman's head, eyeing the dance floor.

"Please," she whined. The tone grated on my ears and the vampire didn't seem happy about it either.

"I said no, blood-whore," he hissed. This was a blood-whore? I wasn't begging for it like this. She reminded me of an addict, the shifting gaze, the tapping fingers . . . I didn't behave that way.

She pawed at his chest, and he shoved her so hard her elbow slammed into me, sending me teetering to the side.

She didn't turn to acknowledge me. Her attention was fully on groping the vampire. She seemed out of her mind with desperation.

"Inconsiderate, eh?"

I whipped my head toward the preppy vampire. He was

conventionally attractive in a stereotypical college-bro kind of way. And he stared at me with deep-set eyes. My skin crawled. This vampire held no humanity in his expression, no emotion.

"Mhm." I forced a smile and straightened from my slouch. His gaze caressed my face and dropped to my body. His body leaned slightly closer, and his nose flared. His pupils dilated and a chill skittered up my spine.

"You seem out of place." I barely held back from wrinkling my nose at the interest in his tone. Swiveling the barstool toward him, I worked on relaxing my shoulders while the urge to run traveled through my veins. I released the excess energy by bouncing my foot.

"Am I that obvious?" I tried for a coy tone. The vampire's lips quirked. He was attractive, there wasn't a doubt about it, but after being exposed to the vampire's next door, his beauty paled in comparison.

"Tell me, how did a succulent morsel like yourself make it in here without a vampire on your arm." His tone lowered like it had when Jax tried to compel me. I slightly lowered my head, not breaking eye contact. Asher coached me on this potentially happening.

"A tall Viking looking guy brought me. Shoulder length blond hair, blue eyes, slight accent."

"Point him out to me." He leaned closer and the overwhelming scent of blood wafted to my nose. I scanned the crowd and lifted a finger in Asher's direction where he had his back to me, head lowered to listen to whatever the woman said. I dug my fingernails into the wood of the stool.

"Did that Crimson slut set a trap in you? Poison your blood? Anything to target me?" His eyelids narrowed.

"No," I answered succinctly and deadpan. His palm snaked

around the back of my neck. I didn't like the smile that curved his lips.

"Has he fucked you?"

"Yes." The truth slipped out, but it sounded like he knew Asher well if he was calling him a slut, so it seemed like shooting myself in the foot if I said no.

He swirled the still-full glass clinging from his fingertips. The dark red liquid sloshed against the sides, the blood's residue creating a film on the sides.

"Come with me." It wasn't a request. These damn vampires seemed to have an aversion to consent. The bland smile didn't reach his eyes. I nodded because if I spoke, it'd come out as a croak. He carefully set the full glass on the bar and stood in an eerily smooth motion.

He guided me to the door to the side of the space, palm flat at my spine. The door creaked and I licked my lips, wringing my hands in front of me at the dark staircase leading down. It was like one of those staircases leading to a basement where a serial killer kept you for a few days before they slaughtered you. I dug my fingernails into my palm. This whole being around actual vampires, not the fictional ones I wrote, was messing with my psyche. I doubted I could ever return to my blissful fascination.

I grabbed hold of my skirts as I descended, to keep me from falling on my face. I stepped onto the platform, and he hooked his arm around my waist, guiding me to the left instead of to the strobing lights down the hall. When he opened the door, soft yellow lighting flooded my eyes.

The only person in here was an elegantly dressed woman with beautiful skin a few shades darker than mine. Her bow lips tipped up at the corners as she stared me down from the elaborate throne she sat on. Curving gold plated legs wound upward in an elaborate design toward the base where her ass rested.

The door creaked shut at my back and his grip suddenly slid over my belly, feeling me up. I yelped, a tremble starting at my hands. What was he doing?

"Don't move," he ordered.

His hands slid up my side and he felt under my breasts. I gritted my teeth, remaining stiff while he fondled my ass, and then slid his hands down my outer thighs.

"Doesn't feel like she has anything on her. Shall I strip her?" He was already lifting my skirts and I held my breath, waiting for him to see the button Jax strapped to my leg.

The woman crossed her legs and waved her hand.

"No need, Matt," she said with a tilt to her words. "She's human, we'd incapacitate her before she tried anything."

My chest pumped erratically but my shoulders loosened. Still, Matt's hands remained on my waist.

"Do they think I'm this stupid? That I don't know they'd try their little tricks?" The female vampire mused, crossing her long leg over the other.

I kept my mouth shut.

"What, did they tell you to spy for information?" A smirk lifted her lips and I blinked, stunned.

Who was this woman? Seemed like her and the guys knew each other well, but there was also a certain disdainful curl to her lips when she spoke of them.

I cleared my throat.

"What are you talking about." My words warbled as they came out, shattering the illusion of strength I was trying to convey.

The woman snickered and she swayed over, the bottom of

her dress dragging on the ground. She was all sharp edges and angles, deadly and beautiful. Her pointer finger lifted my chin. "Tell me, do you know where they've relocated?"

I met her eyes, the intensity intimidating. I licked my lips.

"No," I croaked, forcing my gaze to remain on hers.

"Disappointing." She pursed her lips. "But at least I can dismember you and litter you around the slut's car."

My stomach dropped to the depths of hell.

She grabbed my upper arm and lifted.

I screamed, tears springing to my eyes. I couldn't even reach for the button. Was this how it ended? In a creepy attic and because of some feuding vampire?

"Silence," she drawled. "I quite hate when you humans get too noisy." Then, she twisted my arm again. Shards of agony splintered from the point she held me up to my shoulder and neck. Like she was shoving my bone into the other.

I valiantly tried to contain my whimpers, but I just couldn't, it hurt too much. Her head cocked and she stopped applying pressure to my wrist, she used it as an anchor to force me still. She blurred from the tears leaking down my cheeks.

"Shut up, no noise. Zilch." She shoved up quick and fast. Something popped and I screamed. My head swam and nausea roiled through my gut.

"In all my days I have tortured and ordered humans not to speak, they never have . . ." Her words buzzed in conjunction with my ringing ears. A sob erupted from my throat, and I backed up, cringing into the other vampire standing at my back.

"I can't compel you." Her brows lifted high. She lowered her tall body, peering closely into my eyes.

"Ram your body into the wall until you can't anymore." Christ, that was sadistic.

"Fuck off," I said between pants. All I wanted to do was run and hide, but at least I'd die with a bit of dignity.

I cradled my limp arm with the other, tears streaming down my cheeks. I couldn't move even my fingers.

She suddenly tipped her head back and laughed.

"They've really outdone themselves looking for Ren." She chuckled. "He'll be quite livid when I mock him about this." She knew where he was. She clicked her tongue in disappointment. "Poor girl, you've really embroiled yourself with the most traitorous, violent, sadistic group of creatures you will ever encounter." I didn't know what that meant but it hurt . . . and scared me.

I blinked. *What did that mean?* Nerves tightened my chest, but she released my face and stepped back.

The door crashed open, rupturing as Asher slammed into the room. *Thank God.* His gaze swept the area, hair blown back as he slitted his eyes. Matt's grip on my waist tightened.

"Don't touch her," Asher hissed.

I wanted to crumple in relief at the sight of him. I sprinted right toward him.

He cupped my cheek, and although I could tell he was looking down at me, I couldn't make out his expression because of my falling tears. His palms dragged down my neck and to my shoulder.

I gasped, flinching from pain. Asher hissed.

"I've never seen you so . . . passionate about one of your whores, Asher." A mocking tilt coated the woman's words.

"You bitch," Asher snapped, eyes briefly flashing red. In that moment he reminded me of his brother.

The woman scoffed. I could no longer hold my head up, so

I set it against his chest, using him as a perch. I garnered as much strength as I could. He needed to know about Ren.

"She has Ren," I interjected.

Asher stiffened, his palm settling on my waist.

"Release him, Calliope."

"Nope, he's paying for his sins."

"You, righteous, bitch," Asher hissed. "It's been decades. You're just pissed that he fucked your female. It's not his fault you can't keep a reign on your bitch."

"Shut up," Calliope snapped, eyes flashing. "He tricked her for that bitch of yours."

"How did you get an upper hand on him?" Asher's chest vibrated with his question.

"No. No. No. Trade secret. Kind of like your little human here. Quite a special one." I peeked over at her and found her smirking.

"If you don't—"

"No threats," she shouted. I jolted, startled. "Yes, your coven is stronger than mine. I fucking know." She sounded bitter. "But you must still respect our customs, or I'll let everyone know you've broken the sanctity of territory laws. We would all move against you. You've all collected quite the long list of enemies in making your way to the top."

"*You're* holding him."

"He trespassed on *my* property, breaking vampire decorum. You know this. He cannot leave unless he plays a little game with me." She smirked. "You know how we like our games." She twirled the end of her short hair. "Fortunately for you, I just want to make him suffer a little."

Asher smirked.

"Or, more likely, he'll seek retribution by using the sweet cunt of your female. After all, he's already fooled her once."

Calliope came flying at us. Asher let me go, sweeping me behind him in a rush of movement to block the attack. He met her in the middle with a swipe of his fist.

Matt wrapped his palm over my mouth and dragged me into the hall.

I scrambled to reach my thigh to press the button, but his corralling thigh didn't allow me the movement as he slammed me against the wall. I grunted from the force, yelping from the jolt to my shoulder.

"Wait," I heaved, having a difficult time breathing.

"Asher fucked my Beloved, so I will steal his little human whore." Matt sneered down at me.

"W-what does that have to do with me?" I wheezed and his nose touched mine. My chest moved hard against his as he pressed his dick into me. God, the grip he had on my shoulder hurt. His nose grazed the side of my neck as he sank his teeth in.

I was so tense it hurt. I sucked in a breath, trying to get oxygen through my panic. He sucked and the drag lessened some of the hurt, but not enough. A panic-inducing curtain of pure black undulated at the peripheral of my vision, beginning to steal my sight. Memories clawed to the surface, dragging me back.

"Let me go, please—"

"Your taste . . ." He squeezed my shoulder, and I cried out. Okay, then. I didn't want to tempt him into doing more so I stilled, letting him drink from me. A flame lit in my core and I hated it more than ever as he swallowed my life's blood. His lip curled down at me and he tore my dress from the front. The rip jerked my torso as I was exposed to my navel. I cried out from shock. My heartbeat felt like hummingbird wings. I needed my inhaler.

"I see why he's so protective of you." He hoisted me up easily and spread my legs, hooking them around his shoulders like I was nothing and causing the bottom of my dress to bunch at my hips. I grabbed his head for purchase and an ache shot up to my shoulder. I scrambled to close my legs—

Fangs sliced into my thigh, invasive and painful. My hand shook as I reached for the button, but my lungs couldn't take it. My breathing became erratic and the spots took over my sight.

"Asher," I cried, coughing.

I slumped against the wall as he slid his fangs into another spot by my knee. A low heat dragged from my clit, and it throbbed with each of his sucks. I didn't want to be turned on, but I couldn't help it. A groan wrenched from my mouth and his hands gripped my ass.

The vampire's legs were taken out from under him and I was caught in a tight grip. My body ached on impact, and I groaned, blinking up at furious blue eyes. Light flooded into the hall from the room we'd been in. Now that it was open, I could see.

"I'm here, Pet," Asher rasped and pressed his lips to my forehead. His jaw twitched as he took in my state. His eyes flashed red, and he dropped me as gently as he could.

Asher slammed Matt into the wall and a fissure opened on impact.

"You dare feed from her," he hissed into the guy's face.

I scrambled back at the violence, having a hard time dragging breaths into my strained lungs. Hearing him call me his clenched every muscle in my body.

I tipped to the side, my knees weakening. A hard chest

pressed into my back. Stiffening sent a stab through my shoulder and I bit my lip to keep my cry in. Whoever I'd leaned against swept me up into their arms.

I whimpered, curling into myself. Jax's lips tightened and he lifted me, tucking me tight to his chest. He adjusted me so my legs hung over one arm and his other propped my back while my head laid on his chest.

"Catalina." Tobias's gaze swept over me, his eyes narrowing in on the torn bodice where my breasts were exposed. I curled my good arm in front of me and angled my chest toward Jax, flattening against him to hide everything. Tobias's lip curled. That was the last I saw of him before he disappeared and rammed into Matt, pounding his fist into the other vampire.

"Jax," I whispered. The corner of his eyes were pinched as he looked down at me.

"What is it, Cat?" That was the softest tone he'd ever used with me.

"Inhaler. Asher."

I coughed hard, my body jerking against him. His eyes widened and he set me down. My hand shook as I kept my arm across my breasts. He disappeared and I squeezed my eyes shut while the sounds of fighting continued. A gentle touch ghosted against my neck, calling for my attention.

Jax lifted my medicine and tugged me toward him. My cheek smushed to his chest, and I couldn't stop my heart's erratic thumping nor the pressure in my chest. It was a physical urge—fight or flight.

His hand wrapped at the back of my head to brace me and he pressed the lip of the inhaler into my mouth.

I wilted against him with my head lolled. Calliope observed

from a few steps away, eyebrows arched. She winked and bled into the darkness, seeming to disappear into the walls.

I lifted my fingers over his and pressed to spray it. I sucked in a breath and the tension loosened at my chest. Thank goodness. His hand moved to my shoulder and I groaned from the agony.

"What is it?" he murmured.

"My shoulder," I gasped.

"She still likes to dislocate the bones, then." He sighed and rested his palm against the top of my shoulder and his other went to my arm, in the same place Calliope had gripped me.

I gripped his wrist, eyes widening on his.

"I know what I'm doing."

I nodded, not really having an option but to let him do his thing.

"Inhale on three. One—" He yanked up and a loud pop echoed.

"You said three," I wheezed. His lips twitched.

I gingerly moved it in a circle, and other than some soreness, it no longer hurt.

"Oh, wow," I breathed. "Thank you." A weird expression crossed his face, but as with other interactions with him that weren't anger, I didn't know how to read him. He only grunted in response.

Asher shouldered Jax, jostling me as he snatched me to his chest, the blood splattered all over him smearing on me.

"Tobias, release him," Jax shouted, and I lifted my gaze to find Tobias squeezing the limp vampire's neck. The vampire's face was a bloody mess, but the cuts on his cheek were healing, problem was he was passed out. "Fuck. Killing one of Calliope's children on her territory is a fight we don't need."

Asher didn't respond to Jax's concern and continued petting my hair as he pressed me to his chest. As much as I hated admitting it, I trusted Asher—a vampire.

I exhaled shakily as Jax moved to grab Tobias, but he whirled on him, flashing his fangs.

"Now you choose to lose all sense? For a human?" Jax's mocking words washed over me.

Tobias's eyes narrowed and red flashed in their depths.

"Catalina, call him over to you," Asher whispered in my ear.

"Tobias?" I croaked hesitantly.

His head snapped in my direction and he shook his head with his eyes squeezed shut. Straightening, he stiffly walked over to me.

"I'll take her home." His words rasped out crisply.

"Jax and I have to find Calliope to see what she wants. She admitted to having Ren." Asher flexed his grip before finally releasing me.

Tobias just swept me into his arms. He shook his head, sending the waves of his mussed brown hair out of his eyes.

"Relax, Catalina." Tobias's voice was low and he hugged me to his chest. I tried doing as he said, but it was difficult. They finally had confirmation about Ren, and that was the entire point of me being there. Now that they knew, I was no longer necessary.

I licked my lips and squeezed my eyes shut as I swayed in his arms.

SHE SLEPT SOUNDLY, her pert nose twitching with her inhale. Her nose wiggling in such a manner made me want to curl her even closer. She hadn't roused which proved too much blood had been stolen from her. I climbed up the staircase to the second floor, attempting to keep her as still as possible to not disturb her. Though I doubted she would wake even if I tossed her about.

Instead of turning right on the landing, I took a sharp turn left toward my bedroom through the first door. She had been in Asher's room before, but I wanted to bring her to mine. For her scent to envelope my bed. I set her on the edge of the bed and the wool coat I'd wrapped her in wilted to the side, exposing her bare skin. The ripped dress still clung to her in tatters. It must not be comfortable hanging off her like this.

With a quick tug of the material, the rest of it ripped and I pulled the fabric away from her.

She lay still, with her legs slightly parted and her nudity before me like a forbidden temptation. I tensed, and my member perked up. I should have averted my eyes. There was something so racy about her bare, hairless privates. Although I'd never partaken in indecent behavior, I'd seen enough nude women to know that shaving their privates was a recent development.

I reached to yank the blanket over her, but her sweet bloody scent teased my senses, and I froze. Stretched over her, I had a clear view of her inner thigh.

The marks continued leaking blood from where the ingrate had bitten her. Rage and hunger stiffened my spine. I gritted my teeth. Matt would die by my hand. I didn't know when or how, but I would manage to end his pissant existence.

The wound's edges were torn and ragged, painful looking. In need of healing. Setting my jaw, I couldn't force my gaze away. My fangs erupted out.

No one would see . . . I would heal her, only heal her. I dropped to my knees and with her next breath, my mouth hovered over her bloody leg. The scent of her sweet blood overpowering all sense.

I laved the skin. A shiver coasted down my spine, my cock becoming turgid. Stretching my mouth over the injuries, I cleaned her skin. I'd have to reopen them, so they didn't scar, and I did just that. Her skin gave way to the sharp points of my fangs and her blood burst into my mouth. My moan echoed hers and I dragged in a mouthful of her blood.

She gasped, her chest jerking, causing her luscious breasts to bounce. They were pert and perfect for my hands. Warmth spilled down my throat, rushing through my veins. My cock throbbed and my hips gyrated into the mattress.

Her legs parted. Her smooth womanhood on display, wet, needy, and swollen. Catalina tugged at my comforter, jerking as sweet little moans escaped her mouth. I sucked again, taking more. So much had already been taken from her and if I continued, it would not bode well for my little human.

And I could not have that. I forced myself to still, savoring her taste one last time as I wrestled for control. Running my tongue over my bite, I made sure to coat them with my saliva, so they healed properly.

She whimpered, writhing so deliciously, moving her hips, seeking relief. I pressed gentle kisses up her thigh until I reached her core. Her scent was just as sweet here. My eyes shut, my grip on the bed tearing the sheet. Swaying forward, I lapped the wet offering before me. Her legs immediately widened, her hips jolting up.

As much of a sin as this was, I could not stop myself.

I flattened my tongue against the damp silky folds, sliding my tongue through them to collect everything she offered. All I craved was devouring as much of her sweet nectar as she could give me.

I sank my tongue shallowly inside her entrance, and she convulsed, crying out as her lush channel throbbed around my tongue.

All the while, she remained blissfully unconscious.

I gladly sunk into the pits of immorality, brought to my knees by a human that managed to disarm me.

Her desperate hip movements halted and she sighed, satisfied.

Lifting from where I kneeled, I brushed her long hair out of her face. She turned toward me like a flower turning toward the sun. Her fingers sank into my arm, clutching onto me. I hesitated from pulling away. I did not want to leave her side, so I lowered beside her carefully. Her smaller form rolled toward me where the bed dipped.

She released a satisfied sigh, nuzzling into my neck. I squeezed her as close as possible, taking care with her feeble human bones. Silence and peace . . . as close to heaven as I could get.

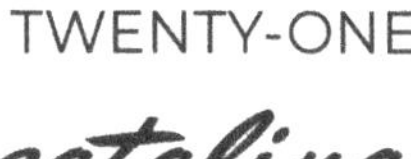

TWENTY-ONE

MY EYES FLUTTERED open as hair tickled my chin. I moved and soreness radiated down my arm, forcing me to freeze against the foreign black silk rubbing against my exposed skin. I wore absolutely nothing. My heart jumped into overdrive as memories flickered behind my eyelids. A familiar sweetness that accompanied the Crimson manor overpowered my senses. A scent that always clung to the vampires. I stared up at the ceiling illuminated by a low golden light shining from somewhere in the room.

Asher dragged his nose over the throbbing pulse in my neck.

"I have you," he murmured into my throat. His arms were snaked around my waist, holding me tight to his torso. I slid my hands to his shoulders, glad I hadn't woken up alone. "You smell better than anything I've ever encountered, Pet." His tongue lashed the crease where my neck and shoulder met before grazing his teeth over my thin flesh. I was addicted to this sensation. The licks, his breath on my neck . . . all of it. I wanted him all over me.

"When did you return?"

"A few minutes ago. I came directly to you."

I lifted my head, seeking Tobias. He'd been the last face I'd seen before I passed out.

"He's not here," Asher said.

I returned my attention to him. "You've been all wrapped around him," he trailed off, irritation coating his words. He cleared his throat. My face heated. I was especially sensitive and Tobias experienced the backlash. I'd have to apologize later to make sure I hadn't made him uncomfortable.

"If I didn't know your motto of 'no commitments' I'd say you sound jealous," I said wryly. "Don't worry, Asher, I'm not expecting anything from you." That wasn't the only reason there could be nothing between us. Another was the obvious him-being-a-vampire thing.

Asher frowned and his pupils dilated, the irises flashing red and just as quickly returning to their normal blue. "You best not think of fucking anyone but me."

I blinked at the sudden order. I was honestly speechless, but I shut down the butterflies going wild in my stomach.

I wrinkled my nose and snickered. Did he not take anything serious?

His eyes thinned. Whatever he was about to say cut off as I gripped the back of his head and pulled him to my mouth. I only had him for a bit longer now that Ren's location was confirmed, so I needed to take advantage of the short-term pleasure he effortlessly wrenched from me. I'd run out of time. These brief memories would be all I had when it came to having a vampire lover because when I was long gone, I was through with the fantasies. He sighed against my lips, pressing his chest into me. With a sudden burst of motion, he scooped me to the side, so my hair fell over the edge of the bed. My body sank into the mattress and Asher used his knee to prod my legs open. I groaned, lifting my hips. I needed his touch and his bite to erase Matt's.

"Is your pussy wet for me?" Asher hummed, the seductive sound shooting strikes of electricity to my clit. Pushing up to my elbows, I peeked at the smooth skin between my thighs, as if there had never been marks. It'd still bled after Matt was ripped off me . . . or I thought I'd been bleeding?

He settled over me, his hips caged by my legs as he sank over me. Asher's lips pressed into mine, prodding them open and dissolving my confusion. His tongue flicked into my mouth and I sucked on it, needing more of his sweet taste. The groan he released caused a wave of moisture between my legs.

Asher reached down and pressed his palm over my pussy, grinding on me. I whimpered and pushed up, arching my back to get closer to the pressure. His long fingers speared inside me. The sudden invasion sucked the oxygen from my lungs in the best way. He swirled the digits in my core, caressing the walls of my pussy.

I clenched around them, heat spreading from my belly and increasing with each swirl.

He retracted his fingers and lifted the glistening digits.

"So terribly wet," he chastised. He brought them to his mouth and licked them clean with long swipes of his tongue. I watched in awe, suspended by desire. "Rivals the delicacy of your blood."

Before I could even think of how to respond, he thrust them back in with shallow pumps.

I gritted my teeth, writhing up to get more of him in me, but he kept them from going any deeper.

"Asher," I moaned, panting so hard my nipples brushed against his shirt with each inhale.

"Yes, Pet?" His teasing tone . . . I curved my fingers into his shoulders, scrunching the cotton. "Tell me what you want."

"Please, Asher. Put your fingers inside me."

He hummed, the sound verging on a purr. I bit my lip, then he offered me sweet relief. Fingers thrust into my core and his thumb swirled on my clit, adding stimulation.

I jolted, the sensation almost too much. A moan crawled up my throat and I writhed against him. He groaned, deep and long as his cock pressed into my thigh.

My hips jerked off the mattress, my heels digging into the foam as my channel throbbed around his fingers. Asher didn't let off on the rhythm, wringing the orgasm from me. I whimpered at the sensitivity, cringing back, but he didn't relent. Asher chuckled at my frantic tugging of his shirt.

"Fall apart for me, Pet."

I panted and stared up at his glittering blue eyes.

"We're not done." I blinked at his smirk, but he slid down, disappearing from sight.

"Since your pussy has never been claimed, I'm assuming my pet has not been licked before me," he murmured in a pleased rumbled.

I squeaked as his tongue flicked against my clit. I gripped his hair, stopping his progression. My chest heaved as I peered down at him. His tongue flicked out again and the barest red flashed in his eyes as he narrowed them. He hummed low, as if making a discovery, but just as quickly the expression passed.

"Yes, I have been," I said breathlessly—lying. His fingers dug into my thighs, and I hissed at the abrupt pain. His expression darkened, but he didn't question me as his red eyes shut tightly and he exhaled sharply.

I tensed. *Had I said something wrong?*

"A-Asher?" Uncertainty bled from my tone. Asher shook his head hard, a short exhale brushing against my wetness.

"You bring out the possessiveness in me, Pet." His lips quirked. "I never thought it'd be possible."

That pleased me more than I could express, but my smugness swiftly faded when his mouth attached to my clit and he sucked.

I screamed, jerking up, but he was relentless, sucking and flicking the bud.

My fingers wove into his hair, and I tugged, whimpering, trying to get him to give me a second. Lids fluttering, my mouth opened on a silent cry as the wave of release crashed into me. Asher chuckled against me, and my toes curled at the vibration. I could not think.

His warm tongue lowered to my slit, and he dipped it into the heat, licking up my juices.

"You taste like heaven, Pet." His fingers dug into my ass as he devoured me like a starved man, elongating my orgasm with shocking ease.

I panted, lifting my head. He stared up at me, his puffy lips wet from my release. I bit my lower lip, unable to handle the erotic sight.

The light in the room glinted off his fangs and my body clenched, lips parting.

"Bite me," I whispered. Unlike with the other vampire, I wanted this one.

His grin widened.

"Beg me, Pet."

"Asher," I whimpered. "Please. Please. Bite me."

His extended fangs sank into my thigh and he pulled at the wound, moaning against my skin. With my fingers curling into the blankets, I panted. A low throb at my core was already starting up again. His tongue licked over the punctures, and he pushed to his knees.

"Jaxon needs to feed, Pet," he murmured, eyes glinting with lust. He hadn't yet fed from me so what did that have to do with me? A hard touch fisted my hair, wrenching a yelp from me. My bare chest heaved as Jax hovered at the end of the bed, his harsh eyes peering into mine. Jax didn't allow me a word as he yanked my head to the left to expose my throat.

I sucked in a shaking breath, my pulse skyrocketing.

"*Mild, hon är mänsklig,*" Asher snapped and although I didn't understand, it sounded like he scolded Jax. His demanding tone calmed my heartrate even though it shouldn't have.

Jax dropped to his knees and bowed over my throat. He didn't even let me get a syllable in edgewise before he struck, sinking his fangs into my throat. Pleasure chased the sting away and I moaned, my hips jerking. Asher's grip held me down.

Jax's grip in my hair stiffened and he groaned against my throat. After another long pull of blood that I felt to my clit, he lifted his head.

"Fuck." He hissed, red painting his lips. He seemed to be battling internal demons; squeezing his eyes shut tight and shaking his head as if trying to dislodge something. I panted, my hips moving side to side in search of relief. His grip on my hair turned painful as he forced my head to the side again, leaving Asher within sight.

Asher's jaw line flexed as Jax struck his teeth into my neck again, more violently. It should have shot fear through me, but fuck. It was delicious. I whimpered and twitched, grinding my hips in needy little movements.

Asher unbuckled his slacks and his thick cock sprung free, the piercings glinting. He gripped my outer thighs and shoved them wide, his glistening cock extended. He reached down and grabbed the base, sliding into me. The piercings massaging my core as he pushed in.

My head lolled at the possession, and I throbbed around him. Asher kept his hands on my ass, keeping me balanced as he pulled out slowly. When his tip was at my entrance, my channel sucking at him to keep him in, he slammed back in.

I grunted at the harsh entrance. He repeated the move, picking up pace with each retreat.

Vampires were fast, but I never thought about how that could be translated in the bedroom. I choked out a sob. Jax's hand lifted to the other side of my throat and he sucked in another harsh gulp. I cried out from the overwhelming sensations sending me to the highest peak I never knew could be reached.

Asher practically vibrated with how fast he moved. The sharp heat tingled up my legs, and I lifted my knees, pressing them into his side as he hammered into me incessantly.

My ears rang as my release washed over me and I panted, goose bumps lifting across my flesh. My stomach cramped from the strain, and another orgasm slammed into me. I lifted my hand and sank my fingers into Jax's hair, sinking them into the short strands. He moaned again and his fangs sank into another section in my throat. My body twitched, gripping Asher's dick and dragging out his release. Asher's head tipped back, and he moaned, his thrusts turning jerky. This level of lust seemed like a fantasy, and I could live forever with pleasure this life shattering.

Asher suddenly pulled his cock out of my pussy and warmth sprayed over my bare belly. The heated liquid continued spilling as he rubbed his hand down his dick until nothing more came out.

He dropped forward but caught himself on his elbows before smashing me under him and in the process, rubbing his cum into my skin. Jax dragged in another mouthful from my throat and it spiked through my clit. Another orgasm swelled and I rubbed Jax's hair between my fingertips, loving the silky feel as the wave climbed. Suddenly he yanked his fangs out with a roughness that pulled a scream from me.

I gawked at him, panting, as he sneered down at me. He swiped the back of his hand across his mouth.

"At least you're of some use." With that lovely comment, he backed out of the room.

Asher's laugh dropped my stunned gaze down.

"Ignore him, he's throwing a fit because you're the most delicious thing he's ever tasted, and he hates that."

Well, then.

Asher crawled over my body so our faces lined up and his forehead pressed into mine as he searched my eyes, brows furrowed. Confusion flickered over his face. I didn't understand why he kept looking at me that way.

He tipped my neck to the side as the tension in my lungs lessened. Asher didn't exacerbate my anxiety, he seemed to calm it.

"My *bitch* of a brother didn't heal you." Asher dipped and laved the side of my neck, ticking the flesh.

I laughed and his chest moved with his amused chuckle.

"Vampire saliva heals everything?"

"Outer shallow wounds. Yes," he murmured into my neck as he tucked me into the curve of his body, spooning me. I sighed, wiggling into him.

It was a wonder my heart hadn't pounded out of my chest.

The door creaked and I lazily opened my eyes to find Tobias placing his removed shirt on the seat as he stepped over to the bed.

"What are you doing in here?" Asher muttered, tugging me tighter to him.

"You're in my bed," Tobias snapped. It was his room? That explained the black bedsheets, Asher's were red . . . Tobias slid into the bed.

My body was too sated to get tense. He settled close, but not touching me. Unlike Asher who curled me closer as if trying to drag me away from Tobias. Even with the distance, I was surrounded, not feeling alone for once. Tobias turned, giving me his back, and I curved myself closer to Asher. I breathed evenly as my eyelids became heavy.

Yet worry wouldn't allow me to be dragged under. Asher's grip slacked and he hummed, deep in sleep. A loud clank echoed through the bedroom.

"What's that?"

"Automatic blinds . . . sunlight," he mumbled, voice heavy with sleep. His arms remained fastened around my waist, caging me. I wouldn't be able to get free until he released me.

"Go to sleep, Catalina."

I startled at Tobias's voice.

"Sorry."

He grunted and said nothing. My eyes traced the muscles in his back, he had a smooth back except for a few beauty marks on his shoulder. I had the oddest urge to kiss them. I fisted my hands, yanking my mind out of the gutter.

"Did I do anything earlier—"

"You didn't."

I swallowed hard at his sharp words. *That was a relief.*

Tobias's shoulders twitched and he rolled onto his back, tossing one of his hands over his eyes.

"Good morning," I whispered, forcing my eyes closed.

The response came many moments later.

"Good night, human."

catalina

GASPING, I shot into a sitting position. A heavy weight on my thigh dragged my attention to my lap. The white-haired dream vamp. Whipping my head side to side, I took stock of my bedroom, and we were indeed in a dream if the faded edges of my sight were anything to go by.

My head thumped on my mound of pillows and I whimpered. How was it possible I was so aware? I was never the type that could recall my dreams this way.

The vampire nuzzled my thigh as he shifted again, but his upper body remained sprawled across my lower half.

He seemed restless.

My fingers popped and I reached down, raking through the long white hair, combing it back from the sharp lines of his face.

A sigh slipped from his lips and he nudged his head into my fingers, asking for more.

I continued running my hands through the silky strands, marveling at his broad features and the bronzed skin that matched mine.

His eyelids fluttered open, red eyes narrowing on me. Oh . . . I'd stopped moving my fingers.

Dream vamp liked when I petted him.

He flopped on his other side so he faced my stomach. Each of his jostles made the bed creak. His nose grazed my belly, and he hummed as I scratched his scalp a little harder.

The vampire dragged his nose over my belly button and my face heated. He was getting closer to my core. His nostrils flared and he grunted as he tipped his chin to the side so his nose grazed over my covered clit.

I sucked in a deep breath, a flush of heat washing over me. He tilted his head, looking up at me, those red eyes eerie. I licked my lips, and before I could drag him off, he licked me again and again, until his saliva wetted the spot between my thighs. I was wet and wanting and I couldn't take it anymore.

Leaning back, I gripped his hair harder as his teeth rasped across my pelvis. A cry slipped free and I wiggled my hips.

He pressed his hot tongue over the seam of my shorts, alternating with dragging his teeth over me, like he was going to bite through and into my clit.

I tensed at the thought and whimpered, arching my hips toward his needy tongue.

He snarled and reached to rip the material off . . .

I sucked in a breath, shooting up. My head spun and I blinked quickly as the vision fizzled away. What the hell?

"Catalina," Tobias whispered, pushing my hair back from my face.

I needed the touches.

I blinked up at him and leaned against him. Exhaling, I sank into his torso.

"Sorry," I muttered and tried scooting away. I didn't want

to overstep, especially since Asher had insinuated he wasn't involved with anything sexual because of his profession as a human. Tobias tensed, his grip remaining fastened around my waist, pulling me tighter so I was flush against his front. The tension radiating his body faded with each second until he was running his hand down my side. Dream vamp left me wet and wanting.

"Where's Asher?" I was so wet it hurt. I needed Asher to fuck me. I needed to get off.

I squeezed my thighs together uncomfortably, biting back a whimper.

"Left," Tobias responded gruffly.

"Oh." It came out sounding like a moan. I sucked my lips into my mouth, biting them. Maybe the stab of pain would detract from the achiness.

I wiggled and a hard length prodded at my belly. Without a second thought, I arched myself closer.

Tobias groaned and his hands spasmed around me. I sucked in a breath, an apology rising to my lips.

Before I could say anything, Tobias grabbed my chin and forced my mouth to his.

"Human," he murmured gruffly against my lips. "I ache for you." The deep voice and accent set off a slew of pleasure receptors I didn't know I had.

I moaned into his mouth, meeting his kiss fervently. He tilted his head, his tongue hesitantly dipping into my mouth. Soon, he had the rhythm and took charge, pressing against me, devouring my mouth with his. He made a guttural sound I felt to my core, and his fang sliced my tongue. His grip on me spasmed and he sucked my tongue into his mouth. I groaned at the pull, and he tugged my leg over his waist so I straddled him.

He thrust up, sucking and lapping at my tongue. His hard cock prodded at my sheet-covered pussy, grinding up in a desperate mimic of sex. I moaned. Tobias was ravenous.

I rubbed my core against the bulge beneath me. He drove his hips up with each of my movements. My God, it felt so damn good. Tobias's head fell back as he panted, leaving me wanting his kiss. I leaned forward and licked the long column of his neck.

"Yes. Love. Just like that."

His encouraging words sent a gush down my throbbing core. The silk against my naked folds slid decadently against my slit. My stomach tightened and I gritted my teeth as a wave crested up my spine, making me cry out his name. He groaned, and jacked his hips up, hitting the perfect spot. My fingers curled into his muscled shoulders as I settled on his dick and rubbed myself against him, riding out my release.

His cock was incredibly hard under me, it had to be painful. I slid my hand down, pausing at the dip of his abdomen, and met his eyes, pausing, asking. I canted my head and the red in his iris faded as he froze.

Tobias yanked himself away, and I landed on the bed on my side. I gawked at his rapidly moving chest. He pushed his fingers through his hair and tugged hard, mussing the brown strands.

My face heated when I saw the damp mark on his khaki pants where I'd rubbed my wetness all over him—and where he'd come. He was drenched.

"I-I'm sorry." I said more from confusion than anything else. The look on his face made me feel bad, like I'd somehow wronged him.

Tobias pressed his lips into a thin line.

I stared at him as he rubbed his face with his palm, then he turned on his heel and left the bedroom. *His* bedroom.

My face heated, embarrassed by my wanton behavior. He seemed into it too . . . until he rushed away from me like I had a disease. I groaned and rubbed my nose with my palm.

It was best I stayed away from him; his mercurial behavior was confusing. Not only that. I needed to get it together. The job was completed. There would be no more vampires in my near future, but why did the knowledge make me want to cry?

tobias

I BUTTONED my fresh slacks and strode out of the bedroom. An imbecile. That's how I'd behaved.

Entering the kitchen, I yanked the fridge door open. My blood was gone. I snatched an empty bag from the side door. Asher could have had the decency to clean up after himself. As soon as I shut the fridge, a fist flew at my face. I braced myself and a sharp burn spread on my cheekbone. I needed that or else I would have turned right around and had my way with Catalina. Every delicious inch of her body would have been mine. Every drop of her blood . . .

My cock hardened from the visual and ache to fuck her even as pain radiated from my cheek.

Asher's nostrils flared and the red evil tint of his eyes faded from sight. That famed relaxed visage returned and he rolled out his shoulders.

"What do I owe such an aggressive reaction to?" I leveled out my tone. Simply put, the aggression was out of character for him. A word vibrated through his head, faint and as if behind a veil.

Mine.

He raked his hair back.

"Her scent is all over you." His fist flew at me again, and I avoided it, but not in time to evade the foot to my stomach. I groaned and slammed against the wall. The sharp sting at my spine lasted a split second before I straightened, brushing the lint from my black jacket with my free hand. "And that's for placing her in your bedroom."

The hard-on I'd had the entire night I'd held her must have broken records, and I hadn't been able to let her go despite the fucking burn.

"Are you jealous, Asher?" This reaction was utterly out of place for him and the fury in his gaze pointed to only that reason. His possessive words and this anger he harbored in his gaze . . . he behaved as if I'd taken his wife—as if he were a cuckold.

But that could not be it, vampires did not love. We did not feel softness, we owned, we possessed, we devoured, we claimed.

There were no 'soul mates' as some deluded humans believed. With creatures such as ourselves, hell-bound and evil, selfish to the core, we were not given such a gift from God. But in my long, ceaseless life, I'd seen bonds formed between pairs, *a Beloved*, the chosen mate to a vampire. Their loyalty to each other was just as binding. He behaved as if she was his Beloved, but that was impossible, a human and a vampire would never work and she could never be turned into a vampire with the vampire illness running rampant. Even *before* blood-madness violated vampires, women could hardly survive the change.

Asher's body tensed, the muscles along his neck becoming taut. *My human,* his thought shouted at me. He staggered back and then he snapped straight as if he hadn't meant to react so viscerally. He masked the slight confusion on his brow with a smirk.

Too late. I'd seen it all.

"I never thought I'd live to see the day," I said, raising an eyebrow.

Asher's eyes narrowed. *Hon var min. Bara min.* The English he was thinking in switched to Swedish, which he well knew I couldn't understand.

"She was mine first, that is all."

"You've never had an issue with sharing." There was a sharpness to my tone. I didn't want to share Catalina if I could have her. I would not give him the pleasure of owning her. Not when they'd all shared Imogen. "None of you have."

"She's different. She's mine." Asher bared his teeth. I'd never seen him so tightly strung or possessive. It angered me. My fangs burned to spring out, but I ground my teeth to keep the show of emotion hidden.

"You know well there is no future for a human and a vampire." I murmured, studying the tension lining his features. Such human emotions flickered over his face. The twins were the youngest of us all, so it would be within reason to believe they could be rash.

"She'll be my blood-whore and if I don't tire of her, I'll turn her."

I scoffed. "You'll end up having to kill her regardless because of the blood-madness." Even if it no longer existed, turning a female vampire had only a twenty percent chance of success.

"Then she'll live as my blood-whore." The corner of his lips tilted up. "She doesn't know it's in the process of happening. Thanks for that by the way." Lying to her about the blood-whore transition time had come much easier than I'd anticipated. She could not know all our secrets. Deceptions and rumors were all that was allowed to be shared with humans. "Or even better, so she doesn't become an addict, I'll share my bloo—"

I narrowed my eyes at him and he cut off.

For us, it was forbidden. There were countless perks the human would receive, but it would open us all to dangers we could not risk.

Sharing our blood was sacred.

"You've been stealing all of my blood bags," I commented offhandedly. The empty package I still gripped slapped Asher on the face. "Come with me to restock since you've drained it all."

He scoffed.

"Send one of my Progeny."

"You know we cannot risk it right now." He knew it too, but he was being difficult on purpose. "For once you're not complaining about having to drink from a bag," I added, hoping to get *something* out of him. But he just stared back at me instead of saying some insipid thing as he usually did. My comment didn't force a reaction out like it would have done to Jax.

The way he watched Catalina wasn't lost on me. He enjoyed her . . . truly enjoyed her, and Asher had enjoyed no one in the centuries we'd all been together. His sly flirtations were all an act. They were all he knew from his past life as a whore. Even with Imogen he was never affectionate as he was with Catalina.

"You've always refused drinking from the bag. What changed?" The answer was clear, but I enjoyed his discomfort.

"Are we going to get the bags or not?" Irritation marred his tone.

I tilted my head and he turned on his heel, the muscles of his back rippling as he stalked toward the garage door located toward the end of the kitchen.

I caught up to him as he navigated downstairs to where our vehicles were housed. Fluorescent lights flickered to life, illuminating the rows of vehicles.

"I saw you too," Asher said. Pulling open the door to the newest Mustang model. "I've never seen you so intrigued by a woman, Priest."

"Don't." The word came out in a snapped tone, much quicker than I could stop it. I wanted to bash my foot into the side door, but refrained with a tug at my vest.

Asher became eerily still.

"Do you realize it's too dangerous to bring a human into our fold? If anyone finds out we—" I paused mid word and slitted my eyelids at Asher. "You. *Hypothetically* own a human. She'll be used against us. No one has the luxury to keep her. You're placing her in danger."

There were selfish reasons for my words. I didn't want her to be with him. Watching him touch her so freely when I craved to do the same ate away at me.

It was too late for me not to desire her, as much as I denied it, there was so much there, but I would continue to turn my back on that. I couldn't face it even if she tempted me unlike any other.

Yet, he got to have her.

My teeth ground as I watched him climb into the car.

No, I couldn't have thoughts like this. I exhaled sharply, closing my eyes. I shouldn't be lusting after anyone. It wasn't something I'd ever needed or wanted. One woman wouldn't tempt me. She wouldn't make me lose my mind.

She already had Asher wound around her finger, and Jax . . . he was on his way there even if he didn't realize it.

It would be wrong of me to want her. She was perfection and I was a monster. She didn't need creatures like us in her life. We would bring doom to her—and her death. My intention at the beginning leaned toward breaking her neck, but everything in me recoiled at the thought now.

"I want to be back before she wakes," Asher snapped, becoming quiet and sullen. He revved the car, and I settled into the passenger seat for the ride. He was acting more and more like Jax as the days passed.

"Are you serious about making her your blood-whore?" His only response to my question was the quirking of his lips. "Leave the girl alone, Asher."

"No," he said mulishly. "You've tasted her blood and her presence. How could you want to be away from that?"

I didn't, but if we kept her, I may lose myself if she was near for too much longer. The descent to hell may be worth it . . .

I gritted my teeth again as Asher navigated the vehicle on the road. The fight against my instincts was a day by day thing, which was why I kept myself away from temptation and Catalina was the only temptation I'd ever had.

I ached for her to where I feared I'd choose her above all else, as well as my vows.

The thought struck horror through me. Obsession would be the downfall of us all.

catalina

MY EYES FLUTTERED OPEN. This time I hadn't woken from the dream like a bat out of hell. After Tobias ran off, I'd passed out, blissed out on all the orgasms. I hadn't thought it was possible to come so much, but I was fortunately wrong. I stretched out in Tobias's bed—utterly alone. Moonlight filtered through the multicolored glass pane, the brown shades enhanced in the shine. I dragged my palm over the silk duvet, marveling at the intricate weavings.

My bladder was especially tight. A yawn stretched my jaw. I kicked the bedding off, and pushed off the high bed, making my way to the restroom. I was so sticky, especially my belly. I thought back to the reason why and my face warmed.

I turned the knob of the shower and water rained lightly across my skin. The cool droplets splashed on my skin and I held my hand suspended until it warmed. Stepping inside, I let the water fall over my head and seep onto my scalp. I squirted shampoo into my palm and scrubbed my head, massaging the cedar-scented liquid into my hair.

Finishing my wash, I tugged the towel from the rod,

wrapped it around my body, and stepped onto the mat to dry my damp feet.

Tobias had to have something I could wear in here. Exiting the bath area, I went to the drawers. Bingo. Combing through a few drawers until I found a shirt, I paused when I caught a glint.

I pulled out a shiny rectangular frame and frowned at the image where Tobias posed beside an elegant woman looking to be his age . . . or the age he stopped aging. *Had he been married at some point?*

The woman's long neck was elegant and it led to a well-endowed bosom and a tiny waist cinched by a corset. Skirts ruffled out around her legs and her hands were prettily set on her lap.

Some strong twisting happened in my gut when I looked at her. Tobias seemed so serious behind her, looming over her like a protector. I ached to ask him who she was, but I feared I wouldn't like the answer.

That nasty twisting rose to my esophagus, and I tucked the image back in its place. Plucking a shirt from the neatly folded stack, I tugged it on, and the hem grazed below my knees.

I didn't want to put those heels back on, but I saw no other way to get around it unless I walked around barefoot. Especially since I didn't know where Asher put the ones I'd brought.

A bang echoed down the hall and I jumped, whirling around. It sounded like it'd come from the hall. What was that?

I shut the drawer and went to investigate. The door had been left ajar. Another louder clang resonated through the mansion and I followed it to the right of the hall, away from the staircase. I passed Asher's bedroom, and then four other doors, stopping at the last one on the opposite side. It seemed innocent enough.

I prodded it open the rest of the way with the tip of my toe to a dark room.

Palming the wall, I felt around for the switch, but there was nothing. The slightest sound reached my ears. Was that a groan? I shuffled a few more steps inside, leaving the door wide open so the light speared across the room in a narrow beam that reached the far wall. It was enough to give me courage to take a few more steps. I rubbed my arms. By this point, I was inside of the room and very much doubting whether I should be in here. A rattle, much lower than what I'd originally heard, bounced around the room. Like metal shaking against metal.

I jumped back so fast, trying to flatten against the wall to sidle to the door, but my hip bumped into what I could only assume was a mattress and then a cold palm wrapped around my wrist. A scream slipped free as I was yanked to something hard.

Panting, I froze, the hands feeling oddly familiar.

I squeezed my eyelids together and felt a light touch on my hand as it was dragged up. My fingers settled on . . . hair?

I gawked up at the male that had moved into the direct line of the beam filtering inside. Red eyes stared down at me, almost expectantly, the same blank aspect to them as in the dream. They lacked humanity. Like I stared into the eyes of a tiger. A large hungry tiger waiting to tear into its bleeding prey.

"You're real," I breathed.

He hissed, pressing my fingers into his long pale, white hair, just like he enjoyed in the dream. He was fucking real? A hysterical laugh wanted to escape but I swallowed it.

My trembling digits dragged across his scalp, scratching slightly. His eyes slitted and he buried his mouth into my neck, biting down hard. I screeched, the sound ripping from my throat.

It was combination of surprise and absolute agony. My fingers curled into his hair, desperately yanking as he sucked in deep pulls.

It'd felt the exact same as when I was held by the other vampire, as if he was pulling too hard and too fast, so much so it burned coming out of me. Like the pressure of blood surfacing was too much to come through the little holes caused by the fangs.

I whimpered, and my mind scrambled.

"Tobias," I shouted, or attempted to. The noise rasped past my throat. "Asher!"

Dots specked in front of my eyes. When I heard nothing I assumed they must not be here . . . the only one here then, was . . . "Jax!"

I cried it out so hard my throat burned.

The white-haired vampire didn't seem to like it. He pulled back and sank his teeth into another spot. My body jerked.

The door slammed open.

"Catalina!" Jax shouted and his entrance caused the vampire holding me to retract his teeth and scramble back, clutching me to his massive chest like I was some toy.

I whimpered in his too tight hold. He was going to pop me. My joints felt close to rupturing.

"I can't move any closer, or he's going to squeeze you to death."

The low words from Jax calmed me enough to not hyperventilate, but there was already tightness in my lungs.

There was a click and light speared my eyes.

"Jax?" I whimpered.

"I'm right here, Catalina. Relax for me, sweetheart."

I whimpered. I wasn't sure if I was more shocked at the endearment or the soft tone. I did as he bade and softened against the rabid vampire. My head bounced on his shoulder as he inched to the corner near the bed.

"Bastien, no," Jax snapped.

Bastien . . .

My back smacked into the mattress and my chest expanded sharply. The simple metal frame the bed rested on creaked as he climbed over me. His nude body pressed into mine and I grunted from the weight pushing me into the plush bedding.

The door banged again and Tobias came into the room at vampire speed. Jax grabbed hold of him as Bastien curved his body tighter over me, blocking me from sight. His wide chest blocked the ceiling.

"Tobias, don't. If any of us come after her, he'll kill her before we get to her." The image of him in my dream, enjoying me combing through his hair filled my mind. He hadn't seemed so bad after he'd initially attacked me.

"We can't allow him to—"

At that point, Asher stepped in and strode forward. Bastien tensed, lifting off me with a hiss. The predatory look on his face shouted deadly intentions. Bastien swiped one of his large hands out and wrapped his fingers around Asher's throat, who grabbed at his wrists. Flesh burst and blood leaked from between Bastien's fingers. Asher hissed, eyes turning red. He didn't seem to be trying to hurt him back, instead he jerked at the arm to get him to release. It wasn't working and the effect was Asher's throat was being torn out as I watched.

Pushing to my ass, I wrapped my arms around Bastien's waist and squeezed. I lifted my hand to the one he was digging into Asher, managing to grip onto his forearm, and I yanked at it.

Bastien turned his attention to me, tilting his head to the side as he flung Asher away.

Asher slammed into the wall, snarling as he pushed up. Jax pulled him back.

"He's territorial with her," Jax shouted in his slightly raspier voice. Bastien swept me into his arms as if confirming the comment.

"Don't worry, Catalina. We'll find a way to get him away from you," Tobias said in a calm tone. I flexed my stiff arms currently squeezing into my side. Bastien continued looking down at me—waiting.

"We should end his torment." Asher's voice floated to me. The low tone strained. My attention narrowed on him.

"We are not putting him down, Asher," Jax snapped. For once, I agreed with the rude twin. "The repercussions are too extensive. We can't afford the loss of his—"

"I said, 'end his torment,' there is no need for drastic measures." Asher huffed.

"I'm in agreement with Asher for once," Tobias added. "We should have put him out of his misery when he became blood-mad."

Bastien pressed down on my sides and a sob wrenched free. He wasn't helping my soreness.

"Fuck," Jax hissed. "Fine, but you two will answer to Ren for this."

The agreement to end the life of the vampire hovering over me didn't sit well.

I pressed the pads of my fingers into his stomach.

"No," I said sharply.

Bastien's brows furrowed and when I squirmed in his grip, he loosened. My heart drummed in my ears.

"He won't harm me . . ." *I should try to sound a little more convincing.*

"Cat, he's blood-mad. He's no better than an animal right now." Tobias sounded closer than before.

Even though he no longer squeezed me close to death, there was tension viced around my lungs. I attempted to suck in a breath.

"Can you get . . . inhaler?" I pushed from my tight chest. The room tilted and my sight faded at the edges.

I wasn't sure how long I was out for but when my eyes fluttered open, Tobias and Jax were arguing, so it must have only been a second. I was no longer upright, my back was flat on the mattress and Bastien's weight was settled over my lower body, pinning my legs.

Asher sped back inside but stopped when Bastien bared his fangs at him.

The medicine landed near my head and Bastien stared as I used it. Now that I was able to breathe properly, I could take stock of my situation and *think* about it.

Bastien wouldn't hurt me. I wasn't sure if it was pure hope spawning the words, but it was a feeling I would go with. So, if he was instinct right now . . . I had to find a way to get through to him . . .

He seemed particularly docile when I wasn't trying to escape. I licked my lips and met his eyes.

He was hyper-focused on me. I swallowed hard and tipped my chin, exposing the column of my throat.

catalina

"CAT. DON'T MOVE," Jax snapped, but I ignored him. My arm trembled as I curled my hand around the back of Bastien's neck.

I relaxed my shoulders and held my breath as his lips pressed against my throat. A wet tongue lashed out and I bit my lip at the erotic sensation. Suddenly, he struck like a cobra and sucked.

My fingers speared into his hair, scraping the scalp slightly. He groaned against my skin and his body fully settled on top of me, pressing the oxygen from my lungs with his weight. I became accustomed to his mass and settled under the vampire. His wide lower torso pressed between my legs as he splayed across me. Now that my thighs were spread, the long shirt I wore pooled at my waist, leaving me embarrassingly bare. The pressure of his smooth, hard abdomen against my core short-circuited my thoughts. That's how big this one was . . . his fangs were embedded deep into the crevice of my neck where my shoulder met it, while his belly button lined up with my core.

Bastien made some sort of rumble in his chest and retracted

his fangs from my flesh. Red stained his lips and his nostrils flared. His palms dipped the bed at my sides, jostling me. What was he doing? I gawked as he slid down my body to bury his head between my thighs.

His tongue lashed out and lapped at my arousal. I yelped at the onslaught, trying to catch my breath. He didn't seem to care about anything but licking away the moisture. My body clenched and his teeth sank into my inner thigh. My back arched off the bed as I cried out. *Dear Lord.* My toes curled. The orgasm blistered through my core, and I panted as my body spasmed from release.

My lashes fluttered as my eyes opened to meet Jax's, Asher's, and Tobias's gazes as they watched my face.

Tobias pushed his fingers through his hair while a flush spread on Asher's face, a multitude of expressions crossing his eyes.

Jax's jaw ticked but he hadn't looked away from me.

Bastien dragged another mouthful of blood and my core gushed again. I felt so damn wet.

"You need to stop him, or he'll drain you," Jax said sharply.

I registered the words, but I didn't want to stop him. That was orgasm brain speaking though. I dragged my elbows back and pushed up, making an effort for my stomach muscles to hold me up. Slipping my hand under his chin, I gripped it hard, but he didn't budge.

"No." I added a little shake with my word and Bastien tensed, red iris's flicking up to mine. I frowned exaggeratedly at him and his teeth retracted, head lifting.

He licked the red painting his lips. His long white hair tickled my arm as I sucked in a breath. I lifted my arm and speared my fingers through his strands, dragging his head down to rest on my lap. There was hardly any resistance and he sank on top of me, allowing me to keep him close.

His shoulder muscles rippled as he adjusted his position and sank onto me in a kind of cuddly, grizzly bear sort of way.

Asher went invisible and Jax's hand dropped. I had no idea where he was but Bastien tensed, a deep, aggressive rumble starting in his chest.

"He knows you're near," I muttered and pressed my fingers into Bastien's shoulder when his hold tightened.

I dragged my palm down Bastien's back, he groaned and leaned into my touch.

"Fuck." Asher reappeared and hooked his hands behind his neck.

"I guess we wait." Tobias sighed and leaned against the wall while Asher paced. Jax remained in place, his attention fixed on my face. I pressed my lips together and lowered my eyes as warmth spread in my cheeks. He was so intense. I couldn't get a feel for Jax. Sometimes it felt like he hated me, but his actions pointed otherwise. Then there was the fact I felt no true danger from him anymore.

From the time I could remember anything, I'd never felt safe. My parents were a bit unreliable and absorbed in their toxic relationship, mix in some drug addictions that landed them dead and by eighteen, Peter and I were on our own. All my life there was work, worrying, and providing.

Then that vampire had taken me and opened my eyes to the supernatural world.

From early on, feeling 'safe' or 'protected' wasn't something I had the pleasure of experiencing. But these vampires somehow brought all of it forward, everything I'd ever wished for.

Bastien nuzzled my leg. I kind of liked this.

Okay, I liked it a hell of a lot more than I should admit. Bastien's thick lashes settled on his cheeks and he stilled preternaturally. From observing the other vampires, I noted they didn't really breathe. The only time I'd seen one of them suck in a lungful of air was during or after something stressful.

It was interesting to be around people that didn't have to do the thing I struggled most with.

Bastien didn't move for many minutes, nothing, not a twitch. If I wanted to get out of his hold, this was my chance.

I scooted more into a sitting position and slowly removed my hand from the tangles of his hair. He gripped my hand.

"Don't—" Jax's sentence cut off at my scream. Bastien continued crushing my fingers as he clutched them to his chest.

My bones ground together, and something snapped. *Mother fucking shit.* A sharp pain radiated up my arm and I whimpered as I collapsed in the bed. Sweat beaded my forehead and I heaved out a sob. He still hadn't let my broken hand go.

Jax was on the bed and at my side, arms wrapped around my upper body while Bastien stared him down with a snarl curving his lips.

"Calm him down, now," he snapped in my ear. Tears trickled my face as I lifted my uninjured hand and rubbed it against his arm as my entire body trembled.

Bastien curved into my hand and settled, even as Jax's legs corralled my sides so I could lean against his muscled chest.

I pressed my cheek against his chest, tears streaming down my face.

"It hurts," I whimpered.

He went on in a stream of curses I didn't understand.

"As sexy as it sounds, cursing at me in your native language right now isn't going to help anyone," I whispered roughly.

Jax stopped the angry cussing and his chest moved once against my cheek in a deep breath. His arms wrapped around me tightly.

"How's your hand, Pet?" Asher paced nearby, his face tight.

"Hurts," I muttered. "Jax, can you put the inhaler to my mouth."

Jax's hand patted to the side and he did as I asked. Better able to breathe and see without spots dancing in front of my eyes, I found Asher inching closer.

A sharp ringing in the room interrupted abruptly and I tensed as Bastien tightened his hold on my hand. I screeched as Jax's lips settled in the crevice of my neck.

"Hold on, Kitten. Just hold on a moment." The words tickled my neck. I lifted my head so I could press my mouth against his cheek to stifle my cries of pain.

"Fuck," Tobias shouted crisply.

"Go, we'll watch her," Asher snapped. "You're aggravating Bastien."

Steps were the next thing I heard. The pain was still stabbing, but I sucked in shallow breaths.

"Move carefully, Pet." Asher inched close, making sure to keep an eye on Bastien. "Switch your hand out so Jax can take a look."

I nodded shakily, focusing on the heavy vampire half-draped across my legs. He hugged my broken limb to his chest like it was some sort of toy. His gaze was hyper-focused on my face to the point that it surprised me holes weren't burning into it. With my other palm, I tugged at his forearm holding my other arm down. Bastien loosened his hold enough for me to slip my crushed hand free. He scooted closer, and his ear pressed to my upper thigh and arms wrapped around my legs. Hopefully they wouldn't be next. I paused my pulling, panting at the pain. Jax gripped my arm and helped me pull it up to him. Each minuscule twitch sent a wave of electricity throughout my fingers.

"Holy, shit," I croaked, whimpering into Jax's chest. Bastien looked up at me, tilting his head. I rubbed my thumb across his forehead.

"Yes, Pet, keep at it. He's responding to you." Asher sounded half-awed and half-excited. With his perverse sense of . . . everything, I was positive that was not a good thing.

Asher knelt by the bed.

"Hurry it up, Jax," Asher snapped, jerking his chin toward my too limp hand. Jax's grunt vibrated against my back. His thumb pressed into my wrist and I tensed up.

"That's hurting her," Asher snapped.

"Yes, well, I need to feel around to know the extent of the damage."

Asher's brows furrowed as he focused on Jax's moving hand. Shards of pain struck my nerve endings, and I tensed up so hard against Jax it felt like my muscles would snap. Asher caressed my cheek with the back of his fingers.

"He destroyed your hand." My throat tightened at Jax's words. Tears flooded my eyes and they trickled from the corners. "It will take you a long time for this to fully heal, and even then, it may not feel right."

I blinked quickly, but regardless of how many times I blinked, the tears wouldn't stop. Exhaling shakily, I trembled against Jax. This couldn't be. I was a writer. My hand was my life. My pulse shot to hell and a panic attack loomed over me.

"Pet. There's another way I can help you—"

"No," Jax snapped, his body tensing.

Asher's teeth clicked together and I pressed my eyes tightly shut until the tears allowed me to see. The twins stared each other down.

"You're not tying yourself to her, Asher."

"Tying yourself to me? What does that mean?" They were acting too weird. My mouth dried up like a raisin.

"When vampires share blood w—"

Jax slammed his teeth into his own wrist in a swift move and then pressed it to my lips. I sputtered against his skin, muttering at him, but his grip didn't loosen.

Liquid trickled into my mouth and a sweet taste spread on my tongue, tightening my belly. I swallowed on instinct and a rush of energy spilled through me.

I moaned, my eyelids fluttering closed as I sucked in another gulp.

"What the fuck was that?" Asher snapped. They settled into a rapid argument in their language.

I lulled against Jax, comfortable and blissful. My belly felt warm and toasty as the blood spread throughout my body. Jax lifted his arm from my lips and tugged out of my grip trying to keep him close. I hadn't realized I'd clung onto him.

My wrist twinged and the ache dulled significantly. Panic obliterated the hazy, lustful blanket that spread through my veins. I sucked in a breath as I lifted my hand, gingerly twisting it in a circle. There was hardly a pinch. My eyes wide, I lifted my stare to Asher. The edges of my vision faded for a split second, and then refocused.

"I feel . . . better," I said, slightly slurring my words while actively working to ignore the sensitivity between my legs biding me to grind against Jax. Asher was still glaring at his twin. I twisted to look at him, making sure not to jostle Bastien too much. "Why did you do that?"

My tone sounded more accusing than I'd meant it to.

Jax's jaw tightened and he pushed me forward. I grunted as I flopped toward Bastien, and Jax slipped out from behind me.

Asher shook his head as Jax exited. A pit balled in my stomach when he disappeared, settling uncomfortably. I didn't feel as comfortable or warm as I'd felt in his arms.

I scowled and pressed my hand to my stomach, fighting the urge to rub between my legs.

Asher sighed. "He didn't give you too much, so you should be clear-headed in a moment."

What did that even mean? I scowled harder. I poked at the furrow between my eyebrows.

"This was why I wanted to give you my blood, I wouldn't have a fit every other second and march off," Asher said . . . mumbled, whatever. I shook my head, struggling to focus.

"What does that mean? You mentioned a connection." I licked my dry lips.

Asher brushed my hair back.

"When vampires share their blood, it heals, but it also creates a bond for as long as it runs through your veins. It's even worse when you've exchanged blood with a vampire. You will feel each other's absence and you will feel when you need each other. It's like a call to one another. A sort of tether. You can also find one another through it."

This must have been how I survived in the cave for so long. The Pale One fed me his blood. And here I thought I'd survived because I'd eaten the damn bugs.

My stomach soured at the memory. Nope. No, time to

block the traumatic memories. Not one of my finer moments but I'd been determined to live so I could get back to Peter.

Turned out I didn't have to do that because he'd been giving me his sweet blood the entire time. Sweet? No! I'd hated it, I hated everything about it . . . but not really. I rubbed my temples. Asher said something about finding—a cold wave washed over my thoughts and I climbed out of the mental cobwebs.

If we could find one another, did that mean . . .

I sucked in a breath.

No. No.

Had he known where I was the entire time?

He'd known how to find me. The whole time he'd known as I ran around like a chicken with her head cut off.

"*Sh. Älskade.*" Asher perched on the end of the bed and pressed my head to his chest.

I was at an odd angle since Bastien weighed my legs down, so I had to twist my torso, which didn't help the shortness of breath.

"What has you so terrified, Pet?"

I squeezed my eyelids shut, unable to get the words out even if I wanted to. No, he couldn't get to me now even if he found me. Vampires seemed territorial and there'd been no other one of them to step foot in their home.

"Distract me, please." The words rasped free, rough and desperate.

"I—" Asher sighed, and I could practically feel the nerves radiating from him. My fingers clenched onto his shirt.

"Tell me about Ren? Or Bastien? Why is he down here? Why is he like this?"

"Ren . . . enjoys chaos. Bastien is subtler. Kills anything that crosses him even when he's not blood-mad." Asher snorted and shook his head.

"What's blood-mad?" Dread tugged at my stomach.

"It's an illness that started running rampant in vampire communities more than three decades ago." Asher dragged his palm down my side. My heart rate was starting to go down and the fingers of the panic attack slowly withdrew. "It drives vampires crazy. The illness eats at their brain and all they want to do is drink blood."

I swallowed hard, nose flaring as images of the Pale One filled my mind. He'd been indiscriminate when he bit me, just as Bastien was. The skeletal monster looked like it'd been vacuumed of anything resembling human, leaving behind a husk of a *thing*. It'd had no care or patience, sleeping or eating practically all the time. A sick cycle that led to feeding me his blood, which, according to them, meant he could have found me this entire time.

How stupid was I?

I'd spent the last few years running, uselessly. If he could find me, then why hadn't he captured me?

Was he playing a game with me?

I rubbed my forehead against Asher's jaw.

"Bastien was always a bit loose up there, though. Where Ren thrives on calculated disorder." Asher chuckled. "Ren and Bastien were known to create the largest number of vampires in one century, which was probably why Imogen wanted—"

He cut off and I frowned, lifting to look him in the face and quirked my brow questioningly.

The corners of his lips tilted up.

"Ren and Jax may have been fooled by her, but the cunt only used us," Asher added. "Bastien would have eventually left

Crimson Coven if he hadn't become blood-mad. I stayed for my foolish brother. Ren looked for alliances that benefited him, but was just as quick to turn on you if something didn't. And Tobias *couldn't* leave." An odd wrenching tore at my chest. That would explain Jax's bitterness toward . . . everything.

"Why couldn't Tobias leave?"

Asher sighed. "That's enough story time, Pet. You need to rest. Don't think I didn't notice you stifle that yawn."

"I just woke up," I said, forcing pep into my words. Another yawn encroached. *My eyelids did feel heavy.*

"Come. Rest against me. I'll keep watch over you."

I pouted and went along with his decree more because he was stronger than me. He settled against the headboard, and I rested against him.

I wiggled my toes, trying to get some blood circulating. My legs were going to be numb by morning with Bastien's weight. There seemed to be tons of baggage accompanying these guys and the one with big blaring lights was named Imogen.

She had a hold on them, even in death, and that soured my stomach. There was nothing positive with thoughts attached to her, but I was sure that had more to do with the jealousy creeping up on me. She had them all seemingly wrapped around her fingers, and I knew now that I had no chance against the memory of her.

As I faded away, Asher's hair brushed my cheek.

"When you're ready to tell me what has you so fearful. I will protect you."

The vow was heaven . . . My shaking subsiding and I slept.

catalina

I GROANED, wiggling my ass to get closer to the hard body pressed against my front. My breasts smushed against the broad, muscled chest and I pinned my hands between us. So comfy . . . and safe . . .

My lashes fluttered and I met piercing blue eyes. Instead of the teasing expression I expected to see, it was serious and searching.

Jax.

My lips parted and I was about to yank back, but he tightened his grip. I blinked at him, my cheek pillowed on his bent arm. I was in a different bedroom, but that was all I could tell from my vantage. Licking my lips, I searched for words, but nothing would come. His gaze lasered in on my mouth.

"What—" He cut me off, swiping his tongue against mine. Hovering over me, he nipped my bottom lip. I sucked in a surprised breath. I expected him to push away from me or spout nonsense about being disgusted—not this. His eyes heated, a sultry look in them that made my stomach dip. Lust flushed my body and I wiggled my hip into the bed. Jax's hold flexed and his palm dragged up my body, lifting my shirt to my neck and exposing my breasts.

I gasped, detaching from Jax's possessive caresses. His thumb and pointer finger gripped my chin and he forced my gaze to his.

"I'm going to fuck you, Kitten." I sucked in a deep breath, my eyelids fluttering from the electricity tightening my throbbing pussy.

His muscles bunched beneath the skin containing them. I tipped my head back to look into his eyes. Jax lifted his hand to my cheek, and he pressed his thumb to my mouth. A wicked grin spread on his lips as he dragged the damp digit to my nipple, then trailed them lower and lower until his large hand engulfed my hip, clasping it tightly.

He flipped me with such ease it took my breath away. My cheek pressed into the mattress.

On instinct, I fought to turn back around, but his palm pressed between my shoulders, forcing my chest to flatten on the bed. My hands pressed into the bed next to my head and I was about to forcefully push up when his teeth sank into my shoulder.

I went limp, moaning as Jax dragged blood out of my body. He lifted his head and lazily licked the wound once. The bed jostled as he pushed to his knees. I remained in place as his hands skimmed down my sides and gripped my bare thighs. His thumbs pressed into my ass cheeks as his fingers wrapped around my hips, teasingly near my pussy. My face was warm from lust and embarrassment, but I wanted to be filled so bad.

Jax dragged me back, forcing my ass higher in the air. I yelped at the sudden movement and exposure of my sensitive flesh. The cool air made my drenched state startlingly clear. Nerves curdled in my stomach and I tugged once to get free, face blistering. There was something so erotically charged about being so vulnerable and at the mercy of the vampire that didn't like me.

He stilled my hips and a sudden swipe of a wet tongue had me sucking in a deep breath and groaning into the mattress. I bunched the sheets in both fists as Jax's tongue prodded my entrance and slowly swiped upward to the bud of my ass where he swirled his tongue.

The suddenness there stiffened me, but he chased it away by slipping his tongue into my wet pussy.

A moan crawled from my throat and my toes curled.

The bed jostled again as he lowered the angle he had me at and his hard cock prodded my entrance, slowly dipping in and out in a shallow thrust, again and again until I was wiggling in his hold. My fingers gripped the bedsheet, and I arched my back, but nothing I did forced him to give me what I wanted.

"Jax," I whimpered.

"Quiet, Kitten."

The order had me pressing my lips tightly together. Stilling, I gritted my teeth. The shallow touch of his dick retreated, and I whimpered. Frustration was about to make me snap. Fortunately, I held my tongue and in the next second he thrust into me so hard I lurched forward. Jax slammed me back on his shaft and fullness overtook my channel.

I sucked in a deep breath as his cock prodded my cervix. The sensation verged on pain, but I wanted more.

Jax didn't leave me waiting for the full sensation. He slid out and slammed back in, hitting a spot deep inside that hollowed my stomach. Dear God, I would willingly give up one of my designer bags to feel this over and over again.

Tears came to my eyes at the pressure, and I whimpered but wiggled for more. I pressed my palm into the mattress to turn to look at him, but he forced my head down. I frowned into the mattress, but my irritation faded as he started a relentless pounding rhythm.

A tremble began at my toes and coasted up my spine. Spikes of pleasure sparked and spiraled across my body. My arms gave out and I flattened on the mattress. His rhythm made my nipples rub against the sheets and the added sensation made my toes curl.

Fuck this felt good.

The pressure tautened and erupted in an explosion of starbursts behind my eyelids with my pussy clasping his dick helplessly. My legs twitched with each and every one of Jax's uneven thrusts. His grunts and moans floated to my ears, heightening my pleasure.

He stilled against me with a ragged breath and then his dick spasmed in my channel, setting off a secondary orgasm.

I panted, slumping against the bed as Jax's chest pressed into my back. He grabbed my chin and squeezed as he forced me to look at him. His lips hovered close and called to me, so I leaned toward him and pressed my mouth to his. He stiffened for a beat and I slid my tongue across the seam of his lips. Exhaling sharply, he gave in, meeting my tongue with his, his hand cupping my chin in a hard clasp.

He groaned into my mouth and lifted; his breath fluttering the hair around my face. I looked into his lustful eyes. Sweat cooled me as my heart rate lowered. There was a comforting warmth in my belly—a fullness. I tilted my head to the side, sweeping my hair over to expose my neck.

"Kitten . . ." The way he rumbled my nickname made my toes curl. His eyes flickered red.

"Catalina."

My name was said in a stiff tone, making me tense up. Lifting my head toward the voice, I found Asher watching with his jaw tight and eyes angry.

There was accusation there. That and unbridled anger. I frowned. *Why did he seem so pissed?* I nudged Jax, but he didn't release my hips and his hardening cock twitched in my channel.

"What are you doing?" Asher snapped. My shoulders hiked at the tone. He was livid. And I was just so fucking confused as to why. Jax tugged me back until he sat with me fully speared on his dick. A moan crawled free and my face warmed. "I thought she disgusted you, Jax?"

Jax's hands at my waist forced me up and down his cock and I sucked my lips into my mouth. This felt so good, but he shouldn't be fucking me in front of his brother, right? That was wrong. Jax repeated the motion and one of his hands slid to cup my breast. I was back to not caring. I wiggled on the hateful brother, body hot and needy.

Jax repeated the motion and I couldn't stop my helpless moans. Asher watched my pussy suck him inside me and lifted to my expression as I ground on Jax.

"Doesn't mean I can't fuck her."

The words slapped me across the head. A really big part of me wanted to say fuck it, but I had pride. What was there not to like about me? I sniffed in offendedly and stilled.

I sank my teeth into my lip until it hurt and forced myself off his delicious cock. Jax's hand pressed into my spine, but I smacked it away. He stared at me stunned as I bounced to the edge of the bed and hopped off. My action stunned me too, but they would have killed me already if they wanted to, right?

I didn't bother saying anything to Jax, I just scooted off the bed, stood with my shoulders squared and walked out like cum wasn't sliding down my inner thigh.

I needed space. And I needed to pee so damn bad. I glared at Asher as I walked by. He grunted, and his hand flashed out. Somehow, I managed to twist to the side and avoid it.

"I'll talk to you later," I mumbled and widened my stride, but he dogged my steps down the hall.

"What is going on between you two?" I ignored the question. "I didn't know you wanted to fuck him." The bitter, petty words boiled my blood, but I didn't turn to face him.

He hounded my heels, practically stepping on them. My footsteps pounded down the steps and I gritted my teeth.

"Pet. Stop a moment."

I careened to a stop at the front door and crossed my arms. My state of undress was made remarkably clear, but I didn't want to run around looking for more clothes. At least the important bits were covered.

"You said you don't believe in monogamy, Asher. Why are you acting upset?"

He raked his fingers through his hair, scraping the strands back.

"I know what I said."

I peered closer at him as his jaw twitched. His nose flared and his chest moved up once sharply. He must be feeling something intently if he had to take a breath.

He seemed to be working through something, but my skin itched, and I was practically dancing in place with the need to pee.

"We'll continue this later," I muttered and yanked the door open. I was down the drive quicker than I'd been before, crows seemingly watching my descent. Smoothing the end of the shirt tightly over my ass, I rushed the distance to my house. The clang of their gate ricocheting off metal echoed to me.

My foot slid over the wood board of the porch and a pinch assaulted it.

"Fuck!" I lifted my leg, hopping the rest of the way to the front door. It was a splinter. It had to be, nothing else was as searing as a splinter. I whimpered. I couldn't wait until I was in the shower, basking in the water—

The doorknob twisted but didn't budge.

Are you kidding me right now?

I squeezed my fists so tightly they popped. Suck it up, Catalina. I half-limped down the steps and made sure to not drag my foot to avoid another splinter and rounded to the side of my fence.

Pressing my fisted hands to my waist, I took in the height. I pushed to my toes and reached my arm over, trying to reach the latch. With my nose wrinkled, I strained, the lip of the wooden fence dug into my arm uncomfortably.

No more splinters, please. I wiggled my fingers, trying to get it to flip, but it was a no go.

"Do you need help?"

I screeched and jumped back, but only managed to ricochet into the fence when the arm of the shirt caught over one of the fence boards.

The breeze against my ass told me just how much I was on display. I squeezed my eyes shut. *How embarrassing.*

A snorting laugh sounded from behind me and a weird half-growl half-huff escaped my mouth.

"Are you just going to stare?" I mumbled and narrowed my eyes at Asher. In a few steps his arm was around my waist and his front was pressing into my back. The strain on my toes lessened when he lifted me effortlessly and unhooked my shirt.

My bare feet settled on the ground, and I peeked up at him from under my lashes.

"How long have you been watching?"

"Long enough, Pet." My hand twitched to smack the slight smirk off his face, and I narrowed my eyes at him. Asher pressed closer to me, and I scooted back, flattening against the wood. My lips parted as I stared up into his shadowed eyes. The blue glinted with restrained fury.

The latch clicked and I fell backward. My arms windmilled. Before slamming into the ground, Asher bunched the front of my shirt.

"You did that on purpose." I yanked free and stumbled into the yard, toward the side door. I stepped a little too hard on the splinter in my foot. Wincing, I passed my threshold into the empty garage.

"Let me in."

"No," I shouted back to Asher and slammed the door in his face. Storming inside and then to my bedroom, I headed directly to relieve the tight pressure on my bladder.

As soon as I was done peeing, I turned on the shower and tossed the borrowed shirt toward my hamper. The pile of clothing was getting to the point of no return. I needed to do laundry as soon as I finished unpacking all my stuff.

"WHAT, DO YOU LIKE ME NOW?" Binx meowed and rubbed against my leg, almost pushing me over with his big body. What was wrong with him?

When I'd come out of the shower, I'd found Binx waiting for me in my bedroom. His eerie gaze followed me around my room as I'd unpacked my measly belongings with a tad more aggression than necessary.

I'd spent hours coming to terms with everything. Most especially the odd warmth I felt when I thought of the vampires next door. For the umpteenth time, my attention narrowed in on the window. Just one little peek. There was no way he was still out there . . .

Crossing the room, I peeked down at Asher still hanging around my backyard. He hadn't budged, in fact, he seemed to be settling in for a long wait. I pushed back my damp hair and looked at Binx.

"He's too much sometimes."

Binx meowed, as if agreeing.

I sighed and moved to my basket of clothing. Yeah,

just as I thought, I was running low. I buried my hand into the pile and pulled out a long men's shirt I'd purchased specifically to sleep in. The good thing was I'd added another to my collection. Tobias wasn't getting his back.

I tugged it over my head and plucked the only two socks available. A fuzzy pink one that reached my calf and a short black one that stopped at my ankle. How I always managed to lose my socks was beyond me.

My steps were softened as I padded to the side door, which was the only way into the back area from the house, the sting of the splinter an uncomfortable pinch. I hadn't been able to get it out while I was in the shower, which explained the prune-look to my fingers.

The sliding door was wide open with Asher leaning against the side of the house, a stubborn twist to his lips.

Asher met my eyes and for the first time since I met him, there was unadulterated irritation. It was as if he'd been body snatched by his brother.

I pressed my lips together. Somehow, I doubted he would enjoy the comparison. Inviting him in wouldn't be a bad idea. It was just Asher after all.

"Since it looks like you're not leaving." I frowned, moving to the side.

"You have to say the words."

"Oh, uh. Asher, come in."

He gingerly stepped over the threshold and I turned my back, knowing he would follow me into the main part of the house. My face heated at my sparse home, but I tipped my chin up. There was nothing to be embarrassed about. Not everyone could live centuries and accumulate a shit ton of money. Plus,

I'd work on acquiring more furniture when my next check came in.

"You're still limping."

"I got a splinter."

"Let me help."

"No, thanks," I responded curtly. I was still a bit upset about his reaction earlier. After ruminating about it for a while in the shower, I'd not figured out what had pissed me off. It had almost seemed like accusations.

Asher swept me into his arms and I yelped, scrambling to grab onto him. I went along with it, knowing I had no chance of fighting against him, but I set a severe frown on my lips so he knew I wasn't down for this.

He paused at the entrance of my living room, and I tried my best to suppress the heat washing up my neck. He only hesitated a second more before setting me on the couch and kneeling in front of me and lifting my fuzzy-sock-clad foot.

He plucked it off my foot with a smile.

"It's on my heel." He hummed and bowed over my foot as he lifted it. My knee pushed up and bend close to my face.

"Don't be upset with me, Pet." The cajoling words made me narrow my eyes at him.

"You didn't have to be a jerk—" I cut off with a snort and my foot kicked out at the tickle, nailing Asher across the jaw. I winced and tried to scoot back, horrified, but he didn't release the hold on my ankle.

He worked his jaw side to side and cleared his throat, a small smirk tipping up the corners of his lips. "I got the memo; I shouldn't have been a jerk."

"I am so so—"

"Not to worry, Pet." His long lashes fluttered as he

stared at me, the grin over taking his face. "I kind of liked it." He winked and I choked on my words. "In fact, if you need to get in a few more licks, consider me a willing participant—"

"Oh. My. God, Asher, please stop." I sank into the chair, snorting back laughter. His finger pressed into that tender spot on my foot and I froze. "Don't."

He smirked.

"Fine. Fine." Asher lifted his hand, pinching something between his forefinger and thumb. He'd gotten the splinter. *Thank God.*

Seeing his smile did bad things to my insides. I wanted him. I licked my lips and squeezed my fists. He blinked at me and placed my sock back on, a severe frown on his face. A polar opposite from how he usually behaved.

"Why are you angry at me?"

The question burst from me, and I pressed my lips together. I couldn't believe I was asking him that. I sounded like a child, worry filling my voice and everything.

"I'm . . . not sure."

Our earlier argument flashed through my mind.

"*You* told me you didn't do monogamy," I repeated my earlier point. "I mean if that's why you're angry."

"Absolutely not." Asher's fists clenched, his jaw working overtime. "I'm not a jealous vampire."

My eyebrows about met my hairline at the haute tone. Well, I felt foolish.

"Asher. I thought you were such an open book."

Jax leaned against the threshold, his head tipped to the side as he watched his brother.

I gasped, shooting straight in the seat. Now that I saw him, I realized that the tether in my chest hadn't strained at all. He must have been around for a while.

"How did you get in? Is it some twin thing?" Where one went, the other could go?

"Something like that," Jax drawled.

"Om du inte går. Jag ska berätta för henne att du är katten."

"Jag ska säga till henne att du tittar på henne som en jävla stalker."

They went back and forth a few times, my brain trying to make sense of what they were spouting. All I could decipher was they were both becoming increasingly close to bickering like children.

"This seems a bit counterproductive."

"Don't get involved, human," Jax snapped, and I shook my head and popped off the seat. I'd leave them to it and go to bed. The events of the last few days were catching up to me, and if Asher wasn't going to give me some orgasms, then I was passing out. Tomorrow I had a long day trying to catch up on my edits and making sure I did some laundry.

I made my way back to my bedroom and dropped on my mattress face down. The cheap metal bed frame I'd had delivered creaked under my weight. I hadn't needed to use my inhaler as much recently and it felt good. Everything felt good. My brain no longer raced with fear and the itchy need to escape. The experiences with these vampires were cathartic, even finding out that the evil vampire could have found me soon after I escaped. That must mean he lost interest in me if he never sought me out—I was free.

A palm slid over my ass and the fingers slipped underneath the elastic of my panties. When I tried lifting my head, a palm pressed me down, forcing my cheek into the mattress.

"Don't move, Kitten. I want you just like this." A gush of wetness spread onto his fingers and I sucked in a breath. *Jax.*

He hated me and I wasn't a fan of him either, but I didn't want to push him away. I wanted to be fucked and bitten.

"Why do the nicknames you two chose have to do with animals?" I rasped.

Jax chuckled and didn't answer my question. That cemented my dislike. Asher would have said something in response. Whatever, I didn't have to like him for him to wring those delicious orgasms out of me.

My thoughts evaporated when Jax dipped his fingers past my panties and into my slit. His touch soft and prodding as he spread the moisture on my clit and to the bud of my ass. It was less shocking this time and goose bumps lifted over my skin.

My stomach tightened and I groaned, pushing my ass toward his touch. Jax tightened the grip on my hip and forced me onto my knees. I tried to push up so I could flip over, but he didn't allow me to. A zipper interrupted the silence and my heart thumped like hummingbird wings. I was ready for him to slide into me. I ached to see his dick, but I'd stopped trying.

Jax tugged my panties over my thighs, baring me to him. He hummed and my entire body clenched as waves of wetness released.

My fingers wrapped into my comforter, and I rubbed my cheek into the cotton. He was teasing me. *Was he even going to relieve the pressure in my core with all this playing around?*

A thickness prodded my entrance and I sucked in a breath as he continued shoving into my channel. My core fluttered around the thick cock and I pushed back into it.

Jax groaned and withdrew, slamming into me again. "Fucking human." His pace quickened, and I whimpered at the pounding of his thighs against mine. The rhythmic slap served to heighten my pleasure. He was entirely too good at keeping his rhythm steady, yet forceful.

My thighs trembled and a moan slipped free. Tingles started at my clit and spread to my entrance where he fed his turgid cock into me.

The walls of my channel fluttered around him, gripping at him. Jax groaned, his thrusts coming quicker and harder and less steady. He was losing control. His fingers slid up my spine and he gripped my neck as he fucked me, bending me to his will. The tension of his fingers around my neck made my heart go crazy. Jax stole my breath from me, but it felt so good. The combination of his dick slamming into me and the lack of oxygen tightened my stomach.

"Fuck!" His shout shot my nerve endings over the edge as his digits twitched around my neck. I tensed, my breathing shallow as I cried out and went over the edge. My lashes fluttered shut as I came, my body bucking against him. He tensed at the movement, forcing my ass to still against him as he groaned. His cock twitched in my core, the jerks of his shaft making me move against him helplessly.

Riding out the wave, I sucked in a breath as it leveled and pinpricks spread across my body. Cum gushed down my leg as it escaped my wet core.

Crap, I was about to collapse. My knees were giving out. Before I could flatten, he slipped his hands below my hips and kept a slow pace. I twitched with each of his thrusts. *How was he not soft?*

"I can't get enough of you, Kitten." A shiver coasted up my spine as I focused on my breathing. It was a miracle I *could* breathe, but the tension in my throat wasn't enough to force me to stop. I loved the feel of his thick cock. Jax kept me seated on him as he lifted me backward. My spine pressed against his broad chest and his tongue lashed against the shell of my ear.

I snorted in a half-giggle and he growled. His palm delved under my shirt and skimmed up my belly until he reached my breast. Jax rasped his thumb across my nipple, sending shocks to my pussy. My belly clenched and I groaned, my head falling back.

"Sensitive little Kitten."

I was becoming very fond of the nickname. My ass wiggled against him and I tried to grind on his dick, but he stilled me.

"No, no, little Kitten. *I* fuck you."

I whimpered.

"Jerk," I mumbled through the cotton feel of my mouth.

"Don't fret too much, Pet. He's always been odd like that." The reminder of their past lover slash lovers wasn't appreciated, but I sucked down the sharp pain vicing my chest. I *did not* care about their past. A hysterical laugh built in my throat, but I swallowed it.

I attempted to turn in the direction Asher's voice came from, but Jax's hand on my breast tightened and he lashed his other arm around my belly, keeping me stiffly in place. Steps neared and Asher stepped into my line of sight. His smile was tight and there was something swimming in the back of his eyes that looked a helluva lot like jealousy.

Jax's grip tightened on me as Asher lowered on the mattress and scooted close until he knelt in front of me.

The way he dressed never failed to remind me of a pirate. A smile spread on my lips and his brows furrowed as he cupped my face.

"What's so funny?"

He spoke to me like I wasn't currently speared by his brother.

Before I could say a word, Jax flexed his thighs, driving his cock into me. I sucked in a breath, my words evaporating. There was no way I could formulate more than a moan. My bed frame creaked from the force.

My head fell back, hitting his chest. If he was a normal-sized being, then it would have fallen on his shoulder, but nope, the vampires I'd met were injected with some sort of make-me-big-as-hell-potion and luckily for me, their dicks were on the same level.

Asher lifted my shirt, the drag of the material forcing me to suck in a breath. I couldn't look away from his feverish eyes as he reached forward and cupped the breast his brother wasn't gripping. Jax's hand smoothed down my thigh, gripping and releasing in hard squeezes. Asher's head dipped and my lips parted at the lash of his tongue. My channel squeezed Jax's cock and he groaned.

I lifted my fingers to shift them through his hair, loving how the gold strands contrasted with my darker skin. Asher swirled his tongue and my chest lifted in harsh tugs. He pulled away, a sly smile on his lips as he hovered less than a foot away from me. His presence radiated toward me, and I wanted him to press into me the rest of the way so I could be enveloped in the twins' contrasting energies.

Asher's teasing touches and flirtatious smile. And Jax's aggression and scowls.

"Look at your nipples for me, Pet."

My head dropped at the command. The tip of the brown nipple was wet from his mouth, the skin puckered from need. Asher rasped his thumb over it and my entire body clenched.

"Fuck," Jax rasped, jerking up into me. The move slammed me forward and Asher caught me as Jax started ramming into me from behind. "Tease her later, Asher. I need her *now*."

My hands flattened on the mattress, and I arched to take Jax's thrusts, the friction curling through my body as the angle of his dick applied pressure to my clit and the walls of my pussy.

It was so good I couldn't think. Asher's cock tented his black slacks and I gripped it, my hand not fully closing around him.

Arching my neck so I could see him, his eyelids fluttered and he nudged against my hand, the length twitching. I dropped my hands to balance myself as Jax slammed into me especially hard. I grunted, my breaths coming quick.

Asher's fingers made quick work of the button and his hand wrapped around himself. Their girth was monstrous.

He guided his pierced cock forward and I licked the bead of cum on the tip before fitting my mouth around the head. Asher thrust forward, hitting the back of my throat. I gagged around him and his head tipped back, lips parted. I worked to swallow past the nausea as he stilled in my mouth. My lips didn't even pass over half his cock and the gold round piercings rubbed inside my mouth, clinking against my teeth at times. I flattened my tongue on the silky shaft.

Asher gripped the back of my neck and he thrust, keeping rhythm with Jax. I worked to suckle him as Jax's fingers spread my cheeks and his searching fingers caressed the entrance of my ass. My body clenched and I whimpered.

"*Det här kommer att döda mig*," Jax said with a hiss. He could have been calling me a stupid cow for all I cared as his rumbling words made me gush around him, my body throbbing as my ears rang. My release slammed into me, and I cried around Asher's dick as Jax rammed into me. My arousal dripped down my thighs, and the wet noises of Jax feeding into my pussy didn't relent. I didn't want it to. My legs shuddered but Jax didn't release me, chasing his own orgasm. The ringing eventually faded and I shuddered against him. I was painfully sensitive.

I ran my tongue over the silky shaft and the skin tightened as I fitted him until he hit the back of my throat again.

"*Bra tjej. Ta mig,*" Asher murmured huskily.

I was discovering a new kink and it was them talking in their language. My entire being was short-circuiting and a sensitive mess. I twitched with each of Jax's thrusts, but I wanted more. I wanted harder.

Asher bunched my hair and the sharp pain of my strands being pulled wrenched a moan from my throat. Asher slammed into my mouth in short quick pumps, the even speed losing rhythm. He moaned and slammed into the back of my throat. I swallowed hard as his delicious cum filled my mouth, overflowing. Cum dripped off my chin and as he withdrew, I licked at his skin, taking in his bittersweet, red-tinged essence. Asher pulled out of my mouth, and I dropped to my elbows as he zipped himself up.

Jax's hand slipped under my body and he curved around me as he reached the bundle of nerves. He swirled the bud, teasing it to maddening heights. My stomach tightened and I ground against him, my ass pressing tightly against his flesh as he rubbed just as hard against me. I wanted to take him deeper and deeper.

Jax tweaked my clit and I sucked in a breath, coming as he jerked against me, his cock spasming. My scream was muffled as I bucked, riding out the release.

I dropped onto the mattress. Jax's weight falling on top of me, his cock still fitted inside, but less stiff.

My body trembled around him and he groaned.

"*Jag vill aldrig lämna.*"

"Me too, I think," I rasped back, having no idea what he said.

He chuckled and the move made my pussy squeeze him and we both moaned. Scooting to the side, he brought me with him to keep me seated on him. I was wet from our mingling cum, but I didn't want him to detach from me.

A hand wrapped around my neck. I opened my eyes and met Asher's. His heated gaze stared into my soul. My stomach filled with butterflies at the intense look on his face. I wrapped my fingers in his silk shirt as he settled flush against my front and I cuddled close, rubbing my cheek against the soft material. He tightened his hold on me as Jax's fingers flexed.

"I know I explained to you that we've shared before," Asher began. A frown slipped over my mouth. While I was blissed on orgasms, I didn't want to hear about them with someone else. "More than once."

"Oh," I rasped, frowning. Jax's fingers twitched.

"You're the only one I've never wanted to share," he murmured the words into my hair.

"Oh," I muttered, not knowing what to say. My face heated. "I felt the same way, but when you told me all that stuff—" Asher pressed his finger over my mouth.

"I don't understand what's happening to me." His lips tightened. "I was—am jealous."

My lip trembled at the vulnerability. Jax's arm tightened around my stomach, but he remained silent. I slipped my hand up and cupped Asher's neck the same way he held me. A soft smile spread on his mouth before he pressed his mouth to my forehead. He exhaled roughly and scooted even closer until I was smushed between them.

I liked him. *A lot more than I should like a vampire.*

I was done for. There was no way this would go anywhere and that *hurt*.

All I could do was bask in this temporary halfway situationship. I faded into sleep and curved myself as close to them as I could.

TWENTY-EIGHT

I WAS HALF-ASLEEP and hard as fuck. It was her grinding that woke me. Kitten rubbed her luscious ass against me. I'd fallen asleep still deep in her cunt because I couldn't bear to detach myself from her and soaking in the soft walls of her channel calmed the bitterness in my gut.

Asher was gone. I hadn't registered when he'd left, but hopefully he was doing what I talked to him about and getting the human some stuff for her home. As much as I didn't like her as anything more than a body to fuck, I wanted her comfortable while I fucked her, and this sorry bed wouldn't cut it.

My lazy thrust turned more demanding as her hand spread on the mattress and she moaned.

Kitten tried to flip over but I forced her forward. I hated fucking face-to-face and that would never change. It triggered something in me I didn't want to confront.

Gripping her thigh, I lifted it so I could see my cock sliding into her drenched pussy. The tight *insatiable* pussy. My shaft was wet and glistening, her juices slicking the way.

I slammed into her, enjoying her little mewls as I fucked her. I wanted to fuck my obsession out of me. This softness that had grown in my gut whenever I looked at her. It was just the fucking bond that started from giving her my fucking blood. It had to be. Since I'd never shared blood with another, it was the only reason I could come up with.

Watching her was agony—an unmatched obsession.

Another ram into her and her channel fluttered around me. She was tightening up, getting ready to explode. My fingers slipped between our legs and I swirled my fingers over her core, playing with the stretched lips accommodating me and dragging the moisture to the clit that would set her off within moments.

"Jax," she whimpered. My balls drew up. The sound of my name on her lips shot euphoria through me. Her body went taut as a bow string and she sucked in a sharp breath. She was so close, and I couldn't keep it in anymore. My spine tightened and my entire body shivered as my release slammed into me.

I gritted my teeth as I shoved against her and my dick shot off with harsh tugs. Kitten's channel squeezed me as I released and she tried to tug away as she came, but I forced her in place, letting her spasm around my dick.

Nothing was comparable to fucking this human. My eyelids twitched and my release staved off slowly, my body slumping in place. Her leg fell forward and my dick slipped free of the home he'd had for the past few hours.

I grunted at the loss but forced myself to fucking relax as she settled. Her breathing returned to normal and a soft snore slipped free. I fell to my back and stared at the ceiling as I sucked in a few breaths.

Odd for me since I'd never worked myself up to the point that I had to breath this much within a short time frame.

Guilt soured my stomach. I'd never been so riveted by something to this point—least of all a *human*. I scoffed in disgust. Imogen would have snapped the human's neck if she knew my thoughts. My stomach burned and I lifted to my elbow to ensure she remained sleeping.

I tensed. It wasn't like she could hear my thoughts. *And why was I more worried about Catalina's feelings right now?*

Asher was right, and it was time for me to move on. And what better way to start than on a human girl.

She was perfectly . . . forgettable.

Right.

I couldn't even lie to myself. I frowned. She was so fucking sweet it made my teeth hurt.

Even though I was an unimaginable dick to her, she never failed to offer me a smile whenever she saw me.

Cat whimpered in her sleep, moving her head back and forth. Her dark hair spilled over her pillow. I pushed to my elbow again and her brow furrowed.

As I was reaching to jostle her awake, she shot up, sucking in a breath.

Her fearful round eyes flashed across the room and her shivering increased. She scrambled to turn the lamp on next to her bed, searching for the inhaler near her head. She grabbed it and rounded to look at me, eyes wide as she launched herself at me, wrapping her arms around my neck and holding me tightly.

I stilled, my stomach somersaulting at the fearful way she clutched me while also enjoying it too much. My hand pressed into her back.

"What is it, human?"

She sniffled and sucked in a breath as she used her medication.

My fingers uselessly pressed into the mattress. I was never someone others came to for comfort. I flattened my palm against her back.

"Human." I bit out, insistently. Her arms tightened more.

"I hate the dark."

I frowned. The manor always had some sort of low light. Even in Bastien's room, but her bedroom was currently dark.

"Why?" The question slipped out unbidden. I shouldn't care. I didn't care, but curiosity bade me to ask.

"I was kept in the dark a long time ago, and ever since then, I've slept with some sort of light on."

My teeth clicked together at her softly spoken words. Viscous rage burned through me, and she grunted. *Fuck.* I'd tightened my grip on her too much. I reached over her shoulder and flipped the bedside lamp on.

"Who?"

"I-I don't want to talk about it."

Every fiber of my being didn't like that, but I gritted my teeth and held her. Such a vulnerable, gentle human. She eventually relaxed and settled her bottom on my lap.

"You'll never have to fear again." The promise fell from my lips effortlessly, but I couldn't stop it. Her little fingers flexed on my shoulders.

"Why are you being so nice to me?"

I grunted in response. I didn't even know the answer. "You're a good fuck." She stiffened and slowly dropped her arms from where they clutched me.

"What are you doing?" The forceful, demanding question slipped free.

"I'm going to go shower," she said without inflection in her tone. My fingers twitched to return her to my lap. I didn't want to let her go.

"I'll come with you."

She coughed out a laugh. "No, I have a feeling it'll be less shower and more . . . other stuff if you come with. You know, since all I am is a good fuck." Her smile remained in place.

I frowned. I didn't want the space from her. At least when I was a cat, I didn't cause her unhappiness like I continued doing, but I couldn't help lashing out at her. It staved off some of the tumultuous emotions in my chest.

"Jax," she muttered and finally extricated herself when I loosened my grip. She dragged the sheet around her, face red as she peeked at me from the corner of her eye.

The corner of my lip twitched at her shy move. Sweet. As I said. When I was a cat, she strutted around in her panties and bra, like there was no tomorrow.

She disappeared behind the slab of the bathroom door, and I peered around, taking in the space.

The metal bedframe seemed close to collapse and the mattress was relatively good, other than the creaky springs. The bedsheets were cotton and the comforter was a cream that was closer to white. Other than the pale lamp on the nightstand beside her bed, that was all there was. She was new to the home, so I wasn't expecting much, but she didn't have much. Either she was living the minimalist life, or she didn't expect to be here long.

My fangs popped out without my prodding. Her leaving wasn't an option. I pinched the bridge of my nose. The bond was fucking annoying.

Footsteps rasped over the ground, and from the cadence, I knew it was Asher.

The need they had between each other . . . I sneered at my brother.

Another emotion I'd never had the displeasure of feeling. I couldn't bring myself to watch her hurt.

It was a spur of the moment decision I regretted, but I preferred to be the one stuck with the repercussions.

Being close to her was the only way I could relieve the tension to my shoulders. She was on my mind constantly. I *worried* about her. She was so fragile and breakable.

My concern for her was all a result of this bond—it had to be. Sure, I had been curious before it and slowly flamed to life with the time I spent observing her, but the bond seemed to wrench reason out of me. Fortunately, it would be gone as long as I didn't share my blood with her again. It would fade from her system. Even sooner, if I kept draining her mind-altering blood, which was my plan. Feed from her until I no longer wanted to gather her into my arms.

I pushed off the mattress and reached for my clothing on the ground, tugging them on as Asher strutted in; his head craned to his phone.

The corners of his eyes tensed with the same jealousy battering my insides. When I'd heard his confession to her, I'd been stunned into silence. My brother never allowed his emotions to cloud anything. He was a whoremonger. A proud one. So his genuine emotion rocked me. No, he must be fooling her. He was never one to give himself to anyone, least of all a human.

catalina

I SET the brown bag of medication on the passenger side as I settled in for the drive home. The pharmacy was fortunately quick when I placed my orders for albuterol. There couldn't be too many inhalers around.

My engine groaned as I sped out of the parking lot, struggling more than usual to get up to speed. But after the slight grumble of the van, it settled. I eyed the freeway exit leading out of the city. I could make my escape now . . . or yesterday, or the day before that . . . but I'd put my plans on pause, running away could wait, right? I worried my lip.

As wrong as it was, I was addicted to how Jax and Asher dominated my body and I couldn't stop thinking of the last two nights with them. They were always gone in the morning, leaving me to my guilty conscience and sated body.

Even if they did have someone tailing me while they were in deep slumber, I hadn't even tried.

I pulled into my driveway and turned the key. The engine hissed as it shut off. I rubbed my palm along the dash. I muttered some appreciation at the inanimate object, then got out of the van and strode to the manor. Based off the purplish hue of the twilight sky darkening by the moment, they should be up.

Maybe we could have something longer between us. Obviously not forever, but the sensuous sex didn't have to end. I wanted to bring it up to Asher, but I feared his response. Riding it out until he told me it was over sounded better. A coward's way, but I was fine with that, especially since there had been no mention of what they would do with me now that they had confirmation that Calliope had Ren.

I eyed the upside-down bat knocker staring down at me as I walked inside. They never locked it. The door hardly snicked as I shut it and padded toward the living room.

"Do you know how many enemies you've made?" I jerked to a halt at the half-hissed words. Asher sounded so angry. I shuffled from foot to foot. Maybe I should sneak back out. It was obvious I'd walked in on some argument, and I didn't want to get in the middle of it, but the other side of me was too curious.

"Me?" Jax scoffed. "Don't leave yourself out of the count, brother. How many women have you fucked that belonged to someone else? That has caused us a good chunk of enemies. Then there's all the fucking people Bastien and Ren have murdered. Tobias is screwed by association." A brief pause. "We're a Coven because we need each other. If we're on our own, sure we could take out some fucks, but together we're unstoppable. We all need to get ourselves straightened out before someone comes looking for us."

Comes looking for them?

"If you two are done. We need to figure out what we'll do if Calliope is holding an event at Saphire Estate—"

"We're not using Catalina."

"Leave the human out of it."

The twins snapped at the same time and butterflies went crazy in my stomach.

"I agree. The original plan was for her to go in as a blood-whore, but I don't want her in danger." They wanted Ren back, but instead, they protect me?

"Calliope knows the human is special."

"Let's just off her."

"And have vampires worldwide turn against our Coven, Asher?" Tobias said, exasperated.

"Calliope won't get near her." Jax's threat reached into my veins and spread warmth. Suddenly, they went silent. I cocked my head, scooting closer to the wall . . .

"I will go alone and attempt to talk sense into her. See if she's willing to bargain."

"Why are you sneaking around, human?" Jax snapped, interrupting Tobias. I worried my lip and steeled my spine as I straightened and rounded into the living room. I leaned against the entrance beam nonchalantly, three pairs of vampire eyes staring at me.

"I'll do it," I offered hesitantly.

Asher sprawled on the couch with his legs spread. He patted his lap and I couldn't help but go to him. His hands slipped around my waist and he pressed a kiss to my cheek, and I sank close to him, savoring the feeling of his arms around me. The tension riding my shoulders since stepping out of my house to shop melted away.

"Let us continue our conversation at a later time," Tobias said, as if I hadn't spoken.

Jax nodded tightly, their attention fully on each other.

"I said I'd do it."

"No," Jax shouted, and I swear a vein popped in his forehead. "You will be protected."

I gawked. Not expecting this reaction. My lips tightened and I huffed, crossing my arms. Asher ran his palm down the side of my waist but kept his lips sealed.

"Overreaction much?" I said under my breath. Asher's chest moved on a silent laugh.

"Pet, you're too precious to place in danger."

"You guys already had me go once," I retorted.

"Yes, and it was a mistake." Asher brushed my hair back from my face and my stomach clenched. I licked my lips and wiggled closer to him. His dick was making its presence very known. "How was your day, Pet? Where did you go earlier?" They knew I'd left. Whoever kept an eye on me had them briefed as soon as they woke.

"I went to go get an inhaler refill." And to call my brother without ears around. I didn't want them knowing about Peter. Fortunately, he hadn't gotten into any more trouble, so I wouldn't need to sell my liver after already selling my soul to these vamps.

The money Jax had deposited to my account had all gone toward tuition and the car situation. I hadn't heard a peep from them since, and I wouldn't until the next bill was due.

Asher caressed my hair as I lulled against him. His lap was comfortable, and he made me feel especially safe. A yawn stretched my mouth. His touches made me a combination of sleepy and horny. And I shouldn't be sleepy since I'd slept for most of the day, but I couldn't help my eyes fluttering shut.

Asher massaged my neck and I groaned, rubbing my head against his chest. He chuckled.

I started this, so I might as well finish it, but I didn't want to be an idiot by going by myself. If I went with one of them, at least I would have protection.

catalina

I WHIMPERED, tipping my head back. I didn't need this right now.

I took a deep breath and licked my lips.

"Come on. Don't fail me now."

Saphire Estate was far and at the speeds I traveled, I was pushing my old van. Why did Tobias drive so fast? He was the most careful, yet speedy, driver I'd ever seen. The way he wove through streets was like a professional.

I pressed on the gas and wove my way into the light traffic, multiple cars behind the shiny Mercedes.

It was weird how hearing that they didn't want to endanger me made me want to risk myself. My fingers flexed on the steering wheel. My lungs were pretty tight, but I was waiting until I got closer to use the medication. I didn't want to overdo it.

I reached down and gripped the handle to lower the window. It may not be anytime soon, but whenever I got the chance, I was purchasing a car without this crap manual lever that seemed to get stuck with every second turn. My arm burned with the effort I had to exert.

The me from a month ago wouldn't have believed I would be here, willingly placing myself in danger because of vampires.

Maybe it was foolhardy. Okay, there was no 'maybe' about it, but Tobias would be there, I'd be safe. Even if he didn't know I followed him.

I got off the next exit and followed him up the mountain. The paved street led into a sharp incline and I followed it as I got higher and higher. Weaving around more curves as I got farther from the main road.

There were no lamps to guide the way as the streets became more lined with tall thin trees. I kept my distance from Tobias, and turned off my headlights, driving slow as I followed well behind the Mercedes. Minutes after driving in the same environment with horrifying thoughts of something popping out at me, I finally curved to the left where he'd disappeared.

My poor van creaked as it went up the winding drive. An estate sat far in the distance. My wheels bounced over the speed bump as I crossed two wide opened gates.

Expensive cars lined the front of the home, including Tobias's car. The large windows were lit with bright yellow light, spilling into the darkness. I pulled over to the side of the house, behind a sports car, and shut off the van. I slid the keys into the vizor. With all these fancy cars around, no one would steal my beat up one. I squinted, focusing on the striking lean figure climbing up the steps of the house. Tobias disappeared inside.

Hurrying out of the car, I slammed the door shut and stepped over the curb. My heels sank into the plush moist grass and I grimaced, inching back onto the asphalt. I'd worn a risqué outfit since I was supposed to be a blood-whore, but it was my only outfit that cost more than my laptop. Spears of light illuminated the lawn from the mansion as I wove my way to the front. Fortunately, the front remained empty, and classical music floated out, increasing in volume the closer I got to the wide open door. Still no Tobias.

I nibbled on my lower lip as I swept my gaze across the landscape, trying to figure out which direction I should go search.

There didn't seem to be any entrances to the sides. But since the front was open and no one was there . . .

Okay, screw it. He was probably already inside.

My heels clicked on the steps as I climbed up them. Fortunately there were only a handful, so I wasn't a panting mess by the time I got to the top. I pulled out the inhaler from the front of my dress where I'd nestled it next to my boob and took a puff before securing it back.

Lungs full, I stepped into the hall. No one turned in my direction as I inched fully inside. The place was like a crystal palace. The teardrop shapes adorning the large chandelier was something I'd only ever seen on television. Candles were all that illuminated the inside. Everybody was dressed in elaborate gowns of all cuts and furs or suits.

Yet, here I was dressed in a gold, skintight dress.

Someone slammed into my arm and I grunted at the force, stumbling back. I sucked in a breath and scooted away as the vampire stormed past, their attention on something over my shoulder. The man strutted directly up to a woman standing in the corner of the room. Her eyes glazed as she stared out into the sea of people. When he stepped in front of her, her blank eyes brightened and she smiled wide, lifting her arms.

I was about to get all soft at the sight but then I noted all the raw bites lining her throat. She couldn't be happier though, as she arched her neck and he sank his fangs into her. A smile flitted over her mouth and she sank into him.

My stomach soured and the ball in my gut grew. Steps clicked behind me and I slipped between the door and two vampires chatting it up in Spanish. They were talking about the massacres they'd executed in Spain . . . *yeah, let me get away from this pair.*

I really shouldn't have forgotten my phone in the car.

Turning down the hallway, it opened to even more space where vampires mingled. The music was lowered in here and chatter fell over the room. Seduction charged the room and it felt like an orgy could break out at any moment. The throuple in the corner were already halfway there.

My eyes widened on a human male beside a vampire standing to my left. He smiled over at him and his eyes glazed as he pressed closer.

"Not right now, babe," the vampire said casually and returned to his conversation with another vampire that looked to be about fifteen. I shivered and my stomach soured.

There were so many vampires, but where was Tobias?

Yep, couldn't do it. I needed to get back to the van. I licked my lips and studied my route with the least vamps, but I didn't have many options. If one grabbed me and started sucking my blood . . .

I shivered, slinking behind a curtain and tipping my head back, breathing deeply. *Get a hold of yourself, Cat.* It wasn't like I didn't know what I was getting into, but I was in over my head. My fingers curved into the raspy curtain material.

A particularly high-pitched laugh brought my attention to

the left. I clocked Calliope perched on a couch and surrounded by a small crowd.

My fingers tightened on the material. To leave or to talk to her. If I went up to her right now, I ran the chance of her just ending me then and there, but if I managed to find Ren, imagine how relieved the guys would be—

I squeaked as a hand gripped the back of my neck.

"Why are you looking at my sire so intently, my dear?" My yelp cut off when he slapped his palm over my mouth. I looked up at the pale vampire, his curly hair falling over his forehead. The smile was deceptively approachable.

"Oh, n-no reason." *Very convincing.* His eyes swept down my body and he took in my outfit.

"I don't believe you belong here." His smile became deadly and he shoved me forward by the neck. I stumbled about five times. A few vampires looked over derisively, but they continued with what they were doing after the disgusted expression, like vampires dragging humans around were a normal thing.

Calliope looked up along with her companions and her eyebrows lifted. Curly Hair brought me to a stop, and pushed on my shoulder. I thumped onto my knees with a wince.

"Crimson Coven human." I straightened my spine and tipped my chin up, going for false bravado.

"Calliope." Some of the vampires surrounding her gasped and she smiled.

"You have guts." Calliope brushed her hair back and smiled at me. "Or, you're just stupid." A woman sat beside her, spine straight as she smiled cheerfully. "Everyone leave."

The three vampires she'd been talking to dispersed quickly

and the one holding my neck tightened his hold before releasing me and melting into the crowd.

"Who's this, Callie?" The brown-haired girl eyed me wearily. She had a small pixie face and even sitting I could tell she was much smaller in height.

Calliope gripped her chin and kissed her hard.

"Just an intriguing nuisance, Freya."

The way they looked at each other was kind of sweet. I shook my head and snapped out of my woolgathering.

"Where's Ren?" I asked low. I couldn't hide my fear, my words trembled on my question.

"Is this regarding my mistake from decades ago?" Freya pouted and crossed her arms. "I told you, Cal, I wasn't in my right mind."

Calliope ruffled Freya's pin-straight hair and stood, approaching me.

"You have strange tastes if you're looking for *that* psychopath, human." Calliope said, lifting an eyebrow. "If you're so intrigued with finding him. I'll take you right to him." I had to angle my neck to look into Calliope's face.

She moved like lightning and my socket pinched from suddenly being yanked to my feet.

I scrambled after her. I banged my arm into a vampire and rushed out an apology as I ran to keep up. There was no glance of Tobias anywhere. This was not good. My lungs did not like me right now. She went through an alcove and the music was practically nonexistent as she guided me down a hall. Where was Tobias?

"I'm sorry—"

Calliope stopped and looked down at me.

"I pity you." My apology slash plea for freedom stopped mid word.

I pursed my lips. "Why?"

"Because you care for them, but you'll either end up dead or a blood-whore."

The words smacked me across the face, and I swallowed hard as the knot in my gut flexed. She kept on her ground-eating pace.

"Why do you think that?" I asked between pants.

"I'm sure they haven't told you about their bitch—"

"Imogen?" I interrupted. "Asher told me about her." Calliope froze in place, and the suddenness jolted me to a stop. She looked down at me, head tilted.

"Interesting." She pulled a key free from her bra and inserted it into a metal door.

"Is that door silver?"

"Yes it is. The whole room is encased with silver." She seemed especially proud about this.

"You want to see him so badly. Let's see how long it takes for him to kill you." Her smile flashed and she shoved me forward. I stumbled into the dark room, my heart already racing from fear.

THIRTY-ONE

THE DOOR CREAKED, allowing some light into the room I was being held in. I remained still, waiting for the perfect moment to strike. I would continue to rot unless Calliope let me the fuck go. The bitch wouldn't kill me, of that much I was sure. We shared too much history . . .

My eyes shut at the blinding light and someone stumbled into the room, thudding on the metal floor. I squinted to see her fall to her knees, her long hair whipping over her face and hiding her features as the door shut and encased the room in pitch black.

"There was no need to be so harsh," a lilting feminine voice muttered, and cloth rustled as she brushed at her clothing. There was no light in the space. It was sealed to perfection. My chains rattled as I crossed my ankles.

The girl sucked in a breath, and the room was so insulated I could hear her heart racing from where I sat. I leaned my head back, the chains rattling with my movement, and waited for the sacrificial lamb to move.

Calliope must know I was deteriorating. With the thirst

gnawing at my insides, I was bound to rip her apart. My meal moved and wafted a fresh wave of her scent toward me. The small bit of blood in me sped to my cock.

My cock hardened and my fangs exploded from my mouth. Just a little closer and I could drag her into my arms . .

.

"Ren?"

She knew my name?

Something hit my shoe and a soft body slammed into my chest.

My body went taut. Palms settled on my shoulders, they felt tiny as they grazed my bare chest through the frayed, torn shirt. *What was she doing?*

Touching me so easily. My cock throbbed along with my fangs. Hunger burned through my veins.

If it was a trick, I'd draw it out as much as I could. I savored playing with my prey.

"You're Ren, right?"

I grunted in response, and she exhaled like she was . . . relieved?

"At least this wasn't for nothing." I was even more confused than when she'd first called my name. And I didn't like it. Confusion meant lack of control. "I know I'm acting like a stage-five clinger right now, but I don't like the dark." Her fingers flexed on my arm and she pressed herself closer to me— so trustingly.

She exhaled shakily. Warmth radiated from her body, and I ran my tongue over my fang.

I lifted her higher onto my lap so her thighs spread wide against mine. I wrapped my hand in her long hair. "You're hurting me." Panic coated her words, exciting me more. Her small hands pushed against my face and I winced when she poked my eye.

"Oh, that was wet. I'm sorry, was that your eye?" she cried out. My teeth clicked tightly together. The human was ruining everything.

I yanked her long tresses to drag her throat to my fangs. She desperately shoved at my chest, but it was no use. With an explosion of breath, she lunged at me, sinking her blunt teeth into my shoulder. I froze as her teeth buried harder into my skin.

She bit me.

Fisting her hair, I pulled, but she held on, her teeth sinking in harder, to the point that she broke skin. Her mouth suctioned at the wound and my cock twitched. I groaned, my hips twitching up toward her ass resting on my lap.

What . . . ?

Her sweet smell warmed my senses and her presence became a thing I could mentally feel, not just physically. So much so that I could practically taste her. Fuck, she'd taken my blood and my brain was so fogged from lack of nourishment that I hadn't had the presence of mind to stop it.

As she lifted, she dragged her tongue across my throat and my cock twitched, forcing my hips to grind up again. "I know you must be hungry, but please be gentle," she murmured, pressing her neck to my mouth. *What the fuck was this girl?* Her hand shook against my chest.

I struck, sinking my fangs deeps into her skin, sucking the savory blood into my throat—the searing, blistering hunger abated. Lessening the burn.

Her arms lifted around my shoulders, but she couldn't get them around properly since she was small. Blood spread on my tongue and the taste seeped into me. She was divine. The best thing I'd ever tasted. *Wagashi, mochi, dorayaki* . . . every savory dessert I could have conjured from my childhood. Food I had not tasted in so long, the taste that had faded since my vampire birth centuries ago.

I tightened my hold when she tried to move, but she just readjusted her position, spreading her legs so she straddled me more comfortably. My dick thickened painfully and I groaned, grinding up between her splayed, straining thighs.

She gasped and moaned, meeting my grinding thrusts. Her fingers speared into my hair and I tensed. I hated having my hair touched, but the feel of them melting into my scalp was gentle, and I clasped her tighter.

My biceps flexed around her waist as we ground against each other, savoring the increasing pleasure. My balls drew tight, needy and aching to release.

If I wasn't shackled . . . If I had her splayed before me, I would litter her skin with bites. She tasted succulent and I wanted more. I pressed my fangs into her harder, opening the entrances in her neck so more blood could freely flow into my mouth.

A moan ripped from my chest and I balled her hair in my hand, arching her back. She cried out and I blanked. *Blood. I wanted it. I wanted her.*

Her little fingers flexing on my arm shoved at me. This taste deserved to be savored, so she would not die today. I'd already taken more than was safe, her shoves were weak and she swayed. I groaned as I laved my tongue across the large punctures I'd created and licked the taste from my lips.

She trembled and buried her head in the crook of my neck.

My cock twitched at the feel of her breath on my flesh. Wetness spread on my skin and she sniffled, holding me tighter.

What the fuck was wrong with this human? Why was she grabbing onto me like this?

"I'm scared, Ren." The warbling tone punched my stomach and I ground my teeth at the uncomfortable pressure crawling up my ribcage. Her sleep-filled words were ended by a soft snore as she cuddled closer, her face resting on my shoulder.

What the fuck?

THIRTY-TWO

"YOU WERE SUPPOSED to keep an eye on her," Asher sneered, getting in my face.

"What are you going on about?" I bunched the front of Asher's shirt, shoving him away from me. His eyes flared red and settled soon after.

"Catalina is gone. There's no sign of her and her car is gone." His words sucker punched me in the throat. The human left? My brain lagged on processing the information, but my body had stiffened to a painful extent. The sluggish muscle in my chest thumped.

"She was sleeping . . ." I trailed off. I didn't think she would leave. I knew it, I shouldn't have trusted the fucking human. Look what it got me.

"You lost her?" Tobias gritted out between his clenched teeth. The accusation was thrown at me. I fished my phone out of my pocket. "What are you doing?" Tobias narrowed his eyes at me.

"Calling V so he can put a freeze on her passport," I said grimly.

"She didn't flee," Asher spat, shoving my shoulder. I returned it with a punch to the stomach.

"Watch it," I growled.

"She was taken," Asher continued, almost desperate.

I pitied my brother. The girl had wrapped him around her feeble fingers and he did not know it. He claimed I was a pussy for Imogen, doing as she bid without complaint, but look at him now. At the very least, I'd followed the orders of someone of our own ilk.

I was ashamed to admit, she had started to sink her traitorous little claws into me as well and if it had been a moment longer, she may have succeeded.

Asher crossed his arms. "She was taken," he insisted again, seeing the doubt on my face. The surety in his tone gave me pause.

"I don't believe she would leave either," Tobias's gaze became unfocused as he fell into his own thoughts.

I was supposed to keep track of her. If she had been taken and she hadn't run away like I initially thought, I'd put the weak girl in harm's way.

No, she'd left without informing us and that was enough to cause doubt.

"It's clear, Calliope must have her," Asher spat. "I'll go look for her—"

"You stay," Tobias shoved Asher back. "You make poor decisions when you're emotional." Asher scoffed at his observation. "Do you think I don't know about the human you killed?" Tobias snapped.

Asher snarled.

"I'll go see if Calliope will meet with me." Tobias's tone remained stiff and matter-of-fact. "Jax, you—"

"I'll check with all my contacts," I said grimly. I'd send word out to our progeny as well. If someone came back to us with information, they would be rewarded.

"If she's dead Jaxon, I wi—" Asher hissed and turned on his heel mid-word, disappearing down the hall. I gritted my teeth, retracting my fangs that had popped out at some point. Pressure compounded on my chest, urging me to find her.

catalina

THE COOL GROUND WAS UNCOMFORTABLE, and why was it so dark? My heart rate picked up and I shot up. My forehead smacked into something hard as rock. A hiss came from said rock.

"Sorry," I squeaked when Ren cursed under his breath.

I wish I could see Ren, but it was still pitch dark. He'd taken so much blood that I'd passed out. *Did the guy have no impulse control?* I frowned at him even though he couldn't see me.

My irritation slipped away and the cool splash of reality slapped me across the face. I was stuck in a dark room. Thoughts of the vampire who'd captured me long ago were going rampant in my head.

I clasped my trembling hands together and scrambled back. There had to be light in here, I was pretty sure I'd seen the switch before Calliope slammed the door.

Unsteadily climbing to my feet, I swayed, disoriented by the darkness. Steps unsteady, I smoothed my dress down and stumbled forward with my hands out.

I pressed my palms on the walls, dragging them over the metal surface.

My fingers bumped into something and relief loosened my shoulder as I nudged the switch up. A buzz filled the room and a dim light flickered to life.

Chains rattled, calling my attention to Ren.

I choked on my spit.

My eyes watered as I coughed and worked to suck in a breath.

Holy crap he was massive. He *felt* massive, but this wasn't what I'd expected. His legs were stretched out in front of him. He was as large as the other vampires, but wider, more like Bastien. It was confirmed, these guys had been injected with some unfair height and muscle genes.

His short hair sat artfully mussed. Strands fell forward, framing his forehead. The chiseled lines of his cheeks had nothing on that jawline, and his plump lower lip stained with blood did *things* to me.

Ink peeked from over the neckline of his torn shirt and stretched down both his arms, but I was too far away to see details.

To put it succinctly. He was fucking sexy, and he watched me like a lion watching prey.

I cleared my throat. Now that it wasn't darker than a coffin, oxygen reached my brain. I dipped my hand into the front of my dress to pull out my inhaler.

"Asher, Jax, and Tobias should come after us once they realize I'm not home, right?" I raked my fingers through my hair and slid to the ground next to him. I pressed my inhaler to my mouth, inhaling a puff.

He hadn't moved and when I peeked up at him, his eyes were eerily blank. Nerves tightened my stomach. I wasn't a fan of that expression . . .

catalina

REN WAS STILL LOOKING at me with that blank expression, and I nervously licked my lips.

When I first came in, I'd allowed my fear to get the best of me and crawled into his lap. But he wasn't Asher. Nope. There was a cruel mocking in his expression that sent shivers up my spine.

I didn't know him. His hand flattened on my thigh, and I jumped at the rough touch. His smirk was what was what got to me, and honestly it scared me more than Jax's scowling.

"What happened to land you here?" I spat the question out frantically. His hand flexed around my thigh and my heartbeat sped up.

His smile widened making my mouth dry up. "A-Asher told me you messed with someone."

He mouthed *Asher* and his brows lifted.

Another inch to the side. I didn't want to make it obvious I was trying to get away from him, but I couldn't just sit still.

Ren tossed his head back and laughed. I startled at the explosive sound echoing off the walls. I scooted more while he was distracted and the larger jolt to the side was my mistake.

He lunged. I screamed, scrambling away, but he captured my ankle and dragged me back. My dress lifted, baring my panties as I battled for freedom.

His cool palm spanned my belly and I sucked in a breath. His fingers dragged up my flesh, caressing the sensitive skin to delve under my dress. I tensed at his movements. Ren's thumb plunged under the front of my bra and he tugged it with a sharp twist. The elastic bounced back onto my skin as material ripped open. I gawked up at him, breasts on full display. The swells of my breast rose sharply.

"What are you doing?" My words quaked. "My dress." I couldn't help the whimper. That cost me months of savings.

"Playing."

I had no idea what that meant, and I didn't want to find out. His eyes were bright and I really didn't want to discover what other things excited *him*. Ren leaned down, but his head stopped over my belly. He snarled as he was stopped by the rattling chains. The silver collar around his neck wouldn't allow him any lower.

He gripped my legs and forced them around his torso, keeping his arms over my thighs. My legs trembled as they bracketed him. With his fingers digging into my waist, he tipped me up so I was arched off the ground and my shoulders pressed against the floor.

He bent down and his fangs pierced my stomach. I sucked in a breath at the sharp incisions. He rubbed my increasingly wet pussy against his chest and the mingling pain bled into pleasure.

Ren dragged his tongue down the trails of blood, lapping

my skin with a deep groan. Blood trickled on my torso and over my breasts.

I struggled against his hold, but he roughly kept grip of my hips and ground my pussy against his sternum. The pressure on my clit lifted the hair on my arms. Ren's teeth sank into my stomach a little higher from the other bite and he suctioned. My lips parted as my breathing elevated.

Drops of my blood trickled over my skin, painting me red. The lines marking me caused my lust to flare.

His arm curved under my spine and he lifted me with ease and hoisted me until my breasts were level with his mouth. He dragged the cup of my bra down and his tongue lashed my nipple. I gasped, my thighs clenching around him.

The tickle of my blood trickled downward from where it'd pooled earlier.

Ren's fangs rasped across my quivering peak and I moaned. My God, every bite tautened me up like a bow string. He met my eyes and struck in a swift movement, the sharp fang sinking into the tip of my breast. I screeched at the sting and then he *sucked*. My body became rigid and I bucked against him, the pressure against my clit combined with him suckling blood from my nipple shot shockwaves throughout my appendages. A wave of pleasure slammed into me, and I cried out in ecstasy, writhing against him as he tightened his hold on me.

He sucked in a hard drag and I whimpered from the onslaught, but he held no mercy. My nipple popped free from his mouth and I cried out as he rasped his teeth against the sensitive peak.

Ren dragged my body down his until my panty-covered core was poised over his hard cock. I was back to staring back up at him, but his face was flushed and he had a glazed look to his eyes. His fingers flexed on my shoulder.

"Such a wet little cunt." The words were growled as he pressed me down. My thighs curved around his waist again and my spine pinched at the position he forced me into. "I want you drenched in blood. To feed from your pussy." His palm pressed between my thighs. I had no doubt I was wet. My face heated at his gaze as he took in my body with uninhibited need marring his expression. There was pure possession in those glittering brown eyes.

His gaze flickered and he slipped his hand between the tight fit where the seam of his jeans met my pussy and rubbed roughly. His knuckles pressed against my covered slit and I whimpered, arching toward the touch as another gush of wetness dripped around his hand. I used abdominal strength to pull myself up to get near him, but Ren wrenched his hand free and shoved me down again.

Ren's irises turned red for only a split second and he sneered down at me as he dug his nails into the sides of my waist.

I screamed at the sharp pain as he sliced me.

Blood bubbled to the surface and panic tightened my throat. He roughly gyrated up against me, and my sensitive pussy throbbed.

It shouldn't feel as good as it did.

He chuckled low. I squeezed my eyelids together, not wanting to see how wrong it was, I simply wanted to feel the pleasure.

"Watch me," he hissed.

I whimpered, unable to move from the mix of pain and ecstasy. He gripped my hair in his fist, forcing my neck to bend.

I slowly blinked as I took in the blood smeared across my

skin. The punctures on my lower abdomen and my nipple trickling blood from them. Ren hadn't made the effort to close the marks.

That was how *that* vampire was. The one I feared. He left me open to bleed sometimes, it was worse when he first caught me. The thick lines of blood going up the sides of my torso.

Ren dragged the tip of his fingers over the red liquid, spreading it over my skin until his hand was playing in blood across my stomach.

He groaned and shuddered at the sight.

Ren gripped the back of my neck and yanked up in a sharp tug. He bit my throat and fed . . . and fed. Taking from me as much as he could.

My sight became fuzzy and I became lightheaded as I struggled sucking in a breath. My chest squeezed painfully.

I went limp against him and then blacked out.

It felt like a moment, but it had to be longer. I coughed, sputtering against the wrist pressed to my mouth. I lifted my eyelids, pulling against the hold on the back of my head forcing me to remain in place. Soreness spread though my neck and I moved to stretch, but he hissed and I automatically stilled. I stared into his pensive expression, unable to do anything other than breathe as my mouth overfilled.

"Keep swallowing."

I whimpered at his order and did as he bade. It was too much.

Pressure mounted in my stomach. This was too much—it

hurt. I whimpered, blood overflowing the corners of my mouth and trickling down my chin.

He kept me in the same position for longer than I could determine. I drank from him as I stared into his increasingly stiff expression. There was no need to force me to drink this much, nor to be so damn aggressive with my neck. I huffed from my nose, glaring at him over his wrist as my stomach rebelled.

I thrashed in his grip until he released me. He must have seen the desperation in my eyes. Tossing myself off his lap, I landed on my hands and knees. My stomach churned and I gagged, blood dripping off my chin.

The droplet on my chest rolled slowly downward, thicker and darker red. I fisted my hands, aching to rail at him for doing that.

Was he trying to drown me? Chains rattled.

I narrowed my eyes at him, lips pressed tightly together. Why did he seem so obnoxiously smug?

Ren's head canted and he reached for me, but I lurched back before his fingers touched me.

I backed into the corner of the room, the farthest corner I could get from him. The chains rattled as he stood, the light from the beam reflecting off the shackles as he stretched. He seemed . . . especially energized. I was sure that only meant I was in that much more danger.

catalina

REN GAVE me his back and looked at the chains attached to the wall, studying them carefully.

"Break the camera," he ordered, his back still to me. "Hurry up."

I found the camera in one sweep of the room. In the top corner, a round lens faced us. It took a few attempts of jumping to grab onto it, but I finally hooked both arms around the plastic. The perch holding it up bent under my efforts and I managed to yank it off. I slammed it into the floor and pieces scattered.

As soon as it was crushed on the floor, he wrapped his hands around the metal attached around his neck and jerked it once. The silver pressed against his skin and it hissed. Letting it go, he focused his efforts on the long chain attaching him to the wall. He set his boot against where it was securely bolted and strained. A hiss echoed and steam lifted on his hands where he held the chains.

A shrill screech rent the room and my eyes widened as the square of bolted-down material peeled off.

My mouth dropped.

Well, then. Vampires were strong, but God damn.

He reached for the chains attached to the shackles of his wrists and did the same, but he was able to rupture the link so there was less of it hanging off the end. The other wrist followed suit and then he was free. Burns coated his hands; a thin layer had been seared off.

In a few strides, he was at the door, eyes studying the metal encased entrance. He slammed the flat of his foot into it repeatedly, but it held up. Ren took a ragged breath. The scent of burned flesh seared my nose and blisters erupted on Ren's arms from where the flailing chains rested against his skin. Winding his leg back, Ren angled his shot toward the hinges, and the slab bent.

He was a psycho, yes. And terrifying.

The bolted hinges ruptured and the wooden doorframe cracked as the slab of metal and ruptured wood crashed to the floor, letting in the hall light.

Ren brushed some broken pieces of wood off his arms as he strode out.

I stumbled after him, moving quickly.

"Wait," I cried out as I stuttered to a stop a foot from him.

Ren paused and lifted a brow.

"Why?"

My mouth parted and I narrowed my eyes up at him. He couldn't be serious. He snorted and turned his back to me. He was about to zoom out of here and leave me behind, naked and bleeding. My heart rammed against my chest and I used every inch of strength I had to jump on him.

I wrapped my arms around as much of him as I could, hooking my arms around his wide chest. He was so massive it was difficult to get a grip, but I wasn't giving up. I used as much strength I could muster to climb up his big ass body.

"Off, human."

I huffed closer to his ear, trying to catch my breath.

"No."

Shouting echoed down the hall.

"You better hurry, or they'll get us in there again."

He laughed like I'd just said the funniest thing he'd ever heard.

Ren shook his head, still chuckling as he made his way down the hall Calliope had brought me down. We weren't too far from the entrance, we just had to avoid . . .

Never mind.

A vampire gawked at us, but before he could take off running, Ren grabbed him and slammed a piece of metal into his chest cavity. The vampire wheezed and lashed out, weakly hitting Ren in the face. I scrambled to hold on for dear life as his shoulders undulated with each of his movements. Ren pushed him against the wall and rammed the metal into his chest again until it caused a cavern of ruptured insides. Blood splattered across my cheek and my stomach lurched. I was going to throw up. Ren tore the heart out with ease and tossed it. The blisters had spread much faster on this one.

"Young vampire," Ren commented with a grunt.

I buried my head in the crook of his neck and sucked in harsh lungfuls of oxygen. I tightened my thighs on his sides, but I kept slipping and having to readjust myself on him. It was his fault for being so large.

He kept walking at an even pace, dispatching the other vampires he crossed with ease. I kept my head ducked because I wasn't being subjected to the stimulating visuals again without vomiting my guts out.

Yellow artificial light filled my closed eyelids and I squinted. We were outside on the porch and it was still dark out. How many days had passed while I'd been passed out?

I loosened my hold and dropped to my ass with a grunt. I winced and pushed to my feet.

Ren squinted out at the lawn, a slight grimace on his face.

I gripped his shirt and tugged. He amazingly followed me as I guided him to my van. The lone vehicle sat where I'd left it. There were no longer any other cars crowding the space other than the sparse few that were at the front of the estate.

"Get in," I whispered.

Ren slid into the passenger side, squeezing his huge body in. Yeah, it was pretty beat down and large but he could have slid into the back where there were no seats which was suited more for his frame . . . I pressed my lips together trying not to burst into laughter. It was like a grown-up trying to squeeze into one of those battery-powered kid cars.

My keys were where I'd left them and I turned my car on without a hiccup and sped away from the curb. I settled in for a long drive and pulled a thin blanket off the floor to cover my breasts by hooking it under my arms.

He leaned his head against the headrest and his eyes slid shut.

"How do you know Asher?"

I jumped at the sound of his deep voice and flexed my fingers around the steering wheel. I'd mentioned Asher, but there had been no further discussion since he'd been too busy munching on me.

"Uh, we're neighbors."

"Neighbors?" He snorted and shook his head as if I was lying. "What are you?"

"Um, what do you mean?" I croaked. "I'm human."

What sort of question was that? The words ached to crawl up my throat, but I didn't want to set him off again. I was very much okay with not going there. I licked my dry lips and put the volume up on my stereo with a trembling hand.

Ren was quiet the rest of the way, so quiet it would be as if he wasn't there if it weren't for his oversized presence.

As adrenaline leaked out of me, my body aches rushed forward. I *hurt*. And the sharp pains from the bite marks especially stung in the aftermath.

What Ren had done to me . . . I shivered at the memory of his bites and touch. I jerked the lever to lower the windows and cold wind lashed across my face. I pressed on the gas to increase my speed and sucked in a breath.

Shaking my head, I refocused on driving. It took me less time to get back to the manor than it did to get to the Saphire Estate, which had to do more with the fact that I'd stepped on the gas the entire time.

I pulled into my driveway and left my car keys on the driver seat. I climbed the steps to their house faster than I ever had with the blanket wrapped under my arms and shoved their door open.

"Asher? Jax?" I shouted. "Tobias!" There was nothing in response. My shoulders tightened at the heavy weight staring me down. I whirled to find Ren striding in my direction with his head lowered—stalking toward me.

catalina

REN SLAMMED me against the wall and slapped his palms near my ears, caging my head. My heart rate spiked and I craned my neck to look up at him, keeping the blanket wrapped around my torso. The intensity of his brown eyes stripped me bare and I fought the urge to take off sprinting, but I was sure he'd enjoy chasing me down. Just like Asher had. I didn't know what to do. Or if I could do anything. A hunted feeling crawled up my neck.

With a move too quick for me to track, he'd wrapped his big hands around my thighs and hoisted me up the wall until my core was level with his dick. I gasped from the sudden grind of his jean-covered hardness against me.

"You like that don't you." He chuckled, eyelids lowered, a sultry expression on his face.

My stomach clenched. The echo of his touch and bites crested up my body and moisture gathered between my legs. I liked the feel of him too much, but to just grab at me? He was crazy. Certifiable and not trustworthy from what I'd noted, but my body wanted him.

His dark eyebrow raised and he thrust against me, shoving his hard cock between my legs. I sucked in a breath and bit back my whimper. The blanket dropped to expose the top of my breasts. He looked down at me with a satisfied smirk, as if he liked watching me squirm.

He wrapped his finger around my panties and continued wrapping his finger as the elastic dug into my skin until it ruptured. I gasped as the sudden pressure loosened on my clit. He still pinned me with his hips and the hand that just ripped the last of what I wore, dragged upwards. His fingertips grazed the top of my breast, and the tip of his nail rasped over the top. He dug harder, dragging his nail into my flesh. I gasped from the suddenness of the sting.

A thin line welled with blood. Ren's smirk faded and his attention fastened on the red.

"Ren. Off her."

Ren tilted his head as he stared in silence. His cock was still flush against my clit and I couldn't help but wriggle. A shiver coasted up my spine.

"She's a responsive little whore Asher, where did you find her?" Ren smiled cruelly, his eyes glinting with avarice.

I gasped, the words slapping me across the face.

He stepped back and I landed on my ass—again. I grunted and a dull pain spread down my thighs.

"You're lucky I don't fuck humans," he smiled, showing more teeth than necessary.

"God!" I snapped and groaned, rubbing the sore spot.

Asher flashed over and lugged me up. My legs wobbled and he pressed me to his body. I used him as a crutch to lean on as he carefully wrapped me in the thin blanket.

Ren snorted and the sound dragged my attention to him. His eyes were narrowed on Asher.

"You've never been possessive over your toys. Makes me want her more than I already do."

"Leave her be," Asher snapped, tightening his hold on me.

I couldn't see Ren's reaction since my cheek was pressed to Asher's silk encased shoulder, but I would bet my foot Ren smirked at the threat.

"Why so tense, Asher? Did the human crawl under your skin?"

"How about you tell us what you were doing getting captured by Calliope." Asher's chest rose once sharply.

"I allowed her to catch me. There's a difference, but she knows nothing about the sudden uptick in infections." So he let her put him in that situation? "Her mouth doesn't get loose unless she feels like she's got something over me."

"And what about killing her children?" Tobias said, steps clipped as he approached.

"He shouldn't have gotten in my way." Ren shrugged.

"She's exhausted, she can hardly keep her eyes open." Tobias crouched before me, tucking my hair behind my ear. "Let's get you comfortable."

Asher resisted passing me to him for a beat, and I grunted at the sharp squeeze to my stomach. He finally let go and Tobias was making his way up the stairs with me in his arms.

"I need a bath," I croaked.

Tobias frowned down at me, gray eyes roving over my blood-stained chest. "What happened?" I didn't even have the energy to respond to that. I set my head against his bicep and my eyes fluttered shut.

Tobias jostled me and the spout to the tub powered on.

I stifled a yawn and he tugged the blanket off me.

"Catalina," he hissed, eyes fixed on my body. I blinked slowly and looked down. Crusted dried blood flaked on my skin. My wounds were pretty much healed. The vampire blood Ren forced down my throat must have started the healing process. He set me in the bathtub and water sloshed over the sides of the tub. The clear water swiftly turned pinkish.

I leaned against the back porcelain, zapped of energy. The water lapped against my waist, and I straightened my legs until they were fully submerged.

Tobias reached over to pull the plug so it could drain as it filled. Then he grabbed a small towel underneath the sink and knelt beside the tub. I blinked as I watched him, a thick knot incrementally growing in my throat. He carefully rolled the sleeves of his cable knit sweater to his elbows.

I couldn't stifle my groan of pleasure at the pressure of the water seeping into my bones and spreading through my body. The heat was heavenly and the view was . . . I shivered, watching Tobias smooth the carefully rolled sleeves. There was something incredibly sexy about his forearms. The muscle bunched with each flex, emphasizing the veins through his pale hand.

Concentration marred his brow as he wet the cloth and brought it to my neck, and in swift swipes across my skin, he cleaned away the dried blood as he inched down my shoulders.

The soft rasp of his ministrations combined with the attentiveness constricted my chest and pressure ballooned as I watched him. Goose bumps pebbled my flesh. Each rasp across my skin stoked a heady heat through my body. This wasn't what I should be thinking right now. Such a bad idea to be lusting after the celibate vampire priest.

He ran the towel under the running water, drenching it. My

gaze stalled on his profile as he wrung the excess water from the material. My fingers twitched to lift and graze down the bridge of his nose to the slightly upturned tip.

Tobias's eyelids lowered, his lips softening. He paused with the cloth at my clavicle and his Adam's apple bobbed. I could hardly hear the plunk of the towel sinking into the tub. The material grazed my thigh. I followed Tobias's gaze to my breast where a drop of blood had beaded. It slowly dripped and plunked into the water.

Where Ren had opened me.

"Ren," Tobias bit out. His jaw twitched.

I lifted my hand to swipe the blood away, but Tobias caught my wrist, his throat bobbing.

"I will heal you . . . if you would like." His words were rough and red hinted in his irises before it disappeared.

I nodded hesitantly, unable to make a sound.

Tobias kept my gaze as he leaned over my breast, eyes unwavering from mine.

My breasts rose sharply with every pant. Pinpricks of anticipation crackled over my skin as his lips neared until finally his tongue flicked out and laved across the skin. My lips parted on a breathy exhale.

The line of his neck tensed, the column tightening enticingly. He lunged forward, pressing into me so my back dug into the lip of the tub. I could hardly feel the pinch since ripples of pleasure danced to my clit.

My fingers speared into his hair, curving into the strands tightly. I whimpered, and the water sloshed as I wiggled needily. His grip became hard—unyielding—delicious.

His lips fastened around my nipple, encasing it with his warm mouth. Tobias tongued my breast, sending electricity throughout my limbs. My thighs quivered and I detangled my digits from his hair. There was no feeling in my arms as they boundlessly slipped into the water to rest on my thighs.

Tobias was incredibly good with his tongue.

My breast popped out of his mouth and his shoulders rose and fell sharply. He set his wrists on the edge of the tub and squeezed his eyes shut, breathing hard twice more. His eyelids finally lifted and he sank his fingers into the water, lifting the wet towel from the clean water. He reached over and turned the spout off and pulled the lever so the stopper would settle into place.

I couldn't take my eyes off of the red cresting his cheek bones.

I struggled to get my breathing under control as he cleared his throat. Tobias handed me the cloth and then lifted to his feet, offering me his back. I couldn't tear my eyes from the bunched shoulders or the way he ran his fingers through his hair. I quickly finished washing myself, trying to ignore the enflamed need. It was a mistake to say yes to him. I knew better, but I let lust guide me, and now, he would likely start avoiding me again.

When I'd finished washing, I stood, and water sloshed over the lip of the tub and ran down my body, tickling as it traveled down.

Stepping out of the bath, I caught my balance so I didn't go flying. Tobias wrapped the large towel around me, steadying me. He wouldn't meet my eyes as he retreated and left me standing in place, drops falling from my hair and splattering on the tile.

tobias

I'D LEFT HER BEHIND, intending to keep my distance from her, and there was less than an hour left until I had to return to my bedroom in preparation for slumber, yet here I was, aching for one more look at her—one moment more in her presence. I stuttered to a stop at the deep, spine-tightening moan. My cock hardened immediately. I stood near the entrance, my nose flaring.

Catalina being pleasured was a sound I never wanted to expel from my head. Her breathy little moans and the whimpers that left her lips . . .

Tension lined my shoulders. I should turn around. Leave.

Yet, my legs moved me forward.

It was useless fighting it. I had tried staying away from her, but nothing I did helped. No distraction, duty, or—

Catalina called to a primitive side of me . . . and I was caring less and less as each day passed in her presence.

Asher's head was bent between Cat's legs, his hair trailing over her thighs. The dimmed yellow light coming from the light fixture over his bed illuminated her beautiful, silky brown skin.

This would be the last time. *Keep telling yourself this, Tobias.*

Willfully foolish was what I was being, but it *was just once more.*

Asher must have heard me with our advanced hearing, yet he remained unfazed. Eating her out with such precision that jealousy seared my stomach. I wanted to be him. I wanted in her.

I sank into the chaise to the right of the door, shrouded in the dark corner. Catalina's neck formed a perfect arch as she panted with her head tipped back, her long midnight hair strewn around her.

Her mouth was parted and sweet little pants expelled from her lips.

Watch me make her fall apart, Priest. Asher's thoughts echoed.

Each noise she made served to tighten my balls until my cock throbbed painfully. I unlatched the metal constraint of my slacks and tugged the zipper down.

My cock sprang out, heavy, thick, and wanting. I wrapped my palm around the thick member and squeezed it. *Just once.*

Blood-tinted pre-cum beaded at the head. My gaze dragged back to Cat as her chest rose and fell sharply. Her bare breasts bounced with each exhalation. Sucking on one earlier had shifted something inside me. My fangs extended, piercing my lip. Flicking my tongue out, I lapped the droplet.

Cat's dark nipples jutted perkily, calling to me—begging me to wrap my lips around them again.

My hand squeezed on my cock, sending a shockwave through my stomach. I burned for her.

"More." Her moaned word sent a shiver down my spine. She was such a lovely, sweet thing.

My balls pulsated and I gritted my teeth as pre-cum dripped down the side of my shaft. Her breathing became more erratic and the pumps of her chest quickened. My favorite part would occur soon and she would come. Her spine arched and my attention latched onto her face. The dark, thick brows furrowed closely together as her release hit her and soft cries fell from her lips. An aphrodisiac to my senses.

Her release ripped mine from my cock and cum spilled over my knuckles as I tightened my hold. My eyes slid shut and a low moan wrenched from my lips.

As she fell back on the bed, panting in the throes of aftershocks that Asher licked her through, I sheathed my cock into my slacks and left the room as I zipped up, swiping my soiled hand on my slacks.

She held too much sway over me.

When she disappeared, I'd *feared*. The worst possible scenarios had gone through my head. I'd been unable to calm Jax or Asher and they were as agitated as me.

I'd never been unsteady.

But I hadn't cared for anything other than finding her. None of us had.

I firmly shut my door.

I carefully rolled down the sleeves of my buttoned shirt and unhooked the cinch at the wrist. Jerking the clothing over my head, I carefully laid all my clothing on the end of the bed.

Bathing was necessary to clear my head and as I did so, I could plan my next steps.

A sojourn to England for a few years may do me good. And now that Ren was back, the guilt gnawing my insides at the thought of leaving would cease. We'd stayed together out of necessity, but realistically, there was nothing I could offer. I was sire to none in all the years I'd been a vampire. Put simply, I was here at the request of Imogen.

It wasn't as if everything would fall apart without me. It would be the most opportune time to leave in the centuries we'd been together because if I didn't, I'd cave to temptation and toss all the beliefs I'd clung to aside.

THIRTY-EIGHT

I PUSHED the shopping cart with one hand as I made my way down the cat aisle. The phone was pressed to my ear, ringing as I sought out food for Binx. He never ate and it was starting to worry me that he could get infected with some disease if he continued eating out on the streets.

"You've reached the shelter, how can I help?" The voice on the other end croaked.

"Hi, I'm one of the volunteers, I've left a few voicemails for George, but I can't get a hold of him." I trailed off as sniffles started up on the other end. "Um, hello?"

"S-sorry." Throat clearing ensued. "George won't be able to get back to you. He was found dead. He was mugged and had a heart attack." I slowed to a stop. "I have to go." The call ended.

George was dead?

I clicked off my phone, a little numb. This was not the sort of information I expected to get in the middle of shopping. My hand shook as I hoisted a cat food bag into the cart. He'd died so suddenly . . .

My phone vibrated, and Erin's name flashed across the

screen. She never called this late unless it was important. I put it to my ear to her already speaking. "—good news for you. I got your manuscript last night with all the edits completed and it looks good. I let the publishing house know we had it set to go. Turns out they lost one of their scheduled slots and want to put your release out."

No words came to mind.

"You still there, Cat?"

"Yes," I forced out and it sounded strained.

"I expected more excitement," Erin chuckled. "Anyway, they're sending over your advance."

"T-thank you," I sputtered.

"That's what I'm here for, lady, to make us money. Be sure to treat yourself. Got to go." The beep of the ended call faded as I dropped my arm. I blinked quickly. Even though I didn't know George all that much and he honestly gave me weirdo vibes, I felt a bit bad feeling so happy right now.

But the fear that used to dog me no longer haunted me. My bank account wouldn't be in pain for long, and I . . . liked someone—or *someones*.

Multiple vampires.

Their presence relieved some of the terror that weighed on me for years. They made me feel safe. Something I'd never had.

Everything had changed. Everything was different. *I* was different. Maybe now, Peter could come visit—

"Excuse me, human?"

"Yes," I whipped my head up with a grin ready. I was still too mind boggled to register that it was not normal to be called 'human'. I yelped and scrambled back until the shelf dug into my spine. My elbow unbalanced one of the cat food cans and it thudded on the rubber floor.

Calliope stared at me with her eyebrow lifted high on her forehead.

"Hello, human," she said in a suspiciously friendly tone.

My lips parted and I shut them again, my mind whirling.

"W-what do you want?" My stomach was in knots.

"He didn't finish serving his time." Calliope clicked her tongue, shaking her head as if dejected, but it was a show. She did it too mockingly. "I came to make a deal with you." The corners of her lips tilted up. My racing mind screeched to a halt. "I'm not like you, you know?" She sniffed. "Sneaking into someone else's house uninvited." She stepped closer, looming over me.

"What do you want?" I said, the words rasping from my throat.

"You owe me. You and dear Ren murdered so many of my children." Her hand settled on her chest with the exaggerated words.

"You're ridiculous."

"Unless you want me to destroy that coven you dearly care about, I would do as I say." I stiffened. "I want you to get something for me in the Crimson manor." She paused in a dramatic fashion. "Nothing much. It's this little black storage vase. Seems inconspicuous and featureless but there are little etchings near the circling lip. You get me that and I'll forget about all about my people Ren slaughtered without cause and I won't turn every single vampire in this country against them."

I struggled swallowing.

"I don't even know where it is—"

"Should be either with the ex-priest, or the angry twin."

I blinked at her. *How did she know that?* I didn't have the guts to ask her. Her request turned in my head.

I licked my lips. This wasn't a good idea. It was going behind their backs and I wouldn't do that but telling that to her face seemed like I was asking to be murdered.

Instead, I jerkily nodded.

I backed up, leaving my cart behind as I gave her a wide berth.

"And Catalina," she called. I turned back toward her and she was suddenly in my face. I sucked in a breath. "Do you want their slaughter on your conscience?"

My mouth dried up and I shook my head. Seemed like her good side was properly tucked away.

"Good." She smiled. "I'll leave you to it. Make sure to give me a call." She tossed my cell phone into my cart. *When had she gotten a hold of it?*

She sashayed away, her hips swaying as her heels clicked on the linoleum. She seemed out of place, like she was plucked from the Victorian era with her wide gown.

Helplessness closed in on me. I slumped back until my shoulders hit *something*. I tipped my head back and squeezed my eyes closed. *What pissing contest had I stepped in the middle of?*

catalina

I TAPPED my fingertips against the sofa cushion. They were taking forever to get back. Asher and Tobias headed out to fetch more blood—whatever that entailed. According to what Asher had said, they were going through them too quickly. As for Ren, I had no idea where he was, and I didn't ask questions about him. Jax was absent, as he'd recently been.

I'd been waiting in their living room for almost an hour now, and the curiosity was close to driving me insane. I'd talked myself out of marching upstairs more than a few times, but incessant questions kept rounding my thoughts: Once I told them . . . what if they didn't tell me what it was Calliope wanted? Or why it was important enough for her to threaten me?

It wasn't like I'd give Calliope anything anyway. I wasn't going to betray them; I just wanted answers . . .

I was already on my feet and climbing up to the second floor. I shouldn't do this, but if I didn't look myself, I doubted they would share everything.

Licking my lips, I shoved open Jax's door. If he caught me,

he'd be so angry, so I needed to search quickly. Once they all got back, I would tell them everything she'd said when she cornered me.

I stepped into the bedroom and flipped the switch. Jax's room was down the hall on the second floor. I'd thought Tobias's bedroom was bland, but he had nothing on Jax. The comforter was an onyx color and he had exactly one pillow on it. Oh, and it was about half the size of Asher's.

There was a dresser on the farthest side of the room and . . . that was it. Even so, I quickly swept over the room and even peeked in the bathroom to check if there was anything, but no. Jax was either minimalistic or had some other secret space where he put everything. He didn't even have a closet or wardrobe like Asher.

After turning off the light switch, I peeked out the door. Clear. The door snicked shut and I made my way to Tobias's room. My steps padded down the hall and I was again engulfed in Tobias's comforting sweet scent. The light was already on, so I quietly closed the door. My eyes stuttered over the vase on top of the long dresser I'd grabbed a shirt from.

I hadn't noticed it before, but I guess I was too busy looking for a shirt to bother looking up. Then once I'd gotten the clothing, I'd been staring at the picture of the woman in his dresser.

I neared the dresser it rested on. It seemed harmless. The black surface reflected the light. I leaned close to study the lid covering the top. Just as Calliope described, there were little engravings that looked like thorns, but the lighting was too low for me to get a good look.

I reached for it and hugged it to my chest. It kind of looked like an urn . . . but that didn't make sense. I reached down and tugged at the knob, but it didn't budge.

I better stop less I free some sort of curse or something. I wasn't even sure if curses existed, but I wouldn't be surprised, considering vampires did.

The back of my shirt was suddenly bunched and I was jerked back. I stumbled and fell to my knees. A painful sting radiated up my legs, but I worked to keep hold of the vase thing. I tugged against the hold and my shirt rode up farther.

"What are you doing with that?" Jax hissed.

catalina

"J-JAX," I whispered. His glare was so intense it hurt to look up at his face. Out of all the times he'd sneered and frowned at me, it was never as severe as right now. My fingers tightened around the vase, and I licked my lips.

"Calliope—" I rasped.

Jax scoffed, a sneer lifting his lips, he snatched the vase from my fingers.

"You're a traitor, then," he hissed and grabbed my arm so tight I yelped. With the same hold, he dragged me down the stairs, my legs giving out halfway. The edges of the steps hit my shins.

I screamed in agony. He tossed me forward and I thumped onto my knees. I winced at the burn and struggled to push to my feet.

My shirt was gripped again and I squeaked, pushing to my tiptoes so I wouldn't choke. I coughed and the pressure relented. I dropped to my ass. Ren stood over me with his eyebrows high.

I couldn't get a word out as I struggled to breathe. I was

already shaking my head, trying to wrap my thoughts around their visceral reactions.

"L-let me explain." I coughed.

"You're a human," Ren said slowly. "Why should I listen to you?" I blinked at him as he tilted his head. The look in his eyes was eerie and spine chilling. "How about I just snap your little neck." He grinned and stepped toward me.

I scrambled back, struggling to breathe. My heart was beating so fast. Everything was too much.

"Jax—help," I wheezed.

His eyes narrowed and he sneered.

"I thought you would protect me," I rasped thoughtlessly. I couldn't get the proper words out. He didn't even let me explain myself before throwing accusations.

"Why would I protect a meaningless human?" Jax's words socked the breath from my body and I froze, hugging my chest.

"W-what?" I gasped. After everything I'd done for them . . .

Just then, Asher sauntered into the foyer, the door leading outside swinging behind him as he gawked.

"What's going on?" he asked when he saw them staring down at me.

"She was trying to sneak out with this," Jax said, lifting the vase. Sneak out was a bit of a stretch.

Asher narrowed his eyes on me. "Where were you taking the urn?"

Urn. My guess was correct.

Horror prodded my chest. And my hands shook as I lifted them.

"I didn't even know it was an urn," I gasped. "What's in there?"

I turned my attention to Asher, not wanting to see the hate in Jax's expression or the unsympathetic aggression in Ren.

"It's Imogen's ashes," Asher said, still eyeing me in a way he hadn't before.

My body went utterly numb. *They were reacting like this to the dead woman's ashes?*

My heart thundered in my ears.

Ren crossed his arms, leaning against the wall as he watched me. At least he was no longer near me.

"Please let me explain myself," I croaked.

"She was sent here by Calliope," Jax accused. "The entire fucking time, she played with us." He gingerly sat the urn down on a step of the staircase.

Asher tensed and turned his attention to me. His reaction was slower.

"Is this true?"

I was already shaking my head. "She wanted to make a deal—"

His expression became icy.

Jax lunged in my direction. My eyes widened so much that it hurt. I scooted backward until my back hit a wall, and I sucked in a breath.

"Human trash," Jax hissed, getting in my face. His fangs flashed in my face and my eyes fastened on them. My psyche was dragged to my horrid memories and my hands shook. Asher pressed his palm to Jax's shoulder to shove him back a few steps.

"Enough," Asher responded sharply when I opened my mouth. They weren't even letting me explain myself.

"Don't act like you're a fucking saint, Asher. Your goal was to turn her into your blood-whore before I gave her my blood," Jax spat. An airbag slammed into my body, tossing me into the dark pit of my psyche. I gasped, my shoulders hitting the wall from my shock. Asher's mouth tightened and that was all I needed for confirmation.

My throat closed up. I thought he cared about me . . .

My watering gaze lifted to Ren and he watched happily, eyes attached to my neck. *That was all I was.* A blood bag. Human. Stupid. Those thoughts swirled in my head squeezing my chest in its vice.

My heart throbbed painfully. They may as well have yanked it out of my chest.

The lack of faith . . . it hurt so very badly, but I should have never had expectations from vampires.

"I thought you knew me," I whispered. Jax stilled, a sneer lifting his lips as he shoved past Asher, stalking toward me. There was no room for me with the memory of Imogen making them react this way. And I knew it was a lost battle. I couldn't and wouldn't fight with a memory. Not that I could win even if I tried.

"Know you?" Asher remained frozen in place while his twin was only steps from reaching me. "Catalina, we trust no one," he said, studying me.

"Least of all a pitiful human girl with nothing to her name." Jax's cruel words speared my heart.

My throat clogged up, tears blinding me. I couldn't breathe.

"Let's end this now." Jax's hand wrapped around my throat and he slammed me on the wall, pinning me. My feet kicked out, and I thrashed desperately as I struggled to drag oxygen through my mouth, but it was no use. Spots danced in front of my vision. An arm wrapped around Jax's throat and Asher pulled him back, a string of sentences in their language spilling out. My knees buckled under my weight, but I used the wall to steady myself.

"Did you attempt to turn me into your blood-whore?" I croaked. Asher's gaze sharpened on me.

"Leave," Asher hissed. He pushed Jax who finally stopped immediately trying to come at me.

"Not until you answer me," I screamed back. The tendrils of my sanity slipping from my fingers.

"Yes," Asher hissed, and rushed at me. He gripped the back of my neck and shoved me toward the door. I lost my footing and slammed to my knee. Agony spiked up my leg to my hip.

Ren's shoe stepped on my hand splayed on the ground and he pressed until something popped. My stomach lurched and I bit the inside of my cheek as tears dripped off my chin. He knelt.

"Don't think of running your mouth to anyone human," Ren said. "And don't go too far. I'll come collect you soon." His foot finally lifted off my fingers and I curled my limp hand to my chest.

I lowered my head, backing to the door jerkily. No one stopped me as I dashed into the darkness with tears streaming down my face.

catalina

I NEEDED to get away from here. Far, far away. A sob hiccupped free and I struggled to see as I slammed myself into my van and scrambled to grab my keys with my good hand. Ren's threat bounced around my head, but I was working off pure adrenaline.

Keys jingled from my shaking hand, and I let out another wrenching sob. Pressure in my chest became agonizing. The engine clicked, not revving on. I relaxed my grip on the key, taking a deep breath.

Come on.

I turned the key again and it roared to life. Relief loosened my shoulders, and I wasted no time as I backed out of the driveway. Ren's threat echoed in my ears, but I had to try to leave. I'd hop on a plane and head to Mexico to collect Peter, then we could disappear. I had the smallest window to get out of here, because it was four of them against one.

My non broken hand shook on the steering wheel. My chest was excruciatingly tight and my nose burned. Sobs racked my body as I pushed on the gas. I used my knee to steady the steering wheel to grab my new inhaler with my good hand. It took me a few fumbling tries but I eventually got the wrapper off. Tossing it to the ground, I lifted it to my mouth, sucking in deeply as I drove with my forearm steadying the wheel.

I took a third puff, but the pressure in my chest wouldn't loosen. Another sob wrenched free from my throat as I reached for the radio, trying to shut off the blaring music. As soon as it cut off, my cries bounced off the windows.

Stop, Catalina.

Yet, the sobs kept coming.

Jax hadn't allowed me a moment to speak. He didn't care what I had to say. None of them had. My lip trembled and I had to blink quickly to clear my sight. *Asher told me to leave.*

As if I was nothing.

Who was I kidding? I was nothing to them. Just a potential blood-whore. How had I been fooled so easily? *Vampires are arrogant prideful creatures. At the core of it we like to play*–Asher *told* me this entire time that it was all a game.

The van chose that moment to sputter and jerk. Something started beeping as it stuttered to a stop and hissed. No, God, you had to be kidding.

I blankly stared out the window before my head thumped on the wheel. A loud honk echoed. Quickly straightening, the eerie honk cut off. This couldn't be my life. It seemed impossible that it could become so shit within a few hours. I sighed, rubbing the bridge of my nose.

My van emitted a concerning hiss and a cloud of smoke spilled from the crevices of the hood.

Tears still streaming down my face, I reached over and pushed open the door. An intense smell of fumes assaulted my nose.

Where was I? I rubbed my eyes with the back of my hand and looked around the lonely and road. The outlines of trees stretched into the dark, starry sky. I could see nothing into the thick line of the woods. A sharp pressure tightened my chest. Such a pretty night for it being so shitty. At least I wasn't a hiccupping mess. I'd gotten a reprieve for a moment.

The engine let out another odd sound and I stumbled away from it. I shouldn't have pushed the van so much.

I needed to do something and not just stand here like a lump, waiting for my car to burst into flames.

A pebble clattered. No, those were steps. I squinted down the long line of the road, trying to make out the distant figure approaching me with too much speed. All I could see was the outline of a male body. That nasty ball in my stomach expanded again. I took an unsteady step back. *No. No. No way.*

Was it the vampire from the cave?

Or one of the others?

My chest pumped and I turned and started running down the road as fast as my feet could take me. My head rushed and I picked up pace, the only sound filling my ears was that of my rasping breaths.

Beams of light suddenly blinded me, and a roar filled my ears. Cold metal collided with the side of my body. My ears rang as I went flying and slammed onto the pavement.

Blistering pain seared my arms, and I groaned. Every inch of my body felt like a big bruise. I tried to push myself into a sitting position, but as soon as my fingers twitched, I screamed. My arm was broken. And my leg.

I whimpered and flattened on the ground of the intersecting road. The bright lights of the car that slammed into me burned my eyes as tears washed down my face. Pain speared my lungs, and I couldn't breathe. Dots flooded my vision. I was going to asphyxiate. I hated this. I hated that I couldn't breathe normally. My own body was against me.

I choked on a sob, my body jerking with the cough that struck agony through my limbs. The light from the vehicle illuminated the outline of the approaching silhouette. My eyes widened and my throat closed. Darkness consumed me until there was nothing more.

Catalina's story continues in Undying Thirst.

Visit my website for more book information and be sure to join my reader group and follow my social media platforms to keep up with my releases.

So many people to thank! Especially my Deadly Cravings ARC team, you guys rock.

Thank you to my author friends for listening to my rambling. Aaron thank you for supporting my dreams.

Como siempre, gracias a mi mamá y mi papá.

Allie obsessively reads books featuring sexy, possessive heroes and headstrong heroines. So, it's no wonder characters just like that bustle to escape her imagination.

When she's not working away at her keyboard, she can be found in bed with a good book or bingeing Netflix.

* 9 7 8 1 9 6 5 3 0 0 0 9 1 *